THE
WEATHER
INSDE

a novel

EMILY SASO

Freehand Books gratefully acknowledges the support of the Canada Council for the Arts for its publishing program. ¶ Freehand Books acknowledges the financial support for its publishing program provided by the Government of Canada through the Canada Book Fund.

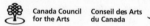

Freehand Books
515 – 815 1st Street SW   Calgary, Alberta T2P 1N3
www.freehand-books.com

Book orders: LitDistCo
100 Armstrong Avenue Georgetown, Ontario L7G 5S4
Telephone: 1-800-591-6250 Fax: 1-800-591-6251
orders@litdistco.ca
www.litdistco.ca

Library and Archives Canada Cataloguing in Publication
Saso, Emily, author
The weather inside / Emily Saso.
Issued in print and electronic formats.
ISBN 978-1-988298-00-9 (paperback).
ISBN 978-1-988298-02-3 (html).
ISBN 978-1-988298-03-0 (pdf)
I. Title.
PS8637.A7538W43 2016   C813'.6   C2016-903511-5   C2016-903512-3

Edited by Rosemary Nixon
Book design by Natalie Olsen, Kisscut Design
Author photo by Anthony Tummillo
Printed on FSC® recycled paper and bound in Canada by Marquis

For Anthony

THE
WEATHER
INSIDE

1

Henry and I've been married one year, but we've been in love for at least six thousand — back when dinosaurs and man roamed the earth together. When I'm trying to be romantic, I rest my chin on Henry's collarbone and whisper our origin story. "Remember? When that pterodactyl stole your hat? When I chased him through the lava field, hiked up the plates of that stegosaurus ..."

A one-year anniversary is extra special, so we're trying to do it in the shower. We tried other places first. On the wingback chair, my horrible rug, the Ikea Björkudden table. Never the bed, though; Henry knows not to bother with the bed anymore. So three minutes ago, he picked me up like a sack of rocks, twisting a knot into his back, and plopped me down in the shower. It's not going well. I've been standing in the same spot for too long. The water is pelting the back of my neck and hurting me like I didn't know water could. I complain, so Henry toggles the head to massage. The water still stings, only now at a predictable pulse. I know when the pang is coming, and where it will hit, and I brace for it. I can't focus. I can't relax. And because of his knotted back, Henry is having trouble holding me up against the black-and-white checkered tile wall, which is what he needs to do. If this is going to work, Henry's going to have to be the strong one.

That checkered tile wall is posing another problem. It's incomplete, a failure at everything a wall is supposed to be. Separate, define, delineate, conceal. This wall does none of that because of a maddening half-inch gap between it and the ceiling that the landlord refuses to fix. Something about failing lath bases and key strength? It would cost him thousands, he says, which we are not worth. I tried to repair it when I first moved in. Bought caulking at Home Depot, loaded the gun, cut the tip off the tube and pulled the trigger. A pleasing flow of wet, messy silicone snaked out. When the length of the gap was filled, I licked my thumb and dragged it along. The seal was perfect, so I left to let it dry. I felt like what a man must feel most days — making a mess then smoothing it over and walking away. By the next morning, though, the caulking had separated from the ceiling and dripped down the wall. Our neighbour — *Canadian Idol* champ Billy Pfeiffer — must have showered, the chemical runoff of his Axe body wash turning the unset silicon into a leaking paste. I should have said something to him, warned him. Maybe I will today, put a stop to the war of our shampoos when they meet in the crack: the tarry punch of my medicinal scalp treatment vs. Billy Pfeiffer's Old Spice musk. Or maybe I'll give up and accept that some holes are just impossible to fill.

Sounds pass through the crack too, the noises of our most private moments. Like right now. When I moan that this shower sex isn't working. When Henry says, "Maybe it would if you took off your bra and underwear and hiking sandals." When I sob against the tile. When Henry crashes out and slams the door. When I leap from the shower to try to lock the door even though there's only living room light and Henry's tense bum shining through the hole where the lock used to be. Henry took a screwdriver to the lock when I moved in. Said it was broken, used to trap him inside without warning, so he pried it out. For my safety. I still reach for a lock, though; it's instinctual. A little button I can press or a dial I can turn, clicking me inside and out of reach.

Henry took the only clean towel so the tracks I make to him are slippery. He's slouched on the futon and drying the crevices behind his ears with intention, as if crevices matter. I join him, sit close to him, closer, snuggle on his lap, graft my limbs onto his like a new kind of tree. He's warm from the shower and the anger and now me. I am three-quarters naked, more naked than Henry has ever seen me in the daylight, but he looks me in the eye.

"Happy anniversary," he says. And I smile and nod.

We've been lying to each other for six thousand years.

2

The Kingdom Hall has staked an enviable plot in our uptown Toronto neighbourhood, a place bloated with condo developments and a subway line bursting at the welds, where the rents are as high and threatening as storm clouds. West of the hall there's a Burger Shack that vents beefy breaths, a Holiday Inn Express, and a Shoeless Joe's with a rub and tug directly above. To the east, a sprawling park. To the south a Daisy Mart and Taekwondo Academy. The hall is in a high traffic area that's fast moving, and yet no one looks both ways.

I stand at the crosswalk, protecting my eyes from the sun with my hands as visors. The light turns red, the walk sign green;

but I can't move. I don't want to move. I picture myself getting hit by an SUV. There is blood everywhere, our street a horror movie set. I've stained the road, turned those yellow traffic dashes orange. I apologize to the owners of Burger Shack. Customers will lose their appetites for red meat. The owners will have to shut down and file for bankruptcy and their children will never go to college. Little Suzy and Billy will turn to a life on the streets. Sell their bodies. Die in the trunk of the same white, windowless van.

I turn around, go home. Save everyone the trouble.

3

Henry and I live in a shoebox—a size fourteen Kenneth Cole. One bedroom with frosted glass French doors. One bath. An enormous street-facing window. Henry has lived here for six years, so I didn't get much say in the interior design. You married me, he says, not my apartment.

Henry doesn't decorate; he tolerates. Only uses furniture when he needs to. His kitchen accommodates the Björkudden dining table from Ikea, matching chairs and a fan of takeout menus. The living room has only what it requires for survival. Bifold futon, leatherette accent chair, heartless coffee table and—my one and only addition—an infuriating geometric throw rug that clings to hair and dust. There's a desk without drawers, piles of my unfinished work stacked on top. In the corner stands a shelf of Henry's recently acquired self-help books, which mean there is something wrong with his life, which means there is something wrong with mine. I was granted permission for a widescreen television and a banker's box for my science fiction DVDs, which was a proud victory. The walls are anonymous white and thin as hospital sheets. No photos or paintings allowed. Our landlord is confident his investment will collapse if his tenants start hammering into it. This suits Henry fine, but makes me ache. There's a perfect spot above the futon and across from the TV for a landscape painting. I try to convince Henry biweekly but fail every time. We could sit together, I tell him, and watch *Planet Earth,* and our lives would be bookended by colour and light.

But I spend too much time here, alone, because of what Henry's been up to.

And I spend too much time here, alone, because I work from home.

I'm an editorial assistant for a vanity legal publishing company, Smith-Coxwell, which means I get paid to enter the professional accomplishments of corporate lawyers like

WRIGHT, MICHAEL, Q.C.
FELPS & PHILLIPS TECHNOLOGIES

Mr. Wright received his undergraduate degree from the University of Toronto (1980), his Masters in English Literature from the University of British Columbia (1982) and his J.D. from Harvard (1985) brag brag brag brag. Mr. Wright has a broad range of experience in commercial, regulatory and cockstroke brag back brag.

into a database and, eventually, into a yearbook that my boss sells back to the lawyers for outrageous profit.

I was trained by a woman named Marnie. She's twenty-six, one year older than me, and has achieved roughly the same level of attractiveness, albeit in a different package. She's a nymph, with hair so blonde it may as well be white, oversized saucer eyes of a cartoon character and skin pimpled just below the surface, blemishes that aren't evident unless you get up real close, or unless you are the kind of person looking for flaws in everyone around you. She is American by birth and therefore loud and confident — every other word she speaks is underlined with the weight it carries.

She warned me about the job in fragments: "too much for one person" and "dangerously repetitive." The combination of those two elements was like a kind of gathering storm, winding boredom with pressure to form debilitating anxiety attacks. The week before she applied for stress leave, Marnie was up to twelve cups of coffee a day but she would still nod off at her desk, dreaming of throwing herself in front of the number seven bus. So she got a note from her therapist and employment insurance from the government, and that was that. She was one person doing the job of two. What did they expect?

I protected myself against turning into Marnie by electing to work from home. The office is far away, two subway line changes and a bus ride outside the city limits in a dissolved municipality called Scarborough composed of miles and miles of parking lots. It is a commute that would compromise anyone's sanity. So I go to the office as little as possible, every month or so to compliment my boss's tie. I spend the majority of my workday sitting in the living room with a hot-running computer resting on my lap. This flexible arrangement, as human resources calls it, doesn't feel as freeing as I'd imagined. Since Henry started sneaking around, I haven't exactly been a model employee. Instead of processing legal biographies, I've been staring out the window, on stakeout, watching for Henry.

Today is no different. My face is pressed up against the glass, the burning wind slipping through the defects of the single pane and super-heating my skin. I consider fainting. The temperature is at record levels, the TV weatherman said, a sweltering system from the eastern United States that will stick to us for weeks. It's thirty-five degrees Celsius, but that feels amplified here in the city. The July air boiled by traffic, pollution and the stagnation brewed between skyscrapers. Our air conditioner is on, but it's never enough. That heat finds its way inside the porous membrane of this building and my body. My stomach swells with it, and I worry about its need to release its contents all over Henry's clean parquet floor. I fight my urges by changing the arrangement of certain things: straightening the furniture, my back, baring my teeth.

Across the street, the Kingdom Hall bends to the will of the fevered summer wind. The gusts shake the hall's mirrored windows in their frames, adding a nightmarish shuddering to everything they reflect back: the traffic, the sidewalk, the Jehovah's Witness handing out magazines to pedestrians hurtling past. I shudder too.

I watch the Witness approach a woman in a dress patterned with sweat stains. She shakes her head and waves both hands from the hip: no no. The Witness backs off, turning already toward a tall guy in denim with his cap pulled low. Cap-Man tosses the Witness's magazine to the ground and kicks over the planters that bookend the hall's entrance. A cheer erupts deep inside of me, reverberating off my bones.

The phone rings and I leap on it.

"Henry?" Every time I want it, need it to be him.

Not even a breath.

"Henry?"

Static takes over the line. Then a female voice. The measured cadence of a robot. "You have a call from a federal prison from—"

"Uncle Bryan."

His voice fills in the blank. Rough from decades of shouting. The robot woman. "Press one to accept the call."

My spine shivers, the whole length of it, every vertebra.

The robot woman is pressuring me. "Are you still there?"

How to answer that question?

"Are you still there? Are you still there? Are you still there?"

I open my mouth. I want to tell her everything about the man she's just connected me to, about how it is that we're connected.

"I don't know," I say.

Only it doesn't have time to come out.

A bitter wind screams through the window. The force of it whips my hair, tossing it around my head, blinding me. My nose drips. My face numbs. My fingers cramp and fist. I feel shorter, tighter, ready to uncoil.

Beneath me, the floor turns to ice.

4

A burly beast with grey curls spiralling out of his head, nose, ears is shaking me, his knuckles covered in grey-black fuzz. He cuts off my scream with hands that taste like Lemon Pledge. "*Gamó!*" he says. "I'm here to help you." His voice is hoarse. His accent thick Mediterranean. "I'm going to move my hand now, okay? You're not going to bite off my balls?"

I nod and he lets go of my face. The room starts to come together, the concussion haze solidifying into walls and window and the floor I'm splayed out on.

"Who are you?" I wheeze.

He wipes my spit off his hand onto his denim thigh spotted with paint. "Steve."

"You? With that accent? Your name is *Steve?*"

"Yes. So?"

"Wait . . . I know you," I say. "Why do I know you?"

He dangles his ring of keys in front of my eyes.

"Of course!" I swipe at his keys like a cat. "You're the super."

"So her brain still works. Good sign." He takes my hand in his and lifts me off the floor. His palm is warm and leathery. Every finger calloused.

My back throbs. I can't stand straight.

"How did you find me?" I ask.

"I was cleaning the windows in the hallway. Heard a loud bang, came in, found you. What happened?"

"It was the floor."

Steve looks at the parquet; so do I. The sheen is gone, as though the ice has melted, sucked itself down into the apartment below.

"It, it —"

"Ah, I see," Steve nods, his hand playing the role of a bottle. "The floor. Yes, of course." He winks.

"No, I was just standing here and then this freezing wind whipped through."

Steve cranes his head so far back I fear he'll fall over. The neck it's attached to is thick as a tree trunk.

"It came out of nowhere," I continue. "And then ice —"

I take methodical steps to the air conditioner. Check it from top to bottom.

"Does this look okay to you?" I ask Steve.

He hobbles over, each step rousing a sigh.

"It's fine," he tells me.

"Are you sure?"

He turns it on and the sweet smell of ozone takes over, its machinated air a soothing breeze. "See? Nothing's broken. The temperature is twenty-one degrees. Perfect."

"What about leaks?" I ask.

"It's a good machine." He's taking all this personally.

I kneel down on the floor. The wood is as dry as a bone. No water stain and, certainly, no water. I lie on my stomach, face pressing against the boards. Even the varnish is undisturbed. "There has to be an explanation," I say.

"I'll give you one," Steve says. "You're too skinny. Next time you drink, eat pasta. The floor might even stand still."

He's laughing as the door slams. A cruel exit.

There's nowhere left to fall from here, so I decide to stay on the floor. My back aches; the blood around my tailbone is co-agulating into a bruise I'll never see. I try to think back to before. I must have fainted from the stress of the call. Uncle Bryan. That pushy robot. Her stupid questions. I must have passed out, hit my head, imagined all of it: the ice, the wind. A bump on the head can explain the mysteries of the world.

5

I stay down here, on the floor, for hours. Fascinating. From this vantage point I see everything that's trapped in my stupid Ikea throw rug. Dust and hair wound up in its modern swirls and bold concentric circles. I breathe in the air at this level, that feet smell tinged with what our home has become with Henry so rarely in it. Instead of his fresh laundry and sandalwood after-shave, my neighbours have taken over. Cigarettes, pot, blackened toast, burnt lint from the dryer that no one will lay claim to. The detritus of lives finding their way through the pores of the walls. I try to cure it by applying strong-smelling lotions to my skin — vanilla, grapefruit, lavender — but they always turn sour, curdled by loneliness. It is a particular brand of loneliness, not the kind a normal person experiences when a roommate moves out or a pet dies. No, mine is intense and displacing. Like it's six thousand years ago, only now I'm by myself in a shoebox-shaped cave. No Henry. No other humans or mammals. Just me and the dinosaurs, and my blood just as cold. When Henry is around, he stares out the window at the Kingdom Hall. And when I talk to him, it's as though the mere act of aiming his ears in my direction exhausts him; each time I open my mouth I see him deflate like a balloon. We fell in love so quickly, easily. Aren't we still in love? Henry?

I only know love, because I have no friends to like anymore. There were the kids I went to Kingdom Hall with in Ottawa, but I haven't spoken to any of them in years. And my roommates in university. We lived in a dorm that was a hop, skip, jump away from the most shot-up ghetto in North York. There was a girl whose name I forget, a lovely thing, a track star. She got molested while out for an evening jog by a man on a bicycle. There was a Mike who grew an ironic mustache and a Myke who wore ironic T-shirts. Naoko, a Japanese exchange student with suicidal tendencies and no tolerance for red wine, and a theatre major, Stacy, who got attacked in the daylight by a boy on a skateboard. To buy affordable milk, luxury toilet paper and vegetables that weren't limp, Whatshername, Mike, Myke, Naoko, Stacy and I had to venture off campus, which was risky — the "priority" neighbourhood and "at-risk" youth worrying to our delicate middle-class constitutions. We had two options: travel to Food Basics on busses filled with failed gangbangers, or take our chances in stolen Honda Civics with the word *taxi* written on the back of a cereal box, duct-taped in the rear window and always marvellously misspelled. Taxee! Tacksi!! Taxsii!!! My roommates and I weren't really friends. We were security.

I don't need friends because I have Henry. But Henry? Yes, Henry needs people, *other* people. He needs engagement, he likes to say — social, intellectual, cultural . . . He used to catch himself before the other word came tumbling out: spiritual. I could hear the click-back of it behind his teeth.

And I can hear his footsteps, right now, coming down the hallway, that wet squeak he always fails to rub out on the welcome mat. He turns his key in our lock and greets me with a hey. I watch him struggle to undo his shoes, breathing quickly, frustrated over laces he always ties too tight.

He kneels down to my level. "What are you doing?"

"I fell."

"Did you really?"

"Of course I did. What does that even mean?"

"Nothing," he says, and he helps me up.

I push my body into his and wait for the calm to take over, the sedation of being pressed against his chest. But my eyeball is locked onto the naked muscle of his arm and the tattoo of my name inside a lace-rimmed Valentine heart. The black outline around the heart is white now, like a burn or a scar instead of ink.

"What's happening to your heart?" I ask.

"Nothing," he says.

"It's like it's disappearing."

"You're imagining things." He rakes his fingers through his hair. I dyed that hair when we first met. He wanted a rebellious look, one that showed on the outside how he felt within. I gave him blonde highlights, which we both decided meant trouble. I spent hours pulling his hair through plastic with a hook. It's brown again. When did that happen?

"My uncle Bryan called me today," I say.

Henry groans.

"But the robot woman did most of the talking."

He tugs on his hair and several strands release. An invisible wind carries them up the wall.

"You still owe me my anniversary present. Henry?"

6

Our community centre is sweltering. Posters for Alcoholics Anonymous (rm. 101), Babysitters Training (rm. 103) and Mommy and Me Yoga (rm. 105) wilt off the paint, double-sided tape no match for this humidity. Henry and I walk down the long, narrow hallway. I marvel at the magic of my hands and arms, able to stretch out and touch both walls at once.

Room 107 hasn't changed. A classroom with lighting that brings out the blue in pale skin, salt-and-pepper terrazzo floors, and pastries shiny with icing and egg-wash on a corner table. The people are the same too, or could be, in suits, ties, skirts, all dry cleaned and pressed, most still coming straight from work, or at least wanting to be thought of in that regard. Truth is, they look as though they've never left their feeble plastic chairs, like they've been enduring lower back pain in this circle for one year, patiently awaiting our return.

"Well well well. Avery and Henry. Welcome back."

"Hi, Nav." I hug him. He smells like vanilla and window cleaner. "I hoped you'd still be running the group."

Henry shakes his hand. Limp, one pump. "And I hoped you'd moved on," he says to Nav.

"Sorry to disappoint, Henry. Still here and still fat." Nav gives me a look and grabs an ice cream sandwich from the table. He keeps them in an insulated lunch box that will be empty in minutes. I used to have dreams about those homemade sandwiches of his. Fresh-baked chocolate chip cookies, soft as bread against the ice cream.

"You know I take credit for your relationship, right?" Nav says. "You're my first Jehovah's Witness Recovery Group love match! Which, I believe, merits naming rights to your first-born."

Henry and I clear our throats. It's an unpleasant duet.

"But, um, we can sort out the paperwork later." Nav wipes dribbled vanilla from his shirt. "You remember Anna, Craig, Mike and Stella."

We collect waves and smiles from around the room. Some disheartened faces, others hopeful. When we stopped showing up at meetings last year they must have made up a life for us, some kind of fantasy that our return has now shattered.

"A few new faces, like Hank over there."

Hank has the body of a wrestler, the kind that breaks backs with chairs. He wears a leather jacket, with a few buckles affixed and an extra zipper that goes nowhere. The poor thing tried its best to stretch out over Hank's beastly muscles, but gave up — gathering in maxed-out creases and folds where his biceps erupt south of his shoulders.

"Now who wants to go first? How about you, Hank?"

"Sure, Nav. I'll spill my guts." Hank's voice is a shocker. High and girly. Steroidal. "But I'd rather spill hers. All over the floor."

"Now, Hank—"

"I'm sorry, Nav, but I'm pissed. Am I not allowed to be pissed?"

"Of course you are, but—"

"Because she took all of my money, this hot Witness chick. She told me Armageddon was coming. This was right around 9/11." He looks around the circle. "You get me? I mean, there were *bodies* falling out of *buildings*, *planes* falling out of, shit, what's that word she used? *Hegemonic* world order. The skies had opened and rained down, she said, the final sign before the end. And I bought it. She got me all riled up. Did I know what team I was playing for because God was coming. She even knew I was into sports and she used it, you know? Anyways, I'm still here, the world is still here, the girl is gone, and so's my money. She said she gave it to some fucking pioneers in the Middle East. I don't even know where exactly. The Pakis maybe, or Indians? Who knows. All I know is I got screwed and I gave her my permission. And now I don't even believe in God anymore. And that sucks. I mean, what's the point to all this shit?"

Henry raises his hand. "I have a question, Nav, if I may."

"Of course."

"What's the purpose of these meetings exactly?"

"Henry," I say. "Please don't—"

"I'm just asking, V." He turns to the group. "It's been a year, so I'm a bit fuzzy on the mission statement."

Nav leans forward in his chair, his portly stomach limiting his angle to roughly sixty degrees. "The purpose, Henry, as you know, is to give former Jehovah's Witnesses a safe place to share their Watchtower Bible and Tract Society experiences."

"The bad experiences, right? Like our friend Hank's?"

Hank crosses his arms. The leather moans.

"Everyone here has been negatively affected by the Watchtower," Nav says. "Including you, if you remember."

"I wouldn't go that far," Henry says.

I scan the room. Door. Window. Drain in the floor. Make note of every available emergency exit.

"Well, most people here would," Nav says. "And the only way to deal with the associated feelings is to talk them through. Because when we give shame and guilt a voice, we take away their power."

"But shame and guilt are God's punishment," says Henry. "You can't just get rid of them."

The window would be a tight squeeze and I'd get splinters in my hips. The drain isn't much of an option because I'm a solid. If worse comes to worse, I could always leap up to the ceiling, wiggle my way through the air ducts.

"And what is your shame?" Nav asks Henry.

"It's not *my* shame."

"Whose shame is it?"

"My wife's."

I decide on the door. If I move inch by inch, maybe no one will notice. I go for it, but the chair scrapes against the terrazzo and blows my cover.

Henry grips my seat. "But she won't talk about it."

"I can relate," says Stella, a secretary in a wool suit. Same suit back when I was a regular, blue herringbone coated in cat hair. "It's like how I felt after I went to see that hypnotherapist. I didn't want anyone to know. But they found out —"

"They always do," says Nav.

"— and I got shunned for it."

A collective sigh fills the room, the enervation of twenty lost souls — or of those without souls at all, or who aren't sure exactly what a soul is, if anything — combined with the overhead buzz of fluorescent lighting.

"They think Jehovah has all the answers," says Mike, stroking his well-kept beard. "Remember when the Watchtower said it had the cure to surface cancer?"

"I read about that shit," says Hank. "Skin cancer and stuff, right?"

"And later they said that vaccinations were wrong. A 'direct violation of the everlasting covenant that God made with Noah after the flood.'"

"Did you hear what they did to the kids? So they'd be allowed into school even though they didn't have their shots?" says Stella. "The parents would use acid to burn marks on their arms so it looked like they'd gotten the vaccine."

"No way."

"That's too far, even for them."

Anna, an old woman who's been fussing with Kleenex in the strap of her watch, rolls up her sleeve. "It's true. See?"

The sound of twenty plastic chairs — compressed by the weight of guilt and anguish and ice cream sandwiches — leaning forward to get a closer look.

"But the best one was in 1967, when The Watchtower banned organ transplants."

"Oh right! They called it cannibalism."

"'Jehovah God did not grant permission for humans to try to perpetuate their lives by cannibalistically taking into their bodies human flesh.'"

"And then they switched positions on that one in the 1980s."

The nearly nonexistent sound of air stirred by the shaking of heads, disbelief swirling like a spoon in an empty mug.

"The truth is ever-changing," says Henry. His forehead vein, twisty as the Mississippi, throbs. "It's like a dimmer switch, and the light of the truth gets brighter and brighter as Armageddon draws near. You all used to know that."

"Before we learned the *real* truth," Stella says.

"No," Henry says. "Before you learned what's convenient."

Nav looks to me with such disbelief that my guilt quadruples. Like it's my fault Henry is doing this. As if I recruited him, promised him seventy-two virgins in the afterlife, strapped a bomb to his back and pushed him into Room 107. I can't stop him, Nav. I mouth the words. But I'll help you pick up the pieces later.

"So you're saying you're better than us, Henry? That you don't sin?"

"We're all born imperfect, Stella," Henry says. "We all sin."

"Especially you," says Mike.

"Excuse me?" says Henry.

"You and Avery only knew each other for a few weeks before you got hitched," he says. "And you're telling me it's a quote unquote honourable marriage?"

"Not to mention, Henry, that now you're singing a new tune," Stella says.

"'Do not be yoked together with unbelievers,'" the old woman recites. "'For what do righteousness and wickedness have in common?'"

Stella turns to me. "I feel sorry for you, sweetie. Thought you married a rebel; end up with —"

"A Joho bitch."

"Hank," Nav says. "Simmer."

Henry puts his hand on my bouncing knee. "You're scaring my wife, Hank."

No, he isn't. It's Henry's touch that's making it tremble.

"Maybe we should go, Henry," I squeak.

"Yeah, go," says Mike. "In fact, why are you even here?"

"Because it's our anniversary," I say.

Hank laughs. "Happy fucking anniversary!"

"I am happy," says Henry, "because these meetings saved me."

Nav catches my eye. Whatever he expects me to do, I can't do it.

"For two years I sat here listening to you all complain about how the Watchtower did you wrong," Henry says. "But the more you whined and cried, the more convinced I became that it was your fault, and that everything our elders taught us is true. Your sadness, your guilt and loneliness, this is the price you pay when you turn away from Jehovah."

"Henry," Nav says, "you don't actually mean that, d—"

"Look around the room, Nav," Henry says. "Look at their lives. Miserable because they each went against God. This is what I don't want for me." His hand tightens around my leg. "For us."

Hank shoves his chair back like it's on fire. "I've had enough of your bullshit."

"Hank, maybe you should take a—"

"No, Nav, he needs to understand: It's insane to think there's a God who gives a flying fuck about you or me. That he's up there handing out punishments and rewards like he's what? Dealing a deck of cards? I mean, it's the craziest fucking idea there ever was!" Hank's orangey tanned face reddens. Muscles behind his forehead, eyebrows, ears—muscles I've never thought about—flex. "As if we're all actually worth anything? As if we were made and didn't just, just happen by coincidence? As if we have a *purpose*?"

"Well, Hank," Henry says. "I never said *you* have a purpose."

Hank throws his chair at the wall. It slams into a poster of graphic Lamaze positions, ricochets and hits Hank in the leg. He squeals like a little girl and limps to the door. Stella jumps up to follow him, releasing a burst of orange tabby fur into the air.

Henry wants to talk. He walks, stands, dances in front of the television in an effort to rearrange my attention, but it's pointless. I should have warned him when we met that first night: if you get between me and the TV, Henry, I cannot guarantee your safety.

"I didn't mean to upset you," he says.

"I'm trying to watch *Battlestar Galactica*."

"Yes, I can see that. I see that a lot living with you. Did you know that on average you watch television for over three hours each day? I did the math, V. By the time you turn sixty you'll have spent ten years of your life in front of the screen."

I turn up the volume. Viper pilot Kara "Starbuck" Thrace smoking a cigar and dealing cards. Her flight suit rolled down to her hips. Her tank top sweaty and soiled with spaceship grease. "*Frak*," she swears, when she loses the hand. She never loses.

"Have you ever heard of the writings of King Solomon?" Henry asks. "In them he says, and I quote, that 'the eating of too much honey is not good.'"

I walk into the kitchen and microwave a sack of popcorn.

"The same principle," he shouts, "applies to TV viewing!"

I shake fake cheese over the kernels to make them taste like something and sit down on the floor. Henry sits next to me, the warm metal bowl wedged between us. He scoops out as much popcorn as he can carry, like he's gathering provisions for a long journey. With his free hand, he changes the channel to the Weather Network. The new weatherman flashes on the screen. Poorly fitting suit, floppy brown hair, beakish nose. He's replacing Kim Tripp, a buxom, pixie-voiced blonde who must have married rich or landed a new job or was suffocated in her sleep by her breasts the size of baby heads.

"Too bad," Henry moans. "Kim's seven-day forecast was so reliable."

I grab the remote and turn up the volume to punish him for thinking about her. *"Signing off for the Weather Network, I'm Calvin Straight, giving the weather* straight *to you."* The tacky line makes me laugh so hard I choke on my popcorn. Henry thumps my back and the murderous kernel shoots Calvin Straight in the eye.

7

Henry is sleeping like a single man. I nudge him. Nothing. Cough. Nothing. Roll out of bed and hit the floor with a thud. Nothing. I don't want to wake him; I want to confirm that I can't.

I pull on my jeans, lock the door and walk across the street.

The park is outfitted with tall trees that were planted full-grown and hills that roll over top of various municipal infrastructural bulges. Subway air shafts and fibre optic cable. Dedicated benches and scattered picnic tables, baseball diamonds and free tennis courts. It's empty tonight, except for a homeless man open-mouthed, drooling. He's dressed for December in July, layers of tattered sweaters, pants and a pair of Sorel winter boots, the laces frayed like ancient rope. I approve of his fashion sense. It seems sensible to me to start with layers and then subtract. Lucky dog. When the moon comes out the park belongs to him.

It's cool at midnight without the eyes of the sun on me. And safe from the Witnesses. From my window in the mornings, I watch them approaching Frisbee and tennis players, picnickers and sun worshippers, interrupting for what trumps it all:

soul saving. Despite the polite rejections, and the fuck-offs and middle fingers, the Witnesses always come back. Every day they patrol the park searching for those vacant spirits, taking the abuse, picking up the flung magazines, praying for that one score that will secure their seats in heaven . . . If heaven's still where they go, that is. It's hard to keep up.

The homeless man is grunting like it's a language, so I move to the tennis court. Lift the latch open. Drop it closed. Safe in a cage. Tennis has always seemed like a straightforward kind of sport. A ball and something to hit it with. No itchy merino wool layers, clumpy glove warmers, laborious waxes, Kleenex stuffed in every pocket, emergency silver blanket in case you got lost in the maze of bowed trees and the endless desert of the Gatineau trails. Back in January, I looked for cross-country trails in this park, digging through bushes in search of those long smooth grooves or groomed sections flattened and clotted by machine. But there weren't any trails, not a one. No one in this city knows how to ski inside of it.

My father hated cities for this reason. He'd made the sacrifice for my mother, he informed me, to live where I was born: Ottawa, Canada's confused capital. City? Region? With a downtown you could bike through or skate around in minutes. Not like here in Toronto, where the vast grid of Harbourfront to Bloor could ruin your day if you confuse north with south, east with west. My father would have suffocated here, but he survived Ottawa. Barely. For a while. "At least it's an easy commute out to the Gatineau Hills," he used to say. All everyone likes about Ottawa is how easy it is to escape.

When we needed to stomp through the snow, my dad and I, we'd hit a park just like this one, with a tennis court just like this one. The most level site there was, perfect for practising the art and science of snow shelter construction. My father was an expert. He had to dig himself into the snow dozens of times over the course of his career just to survive the night. He learned from the Inuit on his early research trips and so used their word for the shelters instead of ours: *quinzhee*. I'd say *igloo* by accident every now and then, it was much easier to pronounce, and would get the "an igloo is the Four Seasons of the snow habitat world, Ave; the quinzhee is the Red Cross tent" speech. He'd usually follow that up with a lecture on the virtues of nature's most misunderstood insulator, as he called it. "It's not the snow you have to be afraid of, Ave. It's you. Your carbon dioxide will kill you, but snow? The snow will save you if you know how to use it." Finally, we'd get to work—our hands in the cold comfort of snow, my dad calling out instructions. "Find a spot that's just right, Ave. Make a pile three times as big as your own body. Pack it down. Firm, Ave, firm. Wait as long as you can. The cold air will harden your pile and then wait fifteen minutes more. Dig a tunnel into the snow, make sure it slopes up. You'll never have a shovel when you need it, so use your hands. Hollow out a domed cave. Sit up to measure its height. Hollow it out more and smooth the roof. Cover the ground with needles, the soft, long ones. And for the love of God, Ave, don't forget to leave a hole in the roof." I forgot. Once. It was a close call, my father told me after I regained consciousness. He told me the next winter, too, and the next and the next.

I lie down on the tennis court and feel the heat from the day trapped in the asphalt. What I want is the cool. The freezing whoosh of winter, that crispness, that metallic flavour on the tongue like blood. The soothing numbness that follows. I'm wearing my sleeping T-shirt, purple with a dinosaur declaring "I just want to hug," so my bare arms are vulnerable against the rough surface of the court. They grow raw as I move them out and up and over my head. Now the legs. Together, apart, together apart. It won't leave a snow angel's impression, but I don't care. My eyes are pointed at the sky. A slice of moon, a satellite, but little else of wonder. Skyscrapers and smog and planes. It's a working sky. No stars. I haven't seen a star since I moved here. It's easy not to think about heaven with a sky like this. It would be nice to have some faith in this moment, though, to think my father is looking down at me from up there. Or wherever. From anywhere.

"When was the last time you thought about God?"

It's dark so I can't make out the face on the other side of the fence. It's not my dead father, though, this voice—a baritone, musical with melodic ups and downs.

"Are you a Jehovah's Witness?" I ask.

"I am."

"I knew it," I say. "I can smell you guys a mile away."

His laugh is hearty and rich like a stew. "What do we smell like?"

My elbows scrape against the court. The pain helps me think. "Like ink. And second-hand clothes. And Scope."

I can make out his form more easily now; my brain is adjusting to the dark. His face is in shadow but for his tooth-paste-model teeth and the whites of his eyes, large as hard-boiled eggs. He is upside down to me, so the effect is both monstrous and gut-bustingly funny. I giggle like I'm high and I hear his jaw clench and then click when it releases. "When was the last time you thought—"

"About god. Yes, I heard you the first time," I say. "I don't think about god. At all."

"He thinks about you."

The homeless man staggers in our direction. He's choking back a can of Molson and, just for a second, I wonder if he'll share. "Crazy bitch," he barks.

The Jehovah's Witness with the voice and boiled-egg eyes keeps talking, unconcerned that we now have an audience. "But you used to think about God," he says. "Didn't you? Years ago?"

"I'm sorry," I say, "but what you're selling — I'm not interested."

"Perhaps you should be," he says. "Perhaps, Avery, you should be very interested." His voice walks off with him into the trees, leaving me with the starless night, invisible snow angels and a crucial new worry — my name breaking through the lips of a stranger.

8

I'm mostly confident about the status of heaven with today's Witnesses: less so about hell. Last I heard, instead of fire and brimstone, all a fallen Witness is left with is nothingness, a friendless grave, undiluted deadness, the consequence for sin. That kind of hell is what I feel as I look out the window and see Henry in front of the Kingdom Hall. He's wearing that awful pinstriped suit from Sears, the one with narrow lapels and pinstripes. It doesn't fit him, it's too short, but he probably thinks he looks handsome, edgy. A fashion model making a winking statement about conformity. Or masculinity. Or the futility of nine to five.

Henry is a tall man, 6'3" at least. It's the oddest thing because I swear a year ago he was 6'1". It's as though he's grown since we got married because there he was, twenty-four hours ago, ducking under the shower curtain rod, bent so his head wouldn't hit when he never had to be bent before. He's been ducking everywhere lately—into the subway, into the elevator, into the closet—and his feet hang over the bed as though he's some giant that no mattress can accommodate. Yes, it is settled: either Henry is growing or all matter is shrinking, including me. He's six years older than me, but his face is lineless, his white skin even-toned; it's the face of a man dedicated to indoor pursuits. He shaves Monday and Thursday and still looks fresh and pore-less in between. He has the features of an aristocrat, defined cheekbones, fragile nose, eyebrows like architectural flourishes instead of overhanging shelters for his eyes, which are almond in shape and navy in colour. He wears glasses, oversized plastic frames, and he is wiry and thin, like those teenage boys whose metabolisms move so fast their mothers can barely keep up with the groceries. His hair is helmet-like. It's forever short because he has standing appointments with his barber, every two weeks. I wish he'd let it grow, just a few inches so some curls would peek from behind his ears, so there'd be trace evidence of a hat when a hat is removed. All these unusual ingredients make him impossi-ble to miss. Does he think I wouldn't notice him standing across the street? That I wouldn't weigh all the unbearable accom-panying choices? I turn away, but not before a janitor unlocks the doors and Henry slips into the hall and away from me.

Henry is gone by the time I reach the Kingdom Hall, so the only wave I receive is my stomach, rocking and spasming in ways I know too well. The rest of my body has always been a vulnerable ship in the sea of my gut, subject to its pitching and tossing, its accompanying high winds, its whitecaps brimming with sharks. Are the spasms showing through my shirt? I look at myself in the mirrored glass of the hall but my abdomen is still as a pond. Whatever's going on is a secret in there.

I step into the hall. The entryway is small and unassuming: a home base for the steps I walk up. The spasms increase when I reach the third floor, so I press my hand against my abdomen like a pregnant woman. I peer through the door and into a salmon-rose room, large windows, plywood panelling, waist-high chair rail, buzzing fluorescent lighting, dusty artificial plants, grey industrial carpeting. The Witnesses are of all sizes and ages, white people far outnumbered. The men all impeccably dressed in suits or khakis and crisp pastel shirts; the women ambitiously and outdatedly styled in chunky two-inch heels, silk blends, even a few shoulder pads. There are sixty or so of them, and they fill the rows of seating that face a stubby stage. I can't see Henry, but I hear his voice. His quietly brash tongue, the accent favoured by Alanis Morissette. All hard *r*s, soft vowels, milk pronounced *melk*.

I'm ready to confront him, I tell myself. I'm ready. I'm not ready. Will never be. I run to the bathroom, lock myself in a stall, thighs on the enamel, ass hanging over the gaping, watery hole. The back of the door offers me its reckless perspective on life.

"Love = Jehovah."
"Carbon-dating lies! The dinosaurs roamed the earth with man!"
"Let wives be in subjection to their husbands as to the Lord. Eph. 5:22"

I choose the empty space next to the hook and pull a pen from my purse.

Henry + Avery = 4ever.

I'm calm now. I unlock the door and walk over to the sink. My phone rings. "Henry?"

"You have a call from a federal prison from —"

"Talk to me, kid!"

I smell Bryan's cigarettes through my phone, whiskey, coffee, stomach acid.

"Press one to accept the call."

I pull my face away. My phone is greasy. Because I am. *I am filthy and nasty and dirty and soiled and disgusting.*

"Are you still there?" the robot asks.

I drop the phone to the counter and run the tap. Squeeze out a handful of soap. Lather, spread the soap like night cream, and splash the water against my greasy filthy dirty face. It makes contact and expands into ice across my skin. An unmovable, numb mask.

"Are you still there?"

I jerk to the mirror. I'm translucent and nightmarish, my mouth a frozen lake. I can't breathe. My fingers tap madly, scratch and claw, but the ice doesn't crack. A tool, I need a tool. Toilet, door, paper towel, sink. No no no no. Fist.

I punch myself in the face.

"—still there?"

Again, again, again.

9

I met Gloria a dozen years ago, at my father's funeral. She was the sweet thing clinging onto my uncle's arm. Blonde curls stacked like vanilla cookies. Cerise CoverGirl lips. Caramel tan. Teeth white as whipped cream. Bubblegum-pink sports coat with shoulder pads thick as pound cake slices. Compared to the vanilla civil servants I was acclimatized to, Gloria was a strawberry sundae.

It's Gloria's bungalow I'm slouching in front of this morning, my head heavy, swollen from yesterday's punches, my back still aching. Her house looks the same, only tired. Chipped red brick, worn and weathered shingles. I pull on a rotting shutter hanging from the window like a rag doll. Shutters that don't shut. Like makeup for a house; that's how Gloria described them to me when she had them installed. A precious Saturday morning spoiled by drilling. A handy neighbour with a tool belt and sweat stains on his jeans. Gloria in a short skirt carrying lemonade out to the stoop.

I ring Gloria's doorbell, her shutter against my hip like a bag of groceries.

"He's not here!" Gloria yells. She must be pressed against the door. "And I don't have your goddamn money!"

"Gloria," I say. "It's Avery."

The door opens an inch. A wide, bloodshot eye fills the crack.

She closes the door. I can hear her fumbling with the chain before she swings the door open. "What on God's green earth happened to your face?"

"It's nothing," I say.

"Nothing? You look like Rocky Raccoon!"

"You're exaggerating. It's hardly noticeable with all this makeup."

"Sweetie, I can see a black eye under twenty layers of concealer. I'm like *The Princess and the Pea* that way."

"What a gift."

"Did you get mugged?"

I nod and it's enough. Gloria hugs me — she still smells like Elizabeth Taylor — and twirls me inside. "Too many fatherless black boys with nothing useful to do," she mutters.

Gloria is dolled up for a party, albeit one that happened yesterday. She's wearing a von Furstenberg knockoff, a wrap dress wrinkled and stained with toothpaste or frosting or something else. Her makeup isn't fresh. Liner gathers in all four corners of her eyes and the powder caking her forehead is missing entirely from her nose and cheeks. Her face still manages to be beautiful, though, despite it all. Young even, with skin as smooth as a wave-worn stone. She doesn't look like a sixty-year-old who spends her weekends in a tanning booth.

"Is this for me?" She snatches the shutter from my hands, and a sliver of wood stabs into her palm. Pulls it out with her red press-on claws.

We stand on the cracked Spanish tiles in the hallway. Which room do we move to? Option one: my uncle Bryan's living room. A black leather recliner facing a twenty-seven-inch Sony Trinitron. Eggshell walls. Drawn crooked curtains. Gloria picks up her drink—whiskey and water and lime—that's been sweating without her. She turns right and sashays into option two: her living room. The ice clinks like bells against her glass. "Let's chat in here," Gloria gestures. "It's so much cozier."

The showpiece of Gloria's living room is a white leather sofa accessorized by red suede pillows. Her favourite spot is clearly demarcated: two rounded dents in the cushion and tobacco stains on the ceiling. Vases and ashtrays carved of clear Lucite give the effect of an enchanted room full of disgusting, levitating things: dead roses and fetid water, cigarette butts and old gum. A red chaise shaped like a pair of lips is set by the window and around it hang velvet paintings of Paris and New York. The space feels smaller than I remember, the air denser with seven years of smoke and cooking odours. But it still looks the same. A set for the kind of porn that women like.

Gloria drops the shutter next to her tube television. Flecks of grey paint crumble onto the white shag. "How does the house look to you? Holding up pretty good, right? Of course it is."

I bang my shin on her Lucite coffee table. The howling sting cancels out the pain from my back and face.

"There are too many Chinese in the area these days," Gloria says. "But at least my walls are thick. Nothing like my old place in Manhattan." She smooths her hair, translucent blonde and dangerously over-straightened. Several strands perk up, as though rubbed by a balloon. "That was a lifetime ago, of course, before I moved here with Bryan. I mean, how coo-coo in love was I? Leaving the centre of the universe for Etobicoke? He was worth it though. My God, hun, he was so handsome." She shoves a Lucite-framed photograph in my face. My uncle, shirtless on Miami Beach, sunburnt like a man who favours tank tops. He's pointing to the sea, flexing muscles he doesn't have.

I push the frame away and Gloria takes it back, gently. Like it's a baby. Or a bomb. "And those people at the Watchtower," she says, "they loved him so much. One of the best pioneers they'd ever seen! Brought in more new congregants than any other in his district, they said. No wonder they recruited him to Brooklyn for that big job!"

"He was a correspondence clerk," I say.

She flips her hair. It's so damaged it hangs in the air for seconds longer than healthy hair would and makes a crunching sound when it finally settles. "It was an important role," she says, "never mind the title."

"He opened envelopes and forwarded the letters—"

"All that concentrating and reading—"

"—and usually to the wrong department."

"Of course, the reading was a real problem in the end," she says. "Poor Bryan's dyslexia. Turned his letters upside down and tangled his numbers into spider legs."

"Maybe if the Watchtower bothered to look beyond his 'spiritual qualifications' they would have—"

Gloria slams the photograph down on the coffee table. "And then those bitches he worked with," she spits. "Said they were tired of covering up his mistakes. Oh please! They were in love with Bryan, but he wanted nothing to do with them. So they went after him!"

I turn to her. "Gloria, he was stealing remittances from the Watchtower."

"They never proved that!" she shouts. "But those jealous hags got the elders talking, didn't they? All day long they'd swoop around Bryan's desk, waiting for him to misfile that one piece of paper so they'd have an excuse to fire him. Is that what good Christians do?"

"I heard my mother on the phone and—"

"But even if he did steal," Gloria whispers, "he was only taking what he was owed. The Watchtower paid him a measly twenty dollars a day. And made him live in some cramped town-house in Flatbush. *Flatbush?* He shared that hovel with fourteen other Witnesses. Can you believe it? A man of Bryan's potential?" She picks up the photograph and rests it in her lap. Strokes it like a kitten. "He stayed loyal to them, even though they turned against him. But all that stress, hun, it does things. There's only so much a person can take before—"

I lean in. "Before what?"

Gloria takes another drink and inches toward me. Her breath is flammable. "Before one day," she sighs, "when you're out pioneering in one of those terrible New York neighbourhoods you see on television, the kind with puddles full of trash and steam coming at you from all angles. And you knock on the door of a drug dealer. But not just any drug dealer, a very bad person—"

"Bryan was the very bad person."

Gloria doesn't react to me. She smiles and her eyes sparkle. She's back in Manhattan, 1980-something, and drifting down the

Hudson like a swan. "I didn't really mind when Bryan was just selling the drugs. He bought Italian suits, a co-op on West 63rd —"

"He bought you."

"— but then, of course, Bryan started *taking* the drugs, too." Gloria's eyes mist over. She lifts the skirt of her faux–von Furstenberg, tents her finger with the fabric and dabs away a tear, taking the angles necessary to protect the structural integrity of her eyeliner. "Sorry, hun," she says, sniffling. "Where was I?"

"West 63rd."

"Right!" Gloria sucks back her drink. She tongues the lime pulp between her teeth. "Our building in Manhattan was a looker. Elegant. But the noise through the walls! We lived next door to the cousin of the founder of Miramax, did I tell you? Lovely woman. But I could hear everything she did. I mean, can you imagine? Paying $985,000 for a condo and living next door to a zillionaire and we could hear each other flossing?"

My shin is throbbing so I dig my fingers into Gloria's never-empty ice bucket and rake some out. I drop the cubes into a Lucite vase and press it against my leg.

"Say my son comes over to visit. Sam. You remember Sam. Here he is, a man who makes forty dollars an hour and I'm going to tell him to keep the TV down because the lady next door will have a conniption? Can you imagine? I mean, goodness. He's a certified forklift driver who makes fifty dollars an hour! Anyways, you look good, Avery. Slim. I used to be slim." She gestures to a cluster of photos. "I've put on some weight over the years. I think it's because he's such a nice guy, your uncle. I don't have to worry with him, you know, if I have an extra slice of pizza or a chocolate bar. I was always skinny with the other ones. I know you two had your issues, but he did his best with you. What with that awful misunderstanding in Brooklyn and the drugs. Then your mother running off like she did, and that mess with your father. Us having to take you in and —"

I'll die here waiting for her to shut up. "Bryan's been calling me," I say.

She scratches an itch on her chest and the wrinkles of her décolletage shift. Aha! She's old there! I wonder where else the years have caught up with her. Aged organs, rusty blood, retired hope?

"Let's catch up a bit first, okay?" She lights a cigarette, blows the smoke out through her nose, mouth, ears, eyes, fingertips. "I mean, hun, I haven't seen you in what? Five, six years?"

"Seven."

"Why straight to business?"

She gestures to her lip-shaped chaise, moving her arm like the showcase models from her favourite game show. I sit in it, my spine conforming to fit the kiss. Gloria offers a chalky wintergreen mint from a Lucite candy dish. I chew, sparks firing off inside the blackness of my mouth.

"Now for my news." Gloria puts out her cigarette, the filter sticking up from the ashes like a tombstone. "Your uncle upgraded my ring!" Gloria forces her finger into my face. Diamonds set in platinum and framed by rubies. The design is kitschy, the gems set to resemble insects kissing. "Bees," she says. "They're a symbol of royalty."

My own wedding ring — white gold, seventy-five dollars — is hidden in my pocket because I didn't want to hear it from Gloria, whatever *it* would turn out to be: concern, judgment, joy. I chew, splitting the wintergreen mint in half, or maybe my teeth.

"I need you to tell Bryan to stop calling me."

She gives me a scathing look, and pulls her hand away. "He wants to see you," she says, petting the bees as though it's their feelings I've hurt. "He wants to make amends."

I chew as hard as I can. Grind and pulverize. My whole mouth bursts into electric blue flames.

10

I have a deadline. I'm trying to work. Twenty bios to fact-check and proofread by the week's end or my boss's production schedule will be garbage. It's a lot of pressure. And my face is throbbing with bruises. A bag of frozen peas presses against my right eye, so I'm relying on my left. It's making me dizzy to look at the world like this, and the nausea it brings on makes me resent

BERGDOFF, ALEXANDRA A.
GENERAL COUNSEL, MADOXX CHEMICAL

Ms. Bergdoff received her Masters in Physics
from Yale (1990) and her law degree from
Osgoode Hall Law School (1993). She brag brag
bragged at the firm of Wanker, Penis and Jerkoff.
Ms. Bergdoff's practice involves strategic labour
relations, trademarks, mergers and acquisitions,
tits and ass, and general corporate matters for
Madoxx Chemical.

Alexandra A. Bergdoff buys three editions of the *Leading Corporate Counsel Yearbook* each year. That's $1200. My boss doesn't know why she buys three, and he doesn't care, as long as she keeps paying for his Porsche's winter tires. But I know why. The first copy is for Alexandra; she keeps that one on her shelf. The second copy is for her father, an illiterate farmer in Guelph, Ontario. She mails the yearbook to him in a bubble envelope. He opens it on his lunch break, glances at it once, at her photo and the hieroglyphics on the page, and throws it on the woodpile. The envelope he keeps. The third copy is for Craig Sanders, a man Alexandra stalked for weeks and sent vulgar emails to from her Madoxx Chemical Blackberry. She cuts her bio out of the yearbook using scalloped scissors from Crafters Superstore. She paints a border around her photo with Chanel Rouge Coco lipstick and highlights her most impressive accomplishments, the ones that enable her to pay for luxury goods and services. She wants Craig to know exactly what he's missing.

Henry hates that this is my job, which is ironic because a year ago he not only got it for me, he taught me how to do it. He showed me which mistakes to hunt for. Oxford commas, omitted periods, glitches in typographical space/time called "leading." He told me about the peace that came from organizing the universe within a paragraph, that you could combat chaos in a column, in a spread, on a page, and that he found true purpose in pointing out the mistakes of others, celebrating them with swoops and checks from his inky red pen. He encouraged me to quit my assistant manager's job at Staples and apply at Smith-Coxwell through his connection. I got an interview. Wore heels that Henry paid for and eyeliner and a yellow blouse with ruffles down the centre that I could only wear once because it refused to iron. The Smith-Coxwell human resources woman gave me a piece of paper to proofread and then left the room. I pulled out Henry's red pen and swooped and checked my way into a more respectable workforce and that much further into Henry's heart. These days though, Henry says my job is a stage for false pride. He wants me to quit, says that his copy editor job at the *Toronto Star* is enough. But it won't always be. I can't believe they haven't fired him yet. He comes home angry almost every night. Like tonight.

"They're supposed to report the news," he yells. "But it's all gotten so political. I can't be part of—"

He's thinking like a Jehovah's Witness again.

He wasn't like this when I met him. The Watchtower was on his shitlist, just like it was on mine. We had wounds in common and we understood each other. We dated for a month. Warm and loving Henry. We got married fast and I moved in. That's when everything changed. He is cold and distant now. That's okay. So am I. And there's no evidence to suggest that I can do any better.

Henry looks at my desk. "Your stuff is everywhere."

"I'm sorry," I say. "But I have to work here."

"It's a mess. A huge, crazy mess!"

I turn around and face it, try to see things from his point of view. His living room has indeed been taken over by sheets of white paper. Like a flock of feeding gulls.

"But at least it's just paper," I say.

"It not, though, V. It's also all the negative workplace energy."

"You're the one who wanted a desk without drawers," I say.

"You want drawers?"

Henry storms into the bedroom. There's a lot of rustling and muttering. He hurries back, a drawer from my dresser under his arm, resting on his hip. He dumps my underwear out on the floor and drops the drawer on his foot. He screams, hops around like a rabbit that's been shot.

I toss him my bag of frozen peas. "Would you please calm down?" I say.

Our downstairs neighbour, the one we call Fish Sticks, knocks against the ceiling.

"Shoot." Henry presses the peas against his foot. "Sorry, Fish Sticks!"

"Just breathe," I say. "Calming breaths."

Henry doesn't breathe. He winces. "This isn't going the way I planned."

"You had a bad day at the newspaper," I say, stepping through all my stuff to get to him. "Is that what this is about?"

"Work is not the problem. It's us."

I palpitate his hand like a heart.

"We're adjusting to marriage," I whisper. "It's normal."

He lets go of my hand. "It's been a year, V. This isn't normal."

"It'll happen soon," I say, and I burrow into him like a baby animal. "See? I'm getting better."

"Dependent and needy affection is not sex," Henry says.

"Don't be weird," I say.

"And by *weird* you mean don't say the word *sex*, let alone have it?"

"I mean, Don't. Be. Weird."

Henry detaches me from his body. "I've been lying to you."

"No, you haven't." I reach for him, but he limps to the closet.

"I have, V, and you need to face it."

He reaches into his bag and presents me with what he's been carrying around. A magazine. *Awake!* A young, modestly dressed couple smile from the cover. They're cooking a roast together, wildly enthusiastic about the rigours of domestic life. I flip through. The paper quality is, at best, one rung above newspaper. The ink leeches onto my fingers. "I'm with the Watchtower again," he tells me. "I'm one of Jehovah's Witnesses."

I look down at my feet. They're sweaty and far away. They leave outlines shaped like the Great Lakes on the floor.

"Did you hear me, V?" He grips my shoulders, shakes me gently like he's trying to wake me. But I don't want to wake up. I don't want to don't want to don't—

"Did. You. Hear—"

"Of course I heard you," I snap.

"And?"

"You're trying to hurt me," I say. "Because I'm a failure as a wife."

"No, V. That's not it."

"Then why?" I cry. "You got out. You were moving on."

Henry holds me, finally, *he* holds *me*. And I'm crushed because all I can do is wish for the strength to push him away.

"I tried life without Jehovah," he says. "I tried the recovery group, and I met you and—"

"We met by the lava flow, six thousand years ago," I say. "A pterodactyl had just stolen your hat—"

"That's a stupid game, V," he shouts. "It's not real." He looms over me. He's so tall he has his own gravitational pull. It's pushing me down but I fight it.

"Okay, okay," I tell him, standing as vertically as I can. "We met at the Jehovah's Witness Recovery Group. We fell in love and a month later we got married and—"

"I don't want to talk about the past."

"You promised, Henry. 'I swear I'll never go back to the Witnesses.' You said that."

"I want to look forward to the future." He gestures to *Awake!*

I turn to the middle pages, to the feature story. *Dinosaurs Killed by Flood at Time of Noah's Ark.* It's the tabloid stuff Henry was raised on. Me too, for a time, before my father's ideas took over. I roll the magazine into a hollow tube and pass it back to him, like a relay runner to a teammate. "You don't actually believe this bullshit, do you?"

He takes it, smoothing out a wrinkle I'd made. "Don't be so closed-minded, V."

I reach for Henry with my inky fingers. I hold him and I mark him. He is mine.

"Hey," he says, "what happened to your eye?"

He is still mine.

11

Henry tells me I have to wear a skirt or a dress. Pants are not allowed for women at the hall.

"Yeah, I know," I tell him.

I pull out my mother's Prada dress. The colour is a stand-out because no one thinks in plum anymore. It isn't just the outside of the garment that holds the rich colour of fruit; the lining of the dress is plum, too, only as it is underneath the peel. That opulent inside flesh, orange like the sun in my dreams, so orange it straddles other colours, too: red, yellow, blue. When I wear that dress I am wrapped in fruit, wrapped in my mother, the sweetness cancelling out her sour. The hem hangs to the knee and its form-fitting skirt hugs my hips like an inverted tulip. It's sleeveless but in a way that covers up that skin in the armpit that always bulges out and it has a low-cut neckline that my breasts rise above. The fabric is of the highest quality, a wool-jersey combination stitched by Milanese hands.

I feel beautiful in this dress.

"Here," says Henry. He hands me a cardigan. Buttons it up to my neck.

The statistics are not good. One hundred and seven cars slam into my body as we cross the street. I am thrown 450 vertical feet and break into thirty-four pieces. It makes for quite a sight. Six thousand litres of my blood streaming down the street and onto the patio at Burger Shack. The owner is clever, though. "Free ketchup!" he yells, and little Suzy and Billy's futures are safe once more. Yet, somehow, Henry gathers me together, juggles me up the stairs and into the Kingdom Hall. The salmon-rose room. I'm smelling it. Scope. The collective washed breath of 100+ Witnesses. He introduces me to none of them because we've just made it in on time. Henry had to sew my limbs back on. I pick at the sloppy stitches on my forearm. Henry has no gift for fine needlework.

We sit down at the back and my spine curves in the plastic chair. It straightens like a rod, however, when a man drifts onto the stage. There is something about him, a magnetism that hasn't been exuded since Tom Cruise in *Top Gun*. The man is short, his chest wide and open, his face boyishly smooth, though he's definitely in his thirties. A fascinating limp in his right leg. Perfect white teeth that shine under the stage lights. Eyes so large he could never need glasses. He is black, which adds to his appeal because black is different for this city, rare, despite our reputation for multiculturalism.

"What is evil?" the man says into the microphone. His voice, I know it. It's a song: the voice from the park. He looks different in the light and right-side up. "Men have struggled with this question for centuries, have gone to great lengths to attempt to control it: burning so-called witches, bringing world leaders before firing squads, imprisoning spies and self-professed freedom fighters. But evil is not so complicated. Evil is—"

Anything that goes against the Word of Jehovah. I know that line well. I've been rapt before evil before, in a different place that was exactly the same, a lifetime ago when I didn't know better. The words absorbed into the sponginess of a young brain. I know what comes next too. He'll call out to us, his brothers and sisters, telling us that we come face to face with evil every day of our lives. For evil is not only terrorism, occultism and the abuse of power! Evil is present in the everyday life of the non-believer! Gluttony, obscenity, greed, lying, drunkenness, apostasy! And it is the non-believers who shall feel the wrath of God!

The hall is electric with the man's oration. A hurricane could strike out there in the city, high winds and hail buckling power lines and grids. Hundreds of thousands trapped in the heat and the subways and the elevators. Trapped in the unknowable dark. Desperate citizens wondering *what if. What if it stays this way forever? What if the power never returns? Will I have to eat my neighbour? Will I have to eat him* raw? But in here, in this salmon-rose room on the third floor, the lights will stay on, powered by the force of this man's will.

"When Jesus spoke about the end of the world, he said nation shall rise against nation and kingdom against kingdom. He foretold disasters: earthquakes, pestilences, food shortages."

The Witnesses clean eyeglasses, cross legs, yawn — so comfortable with these nightmare scenarios. I put myself in their skulls and I see the broken world, laid out before me like a map on fire. The room is warming, my fear driving the thermostat. It's oppressive. I'll burst into flames if I don't do something! If I don't rush the stage and tackle the man and break the spell! But I don't have to because the man lifts me from it. He tells me not to worry, and so I don't.

"Jehovah has also described a future free from suffering and evil," he says. "A time when the ungodly, worldly men and women, shall be destroyed and the earth shall be filled with people who love Jehovah — His Witnesses. It is on that great and glorious day, brothers and sisters, that we, the righteous, shall inherit the earth."

The sermon is over. The man on stage turns off the microphone. It powers down with a crackle and the hum of its electricity I didn't notice until now is silenced. It's too quiet without that hum. Even with the shuffling of asses in seats and the blowing of noses and the rifling through the pages of those limp *Awake!* magazines, there is no sound now except the screaming of my past back into the present. It doesn't belong. I don't belong.

I hustle for the door.

So does the man from the stage. He catches up, reaches for my hand and shakes it with a startling strength — a power surge; my hair stands on end.

"Avery." My name, when he says it this time, has a weight to it like food: a flavour I can't label.

"How do you know my name?"

"I know it because I know your husband, Henry. He's been coming to this hall since we were both young boys. Barring the last few years, of course."

"But now he's back. He's one of you again."

"Yes," he says. "He's fully committing himself."

"That's a good choice of words."

The man laughs. "Henry told me you had a dark sense of humour."

Where is Henry? Why is he leaving me alone with this voice, this face, this suit?

"Henry's over there," he says, pointing.

With this mind reader?

Henry is standing at the back of the room with a woman. She is Chinese, I figure, although I am terrible at making those kinds of assessments. Her hair is shiny and straight and black, the hair of my dreams, all of it held together by a striking red bow. She smiles at Henry, but her skin barely moves. She is glass, I decide. A porcelain statue that grandmothers collect on mantles.

"Her name is Cecily," the man tells me. "In case you're wondering."

Her face is so ghostly white it's hard to get a solid visual grip on her features.

"And my name is Akono," he adds. "In case Henry didn't mention me."

I release my gaze from Cecily. "Henry didn't mention anything."

Akono smiles wide. His teeth look prehistoric reptilian, flat and blunt like a plant-eater's. "Henry didn't mention any of this?" he says. "Or you didn't want to hear?"

I shift where I stand. As though my posture is what's making me uncomfortable.

"You can relax, Avery. This is a safe place." Akono whispers into my ear, shielding the words from others with a carefully cupped hand. "Things have changed since your unfortunate situation."

I want to demand clarification, context—just what do you think you know?—but Henry is saying something to Cecily, and it must have been funny because she laughs. It's a throaty laugh, much deeper than I hoped it would be. He may as well have laid her down on a stack of *Awake!* and fucked her because Henry's jokes are only for me. No one else sees that side of him. No one else knows what he was like before we married and the Watchtower slithered back inside of him like a snake. When I'd open the fridge and the light shone on him and he dirty danced and yelled "Spotlight!" When he unwrapped his birthday present, the first one he'd received in his thirty-one years of life, and he cried with laughter. It was a yoga mat—the runway to Satan. When we stood on the balcony at 2:00 a.m., drunk on wine and each other, and yelled across the street at the Kingdom Hall, yelled everything he'd do that they told him he couldn't. *I'm gonna go to Vegas and gamble! I'm gonna join the Boy Scouts! I'm gonna believe in ghosts and psychics and ESP! I'm gonna get a nipple ring! I'm gonna get a tattoo of a heart with this woman's name in the middle! I'm gonna marry this woman! Will you, V? Will you marry me?*

So when Henry says something again and Cecily laughs, again, I reach my arm into the empty space between us, make my hand into the shape of a gun, and fire.

12

For the record, I know how guns work. My dad was a hunter and a scientist — a wild man with a PhD. Before my mother and I came along he shot what he ate. He didn't enjoy killing; what he enjoyed was having the *need* to kill. To be so far removed from "civilization" he could only rely on his gun and the animals and the snow that revealed their tracks.

My father was a snow acoustic researcher and his work brought him to some of the coldest places in the world: the Yukon, Iqaluit, Greenland, even the Antarctic. Ottawa has brutal winters with snowdrifts as high as front doors and the kind of wet cold that takes you by the bones and shakes you, but it wasn't enough for him. He needed the Arctic lichen beneath his feet, the pine air of the Kootenays in his lungs, the crackling of Iceland's glaciers in his ears. What he got instead were highways crowded with public servants, carpal tunnel syndrome, and a collection of burdens: my mother, marriage and me. It wasn't easy to find steady, family-friendly work in snow if you weren't investigating its disappearance. So when the federal government made him an offer, a desk job in Ottawa, my dad had to take it. Few details about the role were offered up front. It wasn't until he walked into his meeting at Major-General George R. Pearkes Building, an imposing tower that faced a shopping mall and a busy bus route, that he realized his acoustic research had military applications. His expertise was highly sought after, apparently, by a government looking to stake its claim on the disputed territories in the Arctic. They wanted to use my father's research to build a sensor system: something sensitive enough, one general told him, to tell the difference between a Russian light-armoured T-90 four-wheeler and a seal hunter's snowmobile.

I didn't know my father before Ottawa, of course, before the military's money and his love for my mother formed him into the person he never wanted to be. But I could see glimpses of his true self when we went out into the snow together. His favourite part was the quiet, which, he insisted, was much more complicated than it seemed. We used to stand in the middle of the cross-country trails in the Gatineau Hills, sliding back and forth on our freshly waxed skis, listening to the overwhelming silence of the white world around us. "It's the increased pressure," he'd whisper, "sound waves pushing air through the pores in the snow." When the air comes back up eventually, energy has been lost and so you're left with this wonderful quiet. "This peace." Then his smile would fade, his awe along with it, and he'd busy his hands with the zipper on his jacket or the snow on his sleeves. "Pressure changes things."

His coat was a shade of green that he mentioned on numerous occasions. Hunter. I disagreed. Hunter was a classification that did not do it justice. The actual colour had a brightness, a shiny fluorescence that dulled in the real world, but I could see it. If you'd stapled lime peels to the walls, turned off the light and stood back to admire your work, that was the colour of his coat: lime with the lights off. When I was small, I used to sneak the coat from the closet and crawl inside. The hood made me feel like Darth Vader. I would pull it over my head and breathe in deep and loud, as powerful as the kind of person who could destroy whole planets. As long as I was in my dad's lime-with-the-lights-off coat, I was waterproof, windproof yet breathable, infallibly protected from the elements.

The coat was Gore-Tex, the highest performance textile of its kind. My father would often eulogize its merits: an elasticized nylon snowskirt, a drawcord waist, a storm flap over the front zipper, four fleece-lined upper and lower pockets. The guts of the coat were down, a particular kind known as eiderdown, which I'm surprised I could tolerate because I'm allergic to the stuff inside of other stuff. The café au lait–coloured feathers, hundreds of thousands of them, came from a protected migratory sea duck called the common eider, *Somateria mollissima*. Because they cling to themselves and are collected by hand from the nests instead of plucked out of the bird, eiderdown feathers are considered the Cadillac of insulators was one fact my father told me. (The birds eat mussels whole then shit out the shells was another.) There was a problem with the feathers, however: they often burrowed their way out of the Gore-Tex, sharp quills piercing the textile that not even the cold of a Canadian winter could puncture. The feathers always seemed to end up on my body after I'd played dress-up. I'd have flung the coat off hours before, yet there they would be, small and brown and light as air, resting on my shoulders — always my shoulders, the mounds or the blades.

My father tried to figure it out, what the coat company called a phenomenon. *It is normal for the sharp quills to poke holes in the fabric, particularly in newer products, when the down has not yet settled.* Their letters, responses to his own, advised massaging the fabric where the down stabbed through and taking a hairdryer to the area to strengthen the seal, but nothing worked.

The exodus went on for years. It drove my father crazy. "I'll end up with an empty shell of a coat!" he'd declare. But I didn't mind. The feathers kept me warm whether they were inside or out. When I told this to my dad, he laughed and mussed my hair and said, "Ave, you're a heck of a kid." I wanted him to think of me like that forever, so I didn't tell him I'd been collecting the feathers in secret, saving them up. I'd lock the bathroom door and stick them into my skin one at a time, a dozen on each shoulder, where I thought my wings should go.

13

Star Trek keeps me company while I clean the damn rug. The faces on the screen are confused, though. Instead of Kirk and Spock, there are Henry and me. We're astronauts on a mission to Mars, passing the years in a glorious montage: eating space ice cream, writing in pencil, waking to phone call serenades from Beyoncé. Making love is easier here because Henry doesn't believe in god anymore. We're up in the sky where heaven should be, but it isn't.

The ship lands on the red planet with a thud and Henry exits first so he can take the credit. We busy ourselves with rock collecting until a slurping sound NASA can't compute is all we can think about. We turn around and it's Akono, only he's an orange alien, coated in wet, thick skin. *He's probably poisonous,* I say to Henry through my helmet communicator. *Stay away.* He leaves a trail of slime that Henry's compelled to clean up. Cecily shoots by. Silver and sleek, she's a bullet of a creature, pure energy, and she zips around the planet like she owns the place. Henry is fascinated, says he wants to get a better look for the sake of science. He pulls away from me and reaches for the lock on his gold-tinted helmet. I scream and run, but my legs are heavy and slow on this planet. I'm too late. Henry's suffocated. A pile of rusty red dust his grave.

I'm crawling around the damn swirls and circles with duct tape stuck to my hand like a ping-pong paddle when Henry walks into the apartment. He'd warned me not to buy this rug, said that the low-grade fibres would make cleaning impossible, that hair and fuzz and dust would stick relentlessly. He was right, of course, and also immune to the tug of impulse shopping. I love that about him, revere it, because I cannot be stopped from plucking Swedish gum, chocolate and sometimes floor coverings from bins near the checkout at Ikea. So here I am, on my knees with a need to prove him wrong. Hopeless, of course. No matter how frequently or ferociously the rug is vacuumed, hair clings. The best I can do is rip the navy and beige surface bald like a bikini waxer.

Henry takes the tape from my hand, pulling it off like a glove. "I've decided to get baptized again," he says. "As a symbol of my recommitment."

I rip the tape out of his hands, our fingers sticking for a moment.

"You in there, V? You listening?"

"I am," I say. "I just prefer the sound of tape pulling lint and dirt and dust and hair out of the carpet."

Rip. Rip. Rip.

"I'd like you to come with me to the ceremony."

Rip.

"It would mean a lot."

Rip.

"To have your support."

Rip.

"Avery?"

I shouldn't be on my knees. I should be hanging over Henry's head like a cloud heavy with rain and lightning. "And what about me?" I cry. "Do *I* not get *your* support?"

"Of course you do, V." He plants a meek kiss on my forehead. Barely wet. "I'm your husband; I'm always here for you."

"You're *never* here," I moan.

"I'll be here more once you support me on this."

"On the Witnesses?"

He nods. "I won't have to hide anything from you."

The tape wads into a ball as I pull it from my hand. I lob it across the room and it hits the window and sticks. It leaves a gummy mark I'll never remove. "Do you know how many times I've tried to support you, Henry? Tried to acclimatize to this fucking church being in our fucking lives again?"

"Swearing? Really?"

"I couldn't even walk through the doors," I say.

"But you did walk through," he says. "With me by your side, you did."

I wrap fresh tape onto my hand like a boxer, around and around and around. I sever the connection to the roll with my teeth, the act and the sound of it both so primal, and turn my back on Henry. *Rip. Rip. Rip.* Henry stands on the carpet, his feet taking up just enough room to be in my way. It's all right, though. I can work around him. *Rip.*

"Please give this, give me, a chance," he says.

There is so much hair, matted clumps of it orbiting around more hair still. The dust is mixed in and makes my planets of hair look grey. What I see is myself, matted onto that carpet, grey and alone in space.

14

My head is in the toilet, so far down into the bowl that I might as well crawl in. Nothing is coming out of me though everything wants to. My lunch is rude and ungrateful for its accommodations, knocking on my stomach *Hello? Hello?* and begging *Please let me out?* I don't know what's stopping me. One more thing I can't afford to lose? Mine is not a good stomach, even under the best circumstances. It swells and nauseates easily: after exercise, after fried foods and dairy, after extreme bouts of spiritual and marital stress. I'd seen a gastroenterologist about it once, after everything that happened to my father. I had all the tests, the ones on the outside and the ones on the inside. They came back normal. No polyps, no tumours, no gallstones, no hepatitis. I have an irritable bowel, apparently. My Harvard-educated specialist told me to look it up on Wikipedia.

No matter how sick, though, I could never be as sick as my dad's neighbours in the chemo ward. They were sicker even than my dad, at least at the stage I was allowed to witness. Before my dad moved into a distressingly quiet palliative care ward. Before I moved into a social worker's spare room. Before it was one hundred percent confirmed that my mother was missing and arrangements could be made with my legal guardians, Gloria and Bryan. I used to stare at my dad's chemo neighbours most intently when they were distracted by the complimentary juice, their chapped lips wrapped around straws stabbed through aluminum lids. They weren't as hairless as I'd expected, but their faces looked older than their shoes suggested. They stared back at me, red-rimmed eyes roaming as they sipped. Their primal intensity worried me. Willing me to die so they could live. An aneurism preferably, so my major organs could be harvested, my marrow tapped.

The nurse called my father's name and we escaped, choosing two seats in the back corner of the treatment room: he in a cracked plastic recliner and me, a stiff metal chair. The man to our right was old but handsome, like an actor captaining a starship. He had a bald head — by choice — and his hands and feet were wrapped in bags of ice. I assumed that much cold would feel very uncomfortable but he showed no signs of pain. Just stared off into space, dreaming of his next mission.

An obese woman sat across from us, firing off gags like a machine gun: *How many cancer patients does it take to screw in a light bulb? Just one, but it takes a support group to cheer him on. What's the difference between God and a doctor? God doesn't think he's a doctor!* My dad's jokes were mostly observational in nature: "It's packed in that waiting room, huh? Ave! Hey, Ave! How much money do you think I can get for my chair? Think I could sell my *primo* spot for fifty dollars?" The nurses laughed because they were flirts, the generous kind who shake hips and tempt you with extra juice and wink at people with no hair and no virility left to speak of. My dad was sick enough to have a port inserted into his chest on the opposite side of his heart. I was shocked when the nurse exposed it, a monstrous-looking mosquito bite rising up through curls of hair. Dad seemed okay with it, so I pretended I was, too. Further down the ward limped a right-leaning Member of Parliament who made my father growl and complain. The man had scored a private room, one of only two in the ward. Unlike my dad, I thought his special treatment was fair given his celebrity. The patients could be relentlessly chatty, so much so that posters were tacked up next to every recliner begging *Please Do Not Distract The Nurse When Your Pump Is Being Programmed!*

I pull myself away from the toilet. To give it something to do, I place a single sheet of Cottonelle in the bowl and flush. I wish it well as it makes its way through the pipes and the chemicals and into the lake that pushes itself up against the city.

"I should clean you, toilet," I tell it. "Henry has been neglectful."

The bathroom is Henry's chore. Every Sunday morning, a bowl of cereal in hand, my body leaning against the doorframe, I'd chew on whole grains and slivers of almonds as he squeaked the mirror with newspaper and vinegar, scrubbed the toilet until it gleamed and de-molded the shower caulking with a toothbrush. Then I'd shuffle my way to the living room, pick up the glasses and errant popcorn kernels, and rip more damn hair out of the damn carpet.

It's been half a dozen Sundays since Henry last cleaned the bathroom, though, and the cells of calcium, soap scum and various residues have too long been dividing and replicating. It's an experiment of his, I assume, to determine exactly how much filth I can stand. There's no technical reason why I can't clean the bathroom myself, only a psychological one. While I have no fear of dry shed hair, only loathing, I cannot bring myself to touch it wet. There's something altogether terrifying about the act of pulling one's own hair from the drain in an endless, dripping, matted chain coiled tight around itself, strangling what is already dead. Drain hair is no longer hair proper; it's a Japanese horror movie ghost clawing up from a well and vying for revenge. And that's just hair from my head. If I dare gaze at the tub the day after I shave my legs, the ceramic looks hit by shrapnel; splinters of stubble impaling tiles and shampoo bottles that couldn't take cover in time, telltale drops of blood mixed in.

The tub is so filthy I feel dirtier after taking a shower than before, as though the scum and calcium are working together to form a shell around my body. It's only a matter of days, I calculate, three or four more showers, before I am cocooned inside it. So I reach for a sponge, fat it with chemicals and scrub.

I would do anything for love.

I feel the song throbbing through the shower wall before I hear it. More alive and in time than my meek, syncopated heartbeat. The music fills the empty pockets of sponge, the-whatever the sponge is made of, and makes the jump to my fingers, nerves, bones. The notes are more beautiful inside of me because of my hollowness, reverbing through my body as empty as a shuttered cathedral.

I wish Billy Pfeiffer could hear his music like I hear it. If he could, I would feel less of his other sounds through this wall, and that awful gap between it and the ceiling. Fighting then fucking his girlfriend. Cracking his fists against the mirror. *Asshole fucker loser joke* at his own reflection. Hissing at the sting of alcohol on his wounds, down his throat, out his breath. Talking himself back into life.

If he could crawl inside of me, press his triple-pierced ear against my rattling ribs, he'd know his music makes him worthy. He'd know the pleasures of his own voice — warm and cozy, crackling like perfectly seasoned wood. He'd know he plays his guitar like it's an extension of his body; born with it like the rest of us are born with limbs. A left-handed Fender Hellcat was the underwhelming description given by the local news, the first thing he bought after winning *Canadian Idol*. The show was a year ago, but I'll never forget the close-ups. Billy Pfeiffer's strumming fingers, dented by the years of steel strings and cigarettes. His delicate doll-like lips. The fear in his eyes when he won.

15

It's two days after my big baptism fight with Henry and we're in Akono's crappy Toyota. He's driving us to Woodbridge, a vast Italian-Canadian suburb thirty-five minutes outside of Toronto. On every sidewalk a square-bodied, thinning-haired *nonna*. On every lawn an ornament. In every backyard tomatoes. And the halls! For weddings, reunions, first communions, grade-six graduations, birthdays, christenings, anything private basement kitchens cannot contain. The halls grow out of the grass and one is always more embellished than the one beside it. Some feature fountain cherubs that urinate pink water, others boast bridges two-people-wide built over streams yet to be plumbed. And the cars. In every mini-mall parking lot a Ferrari; in one out of every three garages a Maserati, Bugatti, Alfa Romeo. How can they afford them? So many grown-up sons living in so many basements?

I duck out of Akono's car and Henry is quick to take my hand.

"You're not going to run away, are you?" he asks, only half-joking.

I jerk free and march toward the Kingdom Hall, cars hitting me, piercing every organ, smashing every cell, but that's not going to stop me. I'll leave my body in the parking lot. Who needs it? It's never been anything but trouble.

This particular Kingdom Hall is new construction, suburb style: a blank big-box store of a place that prioritizes parking over good taste.

"What do you think?" Akono asks.

"It sure is . . . big," Henry says.

"The developer added those exterior moldings just recently."

"He shouldn't have bothered," I say.

We step inside and are greeted by Tony Davidson. Late sixties with the cheeks of a baby. Stick a needle in his balloon belly, he'll blow up the building.

"I'll be performing Brother Henry's baptism," he tells me.

Prick. As if I don't recognize you, your form and function, the other men from my old life who are exactly the same.

Handshakes. Small talk. Fingers press our backs and coax us into an auditorium. The sight of the people inside takes me by surprise. Witnesses. Hundreds. Packs of them. Chatting teens. Hand-holding newlyweds. Babies bouncing on endless modest knees. Content and celebratory. They take my breath away, the sight of them, the memory. It's as though nothing has changed since my own baptism. The taste of the chlorine fills my mouth, the sting of it in my eyes. My mother warns me to keep both closed, but I don't listen. I want to keep my eyes on my father, to let him know he isn't losing me, that I'll still be his. Wild just like him, I want him to know—I can breathe underwater.

The memory of the baptismal water rushes into my lungs and I start coughing, choking. I can't stop. Dozens of Witnesses crank their necks and stare. Their looks sharp like hundreds of thousands of paper cuts from *Awake!* magazines. Henry drags me, hacking, out into the hallway. We skitter down it until we find a door. A kitchen. We stand inside, Henry patting me on the back until the coughing eases. I look into his eyes, try to find something in them I can recognize.

"Remember how you proposed to me?" I say. "We were at that party. The one in the crater? That night the tyrannosaurus rex got drunk on palm wine?"

Henry laughs. There he is. The man I fell in love with.

A voice booms over the intercom. "Brothers and sisters, if you will please gather in the main auditorium. It's time for the baptismal ceremony."

Henry turns to leave, but I grab his arm. "You chipped a piece of asteroid off the crater wall," I say. "You tied a vine around it, and slipped it on my finger. 'The moon dust shines like the stars,' you told me. 'It shines like your eyes.'"

He smiles, but it's a sad one. A too-little-too-late smile.

"Choose me instead, Henry," I beg.

He pries my fingers off like he's freeing himself from a corpse. "I did choose you," he says. "And this is where you pushed me." Henry leaves the kitchen. He doesn't even look back. It makes it easier to pretend it's a stranger doing this to me and not my Henry at all. I follow this stranger into the main cavity of the hall. He pulls at the chest of his shirt and shakes debris from the cotton. Breakfast crumbs, dandruff, me. Satisfied, he takes a left and I take a right, curling my way up a rickety staircase. There's no seat at the top, only a Juliet balcony to lean over. I can see Henry far away, number eleven standing next to eight, nine, ten. They are gathered in front of a shallow pool fixed into the floor and surrounded by velvet ropes. On a stage facing them bloats Tony Davidson, the world's most combustible man.

"I'm going to ask you two questions." His words come out breathless, like they're holding back a mighty belch. "If you could answer loudly so that everyone can hear you. On the basis of the sacrifice of Jesus Christ have you repented of your sins and dedicated yourself to Jehovah to do His will?"

"Yes!"

"Wonderful! Do you understand that your dedication and baptism identify you as one of Jehovah's Witnesses in association with God's spirit-directed organization?"

"Yes!"

"Your clear answers indicate that you are qualified for baptism as ordained ministers of Jehovah God."

The crowd applauds and Tony "Dynamite" Davidson waddles his flock into a room behind the stage. I press my body against the balcony's railing and envision jumping off. The sweet, young family of five beneath me will be killed — and disappointed. According to the rules of their own church, only one-sixteenth of them will make it into heaven. Henry and the others reappear on stage dressed in shorts and T-shirts. They line the pool's edge. Number ten waves to the crowd. Numbers four through eight laugh and swap high fives. They look like teammates at the world's most prudish swim meet. Except for Henry, number eleven, pale, his lanky limbs far too long for his Gap T-shirt and soccer shorts. Henry just looks cold.

Number one is up. She ties her limp hair in a ponytail, grabs hold of the railing and steps into the pool. Two men receive her in the water, their ties bobbing on the surface. They point at number one's watch but she shakes her head no, her faith extends to waterproofing. The ritual begins. One man holds on to her back and grasps her wrist, instructing her to plug her nose. She takes a breath and bends her knees. Dunks. Surfaces. Applause. Towel. Mop. Next! Over and over.

At last, Henry's turn.

The two men clamp him by the arms and lead him into the pool. Henry scans the crowd, left, right, behind, but not up. He's taking too long. The crowd is growing restless. A swoop. One of the men grabs Henry's wrists and pulls him under water. He returns to the surface, choking.

Applause. Towel. Mop.

I hurry down the staircase to find Henry encircled by his dripping brothers and sisters. They gather around him, a boisterous, chatty forcefield protecting him from his secular wife.

A ball forms in the back of my throat shaped like Henry's name. "Henry!" I yell, to clear it out. "Henry!" He doesn't turn and they shuffle him away before I can get a good look at him, to measure what hasn't been drowned.

As the rest of the crowd follows the swim team, filing to the basement for biscotti, pignoli and Illy coffee, I drift over to the pool. A copy of *Awake!* floats by, its ink leaving a slick like oil on the surface. I tug off my shoes, hoist up my dress and dip my feet, ankles, calves into the water. I slosh back and forth, back and forth. But the rhythm isn't enough; my limbs want to go! So I let my legs thrash with a violence. Wave after wave slops out of the pool. I'm sweating now, and the pool is half-empty. I survey the room. Like New Orleans recovering from the flood. Even the walls are wet, drips crawling down the paint like worms. I am shocked by the damage I've done.

Tony "The Detonator" Davidson is standing over me, a look on his face like he gets it. "Brother Henry just got caught up in the moment," he says. "Don't take it personally."

But I do. It's the *most* personal. It's my husband's rejection, a swift two-handed shove into loneliness. Pain and misery and sickness and living nightmares flood back like the water in this pool and it's stretching and building and climbing higher and wider and burying me and I'm desperate for a release.

TNT Tony considers me, resting his hands on his beer-and-bread belly.

Oh my god I'm going to poke it. I poke it.

No fireball or thermal radiation. Only a whattheheckis-wrongwithyou? from a fire retardant, fat man.

"I'm sorry," I say as he backs away from me—the wild animal.

My phone rings.

"Henry?"

"You have a call from a federal—"

I rush to hang up but hit speaker instead.

"IT'S BRYAN, YOUR LOVING UNCLE WHO TOOK YOU IN WHEN NO ONE ELSE WOULD."

Bryan's voice hurls through the phone and echoes off the water, the lonely room, and the painted domed ceiling I'm seeing for the first time. A fresco, beautiful and strange. The great Noahic flood. Cow, prostitute, tiger and tyrannosaurus rex choking in the punishing seas. A doomed elephant cowers on a rock. I reach up to save him and a wetness hits the back of my hand. A single flake. Snow. What the—? It remains solid just long enough to reveal its crystals. A variation of a sectored plate, my father's favourite. Precise geometry, elegant simplicity. Six perfect crystalline points, surrounding a Trivial Pursuit–shaped pie in the centre. Snow. It multiplies and replicates. Thousands of flakes shake down on me like sifted flour. Fine, soft, delicate. I catch them on my tongue. Salty like minerals. They rest on my eyelids, my lashes, my eyes.

"ARE YOU STILL THERE?"

Snow is all I see.

16

It takes 100,000 evaporated water droplets to build one snowflake. I pull off my wet dress and fling it in the laundry basket. The pool couldn't have induced that effect. Not in that temperature. It's scientifically impossible. I towel-dry my hair. The air conditioner in the hall was running, but nowhere near cold enough for snow. I look it up. A sectored plate crystal forms at minus fifteen degrees.

I turn on the Weather Network. I don't know what else to do.

Calvin Straight flashes on the screen. He's young, my age, and so new at the job he hasn't yet mastered the green screen. He must be wearing a green tie and no one cared to warn him because there's a gap down the middle of his torso, like a chest split by rib spreaders for surgery. Satellite images loop through the place where his heart should be: a hurricane off the coast of Florida and torrential rains beating down Newfoundland.

Calvin apologizes several times over the course of the five-minute forecast for a variety of crimes: coughing into his microphone, referencing one weather system while the screen shows another, and bumbling his words. I can hardly bear to watch. He slips into a British accent at one point, then, laughing wildly, a sort of Arkansas drawl. When the national map pops up he jumps back in surprise and then makes offensively generous circles with his hands, cupping the Great Lakes like a pair of testicles and pinching the Rocky Mountains like nipples. Calvin Straight is the worst TV weatherman ever. But his forecast is undeniable.

"*Sunny and thirty-three degrees with the humidex today.*" He blocks all the graphics from view. "*The rest of July looks very much the same. Unless some unpredictable system comes barrelling down on us from the south. Oops, I mean up.*" He barks with laughter. "*Or the north. Which it won't. I've modelled it; it won't.*"

I Google him and his impressive resumé. A master's degree in atmospheric sciences from Cornell. Five years at Environment Canada. What happened between then and now is anyone's guess. Henry could find out. Call his contacts at the newspaper and dig up the truth about Calvin.

Henry. My Henry. It's midnight, his baptism ended half a dozen hours ago, but he still hasn't come home. I assumed he was mad at me, but what if it's not me at all? What if he inadvertently offended some Woodbridge Mafioso? Scratched a Fiat Turbo? Spoke against a mother or a *nonna*? He could be captive, right now, in the trunk of an Alfa Romeo. He could be breathing through a keyhole, scratching the fibreglass, moaning my name. He could be drowning in one of the pissing-cherub fountains, tomatoes stuffed in every orifice. I can't call the police yet, so I look for Henry the way I look for everything: Google. I type his name into the search bar and only one result pops up. Henry's humiliating time from a 5K run for cancer. He did it five years ago, one week after he quit the Watchtower. "It was a symbol," he told me on our first date. "Of me running away from their crazy lies." He threw his hands in the air. "I mean, really, come on. They don't want us to donate? Why? Because Jehovah will eradicate all cancer in paradise?" I raised my hands to meet his. Weaved my fingers through.

I snap shut my laptop and turn back to Calvin, who's standing in the middle of a rolling storm battering the coast of Haiti. He looks straight into the camera, through it, as though he forgets he's on television, his mind stuck in the storm's centre. I cough to break the tension. Calvin reaches his hand out to the camera, his pinky ring gleaming under the lights, setting off a lens flare. It's a moment, a second only, but Calvin is reaching for me. Then he steps back and resumes his forecast. His chest filling with unstoppable rain and the darkest clouds.

I need to hear the voice of a real person, so I walk to the bathroom and press my ear against the shower tile. The voice of Billy Pfeiffer's girlfriend—high and unsure, every slurred sentence a question. Billy Pfeiffer is mostly silent, his songs replaced with disinterested grunts. The female voice grows angry. Youfuckingassholeloserwannabepussybitch!

A crash.

A sound I can't identify. Marbles maybe? Rolling *up* the wall? OhyeahbabytouchmethereyouknowhowIlikeit.

Sounds like they made up.

I step out into my living room and close the bathroom door, but Billy Pfeiffer's pornographic declarations of love cannot be muted. Of course they can't. This building is constructed of plywood and crumbling vermiculite. And it stinks. Like rotting bananas and sour coffee.

Finally, a problem I can fix.

I wrestle the garbage out from under the sink and drag it downstairs to the garage. The bag is full of things I should re-cycle, work-related documents and cans that pierce the plastic and tumble out.

"You should recycle that." Super Steve. Old, fat, heavy in accent. A Grecian god who let himself go. He steps out from behind the Waste-Co dumpster and picks up my trail of paper and aluminum, dropping each item in the blue bin where they belong.

"I forgot," I say.

"Bullshit. You young kids are lazy. All talk about green this and that, but if it takes a little work, washing out a can, peeling off a label? Give me a break, Avory."

"It's Avery."

"Avory. Like I said."

"How do you even know my name?"

"I'm the super; I know everyone. Your husband, Harry—"

"Henry."

"— signed the lease six years ago. You moved in last year — all of the sudden. I never saw you around before."

"So?"

"So you and Harry got together fast."

"We fell in love quickly, yes, that's true."

Steve looks at me sideways. "If you say so." He points at my chest with my credit card bill. "Speaking of Harry—"

"Henry."

"— did you tell him about your big fall?"

I busy myself with the knot in my garbage bag. Doubling it.

Steve takes the bag from me. "So that's a no." He unties the knots and digs in, picking out microwave dinner boxes, ripping them responsibly in half. "You eat a lot of shit," he says. "Too many preservatives and salt."

"I'm very busy," I explain.

He tosses my actual garbage into the Waste-Co dumpster. "No one is that busy."

My back stiffens. "Listen, *Steve*, I have a job, and a husband, and . . ."

"And what?"

"And I'm not a fucking janitor."

I said it, in a *tone* I can't take back. I'm sick with it. I am trash. *I am filthy and nasty and dirty and soiled and disgusting.* I climb up the side of the Waste-Co and scout for my new home.

Steve laughs. A single shout. The horn of a ship. "I'm not a fucking janitor either," he says. "I'm a super."

He walks away and I throw one leg over the lip of the dumpster. There's a cozy little crevice beneath the unfinished sandwich and diapers and the scratched T-Fal pan.

Steve yells, "Are you coming with me or what?"

17

I trail behind Steve. His torso is perfectly square, his beige shirt tucked into a waist that doesn't exist. He is custom-built to fit through doorways.

He leads me down an unfamiliar hallway that's wonderfully cool and smells like wet cement and gasoline. We turn a corner and Steve reaches for the knob on a door marked "Broom Closet." Neatly stacked cleaning supplies, light bulbs, industrial paper towels, bucket, hedge trimmer, "Caution: Wet Floor" sign, all the tools of Steve's trade inside this narrow storeroom with a naked bulb that hums and swings as my head skims it. But Steve has turned the space into a sort of hideout, the kind where a terrorist might spend his last days. He's squeezed an old recliner in beside the wet vac and installed a kitchenette on the opposite wall: a miniature fridge, convection oven and burner.

Steve offers me a stool, which faces an aerial photo of a fantasy island: eight by twelve inches of far away dotted with perfectly whitewashed houses in perfect rows, like teeth in a mouth of sea. I picture the scene, what lies just outside the frame. Azure shorelines, lemon sails, and almond bodies with cherry sunburnt lips. Mint growing in backyard gardens and green and purple vines climbing the houses perched on the edges of dove-grey cliffs.

Steve opens his fridge and uncovers a sheet pan's worth of golden, dewy baklava, thick as a lasagna. "This is the good stuff. Old family recipe." He cuts me a piece and gently slides it into my palm. I can smell the honey sweetness, can predict the pistachio crunch.

"Are you going to eat it or just stare at it?"

I take a bite and am thrust into gooey heaven.

"Move over to the burner, Avory. I want to show you something else, something even you can cook. Rivithia."

He pulls a bin of chickpeas from the fridge. "Not canned. You buy them dry and soak for a whole day." Into a pot he adds water, rosemary, olive oil, sea salt, onion and black pepper, all

73

of which come from a shoe organizer hanging on the back of the door, each ingredient plucked from its own pocket. He pours in the chickpeas and forces a spoon into my hand. "Simmer for half an hour. Okay?"

"Okay." I stir as he tosses an anonymous spice into the brew. "What was that?"

"That's between me and the pot."

"Why won't you tell me what's in it?"

"You Google generation kids. Need to know everything right now."

"Just tell me."

"A pinch of patience," he laughs. "That's what's in it."

"That photo," I say, "it's Greece, right? That's where you're from?"

Steve grunts. He doesn't look at the photo.

"Why would you ever leave a place like that?"

He squeezes lemon into the pot, his hands strangling the juice out. "Why does any immigrant leave? Because life is hard." He lobs the rind into a compost bin. "For too many reasons."

"But those houses on the cliffs," I say. "And all the colours. And the breeze. Does the air smell as good as I think it does? Like mint and grass and honey? Does the wind taste richer because of the sea salt in the air?"

Steve's eyes are wide as lemons.

I stop stirring, hand him the spoon. "You think I'm weird," I say.

His face relaxes into a smile. "You're right. It's all that." He returns the spoon to me. "But when I was a kid there was war and thousands of fucking Italians swarming the place."

I search through the inventory of wars warehoused in my brain.

"You know the World War was in Greece, right?" he asks.

"The second one?"

"Jesus!"

"Sorry! I'm not that great with dates."

"Dates have nothing to do with it!" He pulls the spoon from me. I have no idea what to do with my hands. "It's your generation! No respect for the past. You're all spoiled! Have it so easy." He aims the spoon at his chest. "I've been working since I was nine years old. Hard work, fishing work. The stink of it. The damn fish gets into everything." Rivithia drips down his shirt. I point at it, but his eyes don't follow my finger. "Scales under my nails. Seaweed in my ears. There's a reason why so many songs and stories are written about life on the sea, okay? It's romance and adventure to you kids, sure, but for us it's mostly just danger and stink. Men trying to out-man each other. Men wringing each other dry."

Steve leans his weight against the makeshift counter: a pine door with the knob and locks jimmied off. The soup works itself up into an angry boil.

"My mother cried every time my father and I went out into the ocean, worried sick that we wouldn't come home. And then when we got home, our nets full of sea bream and sole for her to gut, she cried even harder. Dead son and husband, or a life spent knee-deep in fish shit and intestines?"

Steve stabs at the boiling bubbles with his spoon, popping them with precision. He stops and looks at the photo, finally, as though he's giving in to it. His shoulders surrender, curl inward like a wave. A salty white residue forms at the corners of his eyes. "Anyways, Avory," he says, "I got a toilet to unclog—"

"At midnight?"

"—so if I'll excuse you—"

He plops another sticky chunk of baklava in my hand and pushes me out of his closet.

18

I'm on the futon and my stomach is rumbling, but not over the rivithia I didn't get to eat last night. It's rumbling in the way it does over men.

Henry's left me no clues: not a phone call, not an email, no reference to his exit or his return. But I have a feeling. So I drag the chair next to the front door and sit flipping through a tabloid. The subject of my study is a comparative essay about ass size in Hollywood.

Clunky steps from down the hallway. Henry's.

I move quick. Drag the chair back. Toss the tabloid under the futon. Cross arms. Commit to a passive-aggressive approach.

"Why, Henry," I say, as he opens the door. "How are you?"

"Don't do that, V."

"It's lovely to see you."

"Let's talk about this like adults."

"Eighteen hours without contacting me, without letting me know you're alive? And *I'm* the child?"

"You ditched us first," he says.

"'Us'?"

"Me and Akono."

"Oh so now you're an 'us'? Like Kim and Kourtney?"

"Who?"

I eyeball the tabloid. It's safely hidden in shadow and dust.

"Brother Tony told me what you did."

I drop to the futon. Cross my legs as tight as they'll go. "And what's that?"

"That you poked him in the stomach."

I laugh. I can't stop.

"Why would you do that?" Henry asks.

Just the thought of TNT Tony and his big red baby face.

"It's not funny."

"It sort of is," I gasp.

Henry drops onto the futon. It creaks and wobbles, and then settles.

"You humiliated me, V," Henry says.

"And you left me alone. Again."

He puts his arm around my shoulder and squeezes. There are still traces of Henry.

"I know where you were hiding," I say, "while you were gone."

"Oh yeah?"

"You were in the jungle. Where the thirty-foot ferns were planted —"

"V, stop."

"— the ones the stegosaurus liked for lunch."

"I was at Akono's —"

"You were in the trees throwing coconuts at those chicken-sized dinosaurs. You remember? The ones that barked like dogs?"

He turns to me, holds my face in his hands. "Listen to me, V: I don't want to play that game anymore. I'm not going to make fun of what millions of my brothers and sisters believe."

I pull away from him and my neck tenses. "Fine then. You were at Akono's all night." The muscles are knots, the kind confrontation grows. "And where are you going now? Work, I hope."

Henry pulls out a tube of ChapStick. He has never ever owned ChapStick. Would never think of searching for it in Pharma Plus, paying money for it, keeping it warm and ready in his pocket. He pops off the lid and spreads the balm on liberally.

Top. Bottom. Then reapplies again, smacking his lips together. *Who the hell are you and what have you done with my Henry?*

"I'm not going to work." His words smell like cherry and carnauba wax.

"Why not?"

"Because I quit."

I spring from the futon. "Why? Why would you quit your job?"

"Because I don't need it," Henry says wearily. "The Watchtower has big plans for my career." He stands, wraps his arms around my waist. His hair smells like someone else's shampoo. "You should be happy for me. For us."

I eye what's left of Henry's tattoo. The heart a white scar. And my name? Once locked in jet-black onto his body? Avery. I'm a ghost. "The Watchtower ruined me," I cry. "And you going back to them? It's like it's happening all over again."

Henry presses his thumbs into his temples. My fault, his headache. I'm a low-pressure system. An oncoming storm.

"Ruined you, ruined you, ruined you," Henry chants. "You keep saying that, but you never explain."

I look away from him and through the window. Outside, the sky is waging a war. Fierce snow hurtles down from the clouds—each flake a cannonball firing onto the street. Burger Shack explodes. Taxis melt. The tennis court is crushed into crumbs. It's devastating everything. Yet there, amid the chaos and violence, stands Akono. Snow bombs him, but he remains fully alive and solid, in front of the Kingdom Hall, an *Awake!* magazine in his outstretched hand.

"Henry," I sob. "What's happening?"

19

I wake up, my body drunk with sleep and damp from night sweats. Henry is gone. Our sheets are still flannels, the summer linens buried somewhere we can't recall. Henry sleeps on top so he doesn't mind, but I need to be covered to be safe: from what I can't see, from the dark. Sweat means warmth, which means the snow yesterday—

"The snow was a dream. Just a dream." I put the words out into the world like a mantra.

The lure of a cold drink convinces my body to peel itself off the bed and journey to the kitchen. My thirst is primeval, a desert thirst, so I angle my head beneath the tap and release the flood. I wipe my chin, then stumble to the fridge. No food inside. Not even cereal perched on top that I can shovel in dry. So I dig into the back of the freezer and pull out a cloudy bottle of vodka, a Christmas present from Henry's work.

A buzz. Our buzzer—which hardly ever buzzes except for takeout—is buzzing at seven in the morning.

"Hello?" I groan into the speaker.

No response.

I go back to the vodka, and mourn the loss of future Christmases. No tree or turkey leftovers. No gift wrap or stockings, mistletoe or carols. No cards featuring Henry + Avery wearing matching sweaters and smiles. *Merry Christmas! Love Havery!* I mix the vodka with an expired packet of super-hydrating and mineral-replenishing orange Gatorade. I down the first round, the aftertaste laboratorial. I make another and walk toward the sliding glass doors, step onto the balcony and take in the view. There is no snow, of course, BECAUSE SNOW IN JULY IS IMPOSSIBLE. The summer wind feels unstable and powerful, though, giving me the distinct impression that it could sweep me up and onto the street at any moment. It is this wind that carries her scent up to me, that perfume of hers. Bloodied roses, a rusted fence around an English garden. When I was a child, I could smell it through the whole house, strongest after her morning shower and then again before bed. I can smell it now, even though the wind is bullying the air. There it is and there, consequently, is she.

I lean over the balcony to get a better look at her. Her hair and skin are the same shade of yellow, one fading into the other. She wears a white T-shirt and blue pants cropped to the mid-calf, high enough to survive an insignificant flood, and white running shoes. Her ankles are perilously thin, her arms, too. Her eyebrows, invisible from this distance, leave her eyes all on their own — dark as coffee but cold. My mother.

She shouts up to me, "Avery!" her voice barely audible, the smallness of it overtaken by the traffic.

I shake my head and blink to clear the vision of her away. Still here. It's undeniable. I wish for the snow to blow in from the east and erase her from the landscape. It doesn't, yet I'm shivering. The wind, blustery and warm seconds ago, has turned howling and wintery. My exposed hairs stand on end and my muscles contract inside my body, drawing me back into the apartment.

"Don't leave! Please!" I can hear her clearly, the traffic hushed by two red lights. "We need to talk."

I slam the door and yank the blinds, nearly tearing them from their anchors. It's so dark that I have no shadow, the blackness stripping it away like old paint. The tiny red light of the cable box beckons. I scrunch down on the carpet an arm's length from the television screen, like I used to when I was a kid. We'd drown ourselves in science fiction movies each summer, my dad and I, when there was no snow to escape to. My mother used to stand between us and the box, blocking our view, as though her body could force us to give in and turn it off. It never worked. Instead of her face, I'd look up and see only static: white, black, and grey interference where her features should have been, as though the reception of her needed adjustment. A battalion of warring ants hummed atop her neck, and the harder I looked, the fuzzier she became. Maybe if I taped a hanger to her arm I could see her more clearly? Or if she raised her right foot?

I flip on the television. Colour floods the screen first, then me, then the room. I surf channels until I find *The Empire Strikes Back*, which is always playing somewhere, and there they are: Leia and Han flirting in the carved-out mountainside hallways of Echo Base while Rebel Alliance soldiers scurry. I take such an incredible gulp from my glass, like a whale inhaling krill, that the room spins. The buzzer rings five, six, seven times. I plug my ears with my fingers and wait for my mother to give up. I focus on Leia, wonder what her beige winter vest was filled with: goose down or feathers from an alien species no one thought to mention.

My mother's purse hits the window — she'd failed to double-check the zipper so I watch her pocket-sized New World Translation Bible and her silver compact leap out — but I'm not here anymore, Mother, sorry to disappoint. I'm on planet Hoth. I'm standing behind Luke, looking over him as he freezes on the glacier, a speck of dark in a vast ocean of white. He expects to die, he must, his heart stopping before Han can stuff him inside that awful Tauntaun. My father did the math: a man couldn't survive more than ten minutes inside an animal, so he approved of

Han's construction of a snow shelter. It looked just like ours and performed the same magic: save yourself with the very snow that could kill you.

A pain needles my shoulder. I look behind me, contorting my neck, and a single feather greets me. It's from an Eider duck, its café au lait colour giving it away. It must have leached its way out of a pillow and got stuck in this fucking carpet and then in me. I reach for it and pull, and it feels like nothing on the way out of my body. No tugging inside my flesh, no pain or blood. Clean.

20

My mother left hours ago, and with her, the wind. So I am overdressed as I leave the house, wearing a sort of disguise: aviator sunglasses and an oversized, sparkly grey tunic. It was an impulse purchase, another thing I should have walked away from. I bought it at a tourist shop in Old Montreal. The top is truly ugly, Las Vegas-arts-and-crafts-fair ugly. It makes me look like a wizard.

I pass the homeless man from the park. He's in his other regular spot, his second home, lying over a steam grate like a piece of meat roasting on a grill. No one else seems to notice; they all step over him like they would trash or a pigeon. I bend down. The man is still alive, his breath fetid as the sewer. His boots are loose, offering me a glimpse of his bruised, track-marked calves. I drop two dollars in his hat, the coin on coin sound waking him. "Crazy bitch," he says.

The community centre hops with regional science fair excitement. The air crackles with potato-generated electricity. Mozart blasts at ferns. Baking soda erupts from paper volcanoes. Eggs are sucked into bottles. Kids, their projects hulking over them, recite facts off cards while the pens of judges click like metronomes. Every few seconds an echo, the loud slap of a hand reaffixing tape and Bristol board to a wall.

When I was a kid, I wanted to remind the scientific community of the indelible powers of invisible ink, my words disappearing, leaving only a crispy sheet of paper and the faintest scent of lemon in their wake. But I presented on the Doppler effect instead because my father wanted me to. He was so excited by his only child expounding the virtues of any aspect of the science of sound that I couldn't say no. My mother, no surprise, wanted me to explore another option. She presented her project to me when my father was at the office. "Alternatives to Blood Transfusions," written in elegant scroll on an aptly-chosen, although oversized, red sheet of Bristol board. I knew it would curl off the wall, but I considered her work. Her project outlined a host of choices handwritten on pieces of cream stationary and glued to the board in what I deemed an overly generous application. She would be docked two points for failure to use a computer — the school library had recently acquired thirty candy-coloured iMac G3s — but she would make up for it with her use of technical terms. Nonblood Fluid Alternatives: Saline, Dextran, Haemaccel, Lactated Ringer's Solution, and Hetastarch. A subcategory labelled "How Doctors Can Help" boasted the benefits of iron-containing preparations, synthetic erythropoietin (EPO), blood-conservation methods such as electrocautery, cooling a patient to lessen oxygen needs, hypotensive anaesthesia, therapy to improve coagulation, Desmopressin (DDAVP) to shorten bleeding time, and, my personal favourite, laser scalpels. All of these alternatives were fixed around the thesis of the project, the nucleus of my mother's point and of her life: "What is primarily needed is not blood, but volume. Once volume is restored, shock will be prevented." After I rejected her project, she sulked out of my bedroom and into hers. She didn't mention a word of it until years later, when she pulled the Bristol board out from her closet, dusted it off and presented it to my father and his oncologist.

"What a grand day for science!" a teacher says into a microphone.

I can't agree. This whole scene makes me worry for the future — the same projects are being presented here as they were back in my day, the same mistakes being made, the same "discoveries" happening upon again and again. It's a picture of science so slow to progress, a vision of the kind of world we'd all live in if brains like mine were as good as it got: no computers, no open heart surgery, just a planet full of humans reading invisible ink.

Hank isn't in the room. I'm grateful. Stella and Mike do their best to make up for his absence, though, flinging dirty looks my way.

"Is Henry coming?" Nav asks me.

"No, but he's the reason I'm here," I say. "To apologize."

"It's not necessary, Avery."

"I had no idea he would hijack your meeting like that."

"Don't worry about it. It happens." He pours a coffee, stirs in cream. "You going to take a seat and join us?"

"I should go," I say. "Henry will freak if he knows I came here."

"I wish you'd stay," Nav says. "I wanted to introduce you to a new member of the group." He gestures at the chair next to the chalkboard, the one that's usually empty because everyone thinks they're allergic to calcium carbonate. Right now a girl is sitting in it. She is new to me and young, sixteen or seventeen. Her strawberry-blonde hair hangs next to her face like a pair of curtains, doing its best to obscure her from prying eyes like mine. She smiles when she notices me staring, but I'm not fooled. Something is wrong with this kid. In the middle of a steaming summer in a community centre classroom with no air conditioner and a coffee pot overheating in the corner, she is wearing an enormous winter jacket.

"I think you and Kristie could relate," says Nav.

I've never seen a coat like it. The exterior shell is a green and brown camouflage so convincing it seems trained and ready for battle in the woods or jungle, somewhere more alive than here. The arms are camouflage as well, but the pattern looks off, as though it doesn't belong. The harder I stare, the easier this is to confirm. The forearms are stitched to her coat from another coat, from another body. It's a Frankenstein parka; two halves patched together to make a whole.

"Okay," I tell Nav. "I'll stay for a bit."

I sit next to the girl. Her coat takes up a chair and a half, so I have to sit on a corner of it. The coat is as firm as a sandbag.

"Do you want to share today, Kristie?" Nav says. "The floor is yours if you want it."

Kristie's face turns red. "I just don't know if I'm, like, ready."

The group urges her on. Their intentions are good, but the air is electric with the anticipation of gossip. The signs are here, just as they were then, when I was the subject of their pack-like curiosity. Backs stiff, hands perched on knees, eyes eager for a show. Not a sip of coffee swallowed, not a bite of pastry or ice cream sandwich taken. I look at Kristie and hope with all my might that she will fight the pressure to rip open her deepest scars for them. Whatever she has to say, whatever bad blood she needs to let spill, it will only satiate a need in the vampires around her; it will fix nothing for Kristie. Use this group like I did, I want to tell her: for listening to other people's problems to soothe your own. For finding a man who you think can relate. Don't use it for sharing your pain aloud; that will only give the pain oxygen. And oxygen feeds fires.

I am about to say all of this when the words burst out of her.

"I was disfellowshipped for having sex I knew it was wrong but I did it anyway I couldn't help it I thought I loved him still think I do but she found us my mother I thought she was at work and like the rest happened so fast a tribunal with the elders to testify about my conduct 'unbecoming a Christian' I never wanted to leave the church it was my life I went to all the meetings got baptized was a pioneer after school and on weekends but now? My family doesn't talk to me and none of my friends will even look at me." She folds up inside that jacket. Breathes sticky breaths. "It's like I've got some contagious disease. It's like my life, my life now? It's just so . . . quiet."

Her shoulders are first in the chain reaction, shaking the tears out, the ones she's been denying for months.

I look away and reassess the pack. They are satiated now, by Kristie's pain, and so return to crossing legs, shifting in seats, blowing on coffee, getting up for milk and sugar. Not Nav, though. He is fully engaged with Kristie, his professionalism rising to the top like cream. He kneels in front of her. Whispers something and hands her a tissue. She blows her nose and asks for more.

"Would you take her to the ladies' room?" Nav asks me.

I lead her to a stall. While she blows everything out into toilet paper, I lean against the wall, my face too close to the graffiti to read it.

"Thanks," she says, when she is empty. She flushes, the toilet sucking in her shame, and steps out. Her nose is raw and red. Flecks of toilet paper dust her upper lip. "That was harder than I thought."

"Talking about it is the worst," I say. "Except for going through it."

"Did some of my stuff happen to you?" she asks.

"Sort of," I admit. "The elders."

"Did they ask you awful questions?"

I look at the cleaning schedule on the wall. The bathroom hasn't been attended to in weeks. I didn't notice it when we walked in, but filth is everywhere. Clods of paper towel by the sink. Trash cascading from the can. Toilet paper rolls rolling across the floor. Smears I don't want to contemplate.

It is filthy and nasty and dirty and soiled and disgusting.

"'Where did he touch you? Did you touch him back? On his penis? Were you completely naked? Did he ejaculate? Where? Inside you or on you? Did you enjoy it? Did you orgasm? What did it feel like? Did you tell anyone? Anyone at all? Do not tell, Avery. If you tell we cannot save you.'"

"Stop!" yells Kristie. "Please!"

"Sorry," I say. I think I say. I hope I say.

"Did the elders, like, blame it on you, too?" Kristie asks, head bent over the sink.

"Eventually. But first they made me feel like, if I just told the truth, it would be all right, that they'd take care of it — punish him, give me some form of justice. But it didn't work out that way. They took his side. He didn't want to do it, they said, but I tricked him, tempted him."

Kristie deflates with relief: the deepest kind of breath. "Nav tells me I'll be stronger because of everything bad that's happened to me." She looks at my left hand, touches my wedding ring. "Are you?"

"I wouldn't say I'm stronger. I've just become good at self-preservation."

"How do you do that?"

I look up at the water-stained ceiling. A crack spans the length of the bathroom. Asbestos pores are probably leaking on us as we stand here. And yet I care so little.

"I sort of pickle my mind," I tell her. "Jar it in a brine of work, husband, movies, TV."

"TV is not a solution," she says, reaching for my finger, tugging off my ring. "TV is a compulsion."

"Like you're one to talk," I say, pulling my ring back before she slips it on. "You're wearing a coat in the middle of summer."

Kristie's face scrunches like she smells a bad smell, and that bad smell is me. "What coat?" she says.

Footsteps echo down the hall.

"Nothing," I say. "Never mind."

A woman hurries into the bathroom. She's wearing a frilly summer dress and a bicycle helmet, her red hair sticking up through the vents in the resin. She steps into a stall and closes the door.

Surprise has taken over Kristie's face like a sunburn. Crazy, she mouths silently. I decide the word is meant for the strange woman and not for me.

"How did it end?" Kristie asks, eventually. "With the elders?"

"They told me to beg for forgiveness," I say.

"And did you get it?"

"From who?" I ask her.

"God, of course."

The toilet flushes. The woman in the bicycle helmet walks out of the stall and runs her hands under the tap. She takes her time, making sure the water flows slow and quiet. Her legs are slightly bowed, bent like the pipes. She is washing and washing the bathroom germs off her hands so she can absorb mine and Kristie's instead. The collection of the psychic grime of others. I focus all my energy, the force of the velocity of my own blood, to will the universe to crack her helmet in half and dump the broken ceiling on top of her. "I stopped believing in god the second those men opened their mouths."

Kristie takes my hand. "That's the saddest thing I've ever heard."

Outside in the atrium, a teacher warms up the microphone. "We have a winner!" he announces. "Melanie Fitzgerald, from Forest Hill Academy!"

I remember that project; I walked right by it. First place to a Rube Goldberg machine that burns toast.

21

I walk into the apartment and find Henry sitting on the floor trying to roll the hair out of the carpet like a Cuban cigar maker. He's making progress. His palms must be sweaty.

"Why are you doing that?" I ask. "You never do that."

"I'm thinking. Cleaning helps me think."

"About what?"

"You went to a meeting, didn't you?"

"Are you spying on me?"

"V, you promised me that if I went one last time, that that would be it. You'd be done with those people."

"We met because of *those people*."

"Don't remind me."

"Don't remind you of what, Henry? That we fell in love at a support group for former Jehovah's Witnesses —"

"Stop it, V."

"— or that you quit the Watchtower? Finally saw through their bullshit?"

"That was before I realized how miserable life is without Jehovah."

"You mean how miserable life *is* with me."

We're having two separate conversations. In two different apartments. On two different planets.

"How empty and futile all this is —"

"You don't love me at all, do you Henry —"

"— how pointless without a Creator —"

"— you hate me —"

"— how corrupt the mind becomes without His light —"

"— you think I could never do better than you, that no one will ever love me again, that I'm pitiful and useless, a failure as a wife —"

"— how totally meaningless and sad."

"That's what you meant at the baptism," I say. "When you said I pushed you back to the Witnesses. You think my life is meaningless and sad!"

Henry levers himself into a clumsy standing position. His right leg has fallen asleep so his long body looks precarious as a rented crane. He pulls me to his bookshelf, which, just days ago, used to house actual books. *The Secret. God Wants You Happy. Loving-Kindness Meditation. A Seeker's Guide to Self Freedom. Men Are from Mars Women Are from Venus.* Now there are hundreds of *Awake!* magazines piled and squashed together. He must have burned his books when I wasn't looking. In a drum in the park. Henry and Cecily and Akono and the homeless guy dancing naked around the fire.

"I have a library of help right here." Henry points at the stupid magazines. "But do you read any of it? No. You just watch TV and go to meetings run by heretics and losers."

A groaning noise vibrates directly above me, as though the upstairs neighbour, the one Henry and I call Cowboy, woke up drunk and sick on the floor. I've never trusted that ceiling. When Cowboy has parties it sheds bits of its popcorn finish into my hair. I look up. The ceiling is expanding and contracting like a lung.

"Did you see that?" I ask Henry.

"V, please," he says. "I'm trying to talk to you."

A bulge forms next, a wet bubble pulsing with the life of a heartbeat. The joists and floorboards can't withstand this kind of moisture—it's only a matter of time before Cowboy falls through.

"Are you listening?" Henry asks. "I need to know you're with me."

"Tell me you see that," I say, my neck craned.

"V, would you stop? Concentrate, please. On me."

I pull my focus away from the bulge and back to Henry. His forehead is mapped with worry lines. That neck vein is thumping.

"I can't do this anymore," he says.

Henry's fingers are trembling and jutting out an inch from his too-long sleeves. Always the sleeves. As if he thinks he has monkey arms. I try to make eye contact but his gaze is fixed on the rug's swirls.

"I can't pretend anymore," he says. "I can't pretend that you're enough."

"Henry—"

"I'm going to New York."

"As in the city?"

"As in the state." Henry straightens his posture. He towers over me, inches taller than he was yesterday. His shadow stretches the length of the room. "Wallkill," he adds, proud when he should be defensive.

I snort. "You can't be serious."

"I got a job offer in their publishing division, and I'm going to take it."

I follow Henry into the bedroom. He arranges his clothes in a gym bag that, as far as I know, never once saw the inside of a gym. He moves to the bathroom and assembles his shaving kit. He looks quizzically at his toothbrush and rummages through the cabinet. Unsatisfied, he rounds the corner to the kitchen and opens the bottom drawer next to the stove. He pulls out a sheet of cling wrap. The plastic sticks to itself in a disorganized manner. He rips off the offending sheet, stuffs it into the drawer, and tries again. This time the wrap comes out flat and smooth, and when the tiny metal teeth rip their way through this new sheet, they rip through me, too.

"Don't go," I beg. "Henry, please."

Henry reaches down and touches my shoulder. An electric current from the rug passes between us. He snaps his hand away.

"Then come back to Jehovah with me," he says.

"How can you ask me that? They ru—"

"They ruined you, I get it," he says, his hands slapping down at his sides. "But these are different people, V."

"They're all the same."

"Blame specific people if you want, for whatever happened to you, but not the entire religion. And certainly don't blame God."

The ceiling moans again, like an old man overstuffed on dinner. I have to look at it, it's inhuman not to, and when I do, the bulge expands. Frost grows on its belly and an ancient urge comes back—that primitive part of me that wants to lick it. The bubble retracts and then puffs itself right back out, a toad on the verge of a mighty croak. The frost expands with it and as the whole monstrosity moves, a few crystals fall to my feet.

"I'll send you the annulment papers to sign," he says. "It should be fast. Since we've never had sex."

I'll never know how Henry left; I was watching the crystals melt. He probably ducked out the door and paused, hand still on the knob. Probably looked back at me and sighed, then ran down the stairs, his bag swinging. But maybe not. Maybe he unbound his secret set of wings and flew out of the apartment. Yes, that's it; I can see him now. Henry, soaring through the open window at full speed.

22

The bulge is growing. A tumour in the ceiling that seems untreatable. I stand on the coffee table and tape plastic bags around it to contain the frost that flakes off, but no tape sticks. I point my hair dryer at it but the heat only feeds it. I kick a bucket beneath it and poke it with a fork, hoping to alleviate some of the pressure in a controlled setting. The thing won't burst. It just keeps expanding and moaning, a hideous beach ball in distress.

I sidestep down to the basement, ducking under pipes and passing signs that have been warning wet paint for weeks. The stairs are narrow, with an unevenness that always takes me by surprise. Each step is just a quarter-inch too short, but my body can still tell the difference. My foot lands a quarter of a second too soon, radiating shock from heel to head.

Steve's broom closet is open so I reach for the wet vac, yanking the trunk of it free from a ladder it was wedged against. I pull too hard, the force taking some paint cans down with it, a canister of carpet cleaner, a bucket full of rags, a screwdriver and a million screws. Whispering apologies, I stumble around trying to tidy.

"They were born in a broom closet—"

I jump.

"—so they don't speak English."

"Sorry about this, Steve." I gesture to the tangle. "I was trying to free that thing."

"The wet vac? What did you spill?"

"Nothing yet."

Steve smiles. "This is for some sort of premonition then? You're an oracle? A seer of leaks and floods?"

"No."

"Well, this is property of the management company. Very expensive machinery. I can't just give it to residents with supernatural powers."

"In that case, I did spill something."

"Too late."

"Please?"

"I tell you what, we'll make a deal. You let me cook in your kitchen now and then and you can use the wet vac whenever you want."

"But you have a kitchen right here."

"I mean a real kitchen."

"You don't have a real kitchen?"

"I do but it's no good."

"What's wrong with it?"

"None of your business, that's what's wrong with it. Deal? Or no?"

"Fine."

"Say it."

"Deal. We have a deal."

We shake on it.

The vacuum roars to life. I aim it at the bulge and it sucks off the popcorn finish. The bulge moves with the suction, smaller protrusions jut out and follow the pull, but it doesn't release itself, doesn't let its liquid flow, controlled and civilized, into the wet vac like I hope. It grows. To twice its size.

I turn off the vacuum and my phone rings. It sounds tired, as though it's been ringing for some time.

"Henry?" I say.

"It's your mother."

The bulge grunts and gives birth to a smaller bulge, expels it from its mass.

"What the hell do—"

"Language, Avery, please."

"What do you want?"

"To know how you're doing. To ask how married life is treating you."

"How do you even know I'm married?"

"You're my daughter. I make it a point to know."

"But not to call?"

"I'm trying to rectify that now."

"I haven't heard from you in thirteen years!"

"I know. Believe me, I know."

"Where were you?"

"I'd rather not talk about that right now."

"Well, this is your only chance so—"

"It's not the right time—"

"What are you after then, Margaret? Do you want to catch up? Pick up where we left off?" My mother makes a wet, hollow sound, like there's a straw shoved down her throat instead of a tongue. "How were the early 2000s for you? Did you abandon any other children? What about sick husbands?"

"And what about you, Avery? Still watching space movies and hiding from the world? Even though science fiction is dangerous witchcraft?"

"That's funny. Because your religion is science fiction witchcraft—"

"Those movies are spiritism of the worst kind. They invite the demons in."

"All those numbers, Armageddons and prophets coming back from the dead."

"If my religion were science fiction, Avery, you'd be as devoted to it as you are to *Star Wars*. And you wouldn't be sitting there alone without your husband."

"Wait . . . How do you know—"

The smaller wart shifts, burps, and a leak of snowflake drips to the floor. I nudge the bucket beneath it and peer inside. Depending on which classification system you prefer, there are forty to eighty types of snow crystals. For my father's tastes, Nakaya's system is the best. Unlike a lot of other researchers, Nakaya didn't just classify the prettiest, most symmetrical crystals. He noted every single one he came across, from bullet rosettes to radiating dendrites. Nakaya was a nuclear physicist; that's how important snow is.

The snow in the bucket looks normal enough, like any one of the classifications my father had gathered in a collection of hundreds of photographs of snow: simple prisms and stellar and sectored plates, fernlike stellar dendrites and radiating dendrites. My favourites were his Photographs of Rare Snow Phenomena. I used to curl up with him and flip through the giant hailstones, snow rollers and eighty-pound ice bombs. I'd fall asleep on his lap dreaming about virga, the evaporating ice crystals that leave trails dangling down the sky, like jellyfish grasping for ground.

"Avery? Hello? Still there?"

My favourite by far though is the coloured snow. Most common in Greenland, Antarctica and Alaska. Caused by algae: *Chlamydomonas* for green, *Chlamydomonas nivalis* for pink, red and orange. But I can't remember seeing a thing about the kind of snow I'm faced with now.

"I have to go, Margaret."

"I need to see you. It's Jehovah's will."

I hang up the phone and head to the kitchen. I mix a vodka and Gatorade and drink it down, pour another, and walk it over to the futon, my body making whatever small adjustments in geometry and physics it needs to keep everything level. Everything is not level, though, because there, on the futon, sitting up independently as though a body is inside of it, is my father's parka. Lime with the lights off.

My glass plummets, landing on the rug, so it doesn't shatter or stain, the orange liquid just seeps into those greedy navy fibres. I feel my mouth twist into a shape I'm glad I can't see, and my heart stops, speeds up and takes off. So this is what horror feels like.

One green sleeve stretches out, as though aching for me, the coat pulsing with a promise of warmth. I pull it on top of me and zip myself in. It's stiff on the inside — not soft and forgiving as I remember. My reflection winks at me from the window. The coat has swallowed me completely, like it swallowed my father in his coffin — his body no longer a body at all, but a corpse. The funeral home people should have pinned the coat strategically. Or filled my father with extra formaldehyde and humectants.

"This parka," I say, the truth reaching into my throat, pushing out a voice I don't recognize. "I buried Dad in this parka."

I scream and unzip, but the parka clings to my arms, strangles my waist. I fight and pull and strain, fling it off and throw it in the corner. Watch it slump into a pile.

A thousand nightmares swirl. My head so heavy with them that I can't hold it up. So I trip down the stairs, overreaching by half a step. The door to the broom closet swings open when I kick it, but Steve isn't inside. I turn back and run to the end of the basement hallway where the lighting is only half-functioning and wet paint signs cover the walls. Another door. A different sign. "Superintendent." The letters are small, the font size of a man who doesn't want to be disturbed.

I knock three times, hard and fast, wait, knock again.

"Steve!" I call. "Are you there? Let me in!"

Steve opens the door just barely. He slides his body through the narrow gap and closes the door behind him.

"Wolf chasing you or something?"

"I'm sorry but I think I'm losing my mind either that or something very wrong is happening something I can't —"

"Can you calm down?"

"— because my father's jacket is here but he's dead and so is the jacket and the snow and oh my god Henry Henry said he wants an annulment he said that he actually said that. I can't breathe oh —"

I crumple; there is nothing I or even Steve can do to stop it.

Steve steers me inside, his gold necklace jingling as he sets me on his couch.

"You okay? You look less white. Still white, though, because you are a very white person. When was the last time you got some sun?"

His living room is a maze of patterns. The floor tiled in yellow and brown hexagons, with smaller hexagons inside and on and on like a Russian *matryoshka* doll. The bookshelves, with their glass doors and legs spun tall and intricate on a lathe, look like empty trophy cases. The coffee table is ornate as treasure, the legs golden, the Plexiglas tabletop cut like crystal. There are two columns, Grecian, non-load-bearing, which myself and the sofa — upholstered in a brown floral fabric accented by swirls — are nestled in between. It must be a source of great pride and anxiety, this sofa, with plastic sheeting stretched over top, every corner tightly tucked. My arms stick to it and make a sucking sound when I peel them free. I sit upright and face the kitchen. It's a professional-looking galley, the type you'd expect on a yacht. Ancient copper pots hang over the stove like grapes on a Grecian trellis. A Viking range with six burners and a grill. All the surfaces are stainless steel, shiny yet dull. They reflect my body back as an indecipherable wisp.

"You have an amazing kitchen," I say.

"Of course I do; I'm Greek."

"So why do you need mine?"

"Why do *you* need my sofa?"

"Because I saw something, something very wrong, impossible, and I needed —"

He puts his finger to my lips and actually shushes me. "We have our reasons." He takes his finger back, leaving the scent of Windex on my upper lip. An alarm wails from Steve's wristwatch. "*Malaka.* I have to go meet with the management company *bástardos.*"

I try to stand but I can't. My body refuses to budge. The plastic has won. I am stuck on this sofa for eternity.

"Stay here as long as you need," Steve says. "Don't move until you're ready."

The door closes behind him. A period to our conversation.

I roll to my stomach and let the hexagon floor tiles hypnotize me to sleep.

23

The scent of roasting fat. Banging pots. Oh god oh god. I turn the key and my stomach turns with it.

"Henry? You came back!"

"It's me. Our deal, remember?" Steve ducks out from my kitchen, a butcher's knife in his hand. "Harry—"

"Henry."

"—was just here, though. With a short black man."

I cry out. "Why didn't you come get me in your apartment?"

"I thought *he* was why you ran away to *me*." Steve points to the living room with the knife. It's an appropriate choice. "Because of all this."

The futon is gone. In its place is an outline of dust mimicking its shape and a narrow scrap of paper, a Post-it torn in half down the middle. Henry had tried to scratch out some of his words, the ones that would have turned his note into a poem.

> *I came back for the futon.*
> *There's no bed ~~for me~~*
> ~~apparently~~
> *where I'm going.*
> - Henry

His CDs? Gone. Books too. The living room has so little living left in it. I can't bear it. I flee to our bedroom. The bed is still there but all of Henry's bedroom things, his trunk, his radio alarm clock, his backup glasses, all the clothes he could carry—gone. Our wedding photo remains—an eight-by-ten of the two of us standing in front of a grey curtain, the best that Toronto City Hall has to offer in the way of decor. It was only a year plus one week ago, he was thirty, but Henry looked so much younger, childlike, as if his body was still growing into his sizeable feet. I stood next to him, smiling nervously, my posture faintly stooped, submissive, in a white imitation-silk shift dress, the seams puckering down my thighs.

I walk to Steve, my chest burning with what it feels like to bury a scream. I take his knife and launch it up into the ceiling, piercing the bulge like a watermelon, making that squelching watermelon sound.

"Feel better?" Steve asks.

He climbs on a chair and reaches for the knife. What will come out? I have visions of blood — it makes as much sense as anything. Only somehow the blood will be mine.

I stop him, pull him down. "No," I say, "I do not."

"Is your Harry a *kunistós?* Is that what all this trouble is about?"

"A what?"

"A rocking chair."

"What are you talking about?"

"Is your husband a queer?"

"Of course not. Why would you say that?"

"Who was the black man then?"

I fill a glass with water and drink deeply. Something to extinguish the searing pain.

"Who was he?" he repeats.

"A Jehovah's Witness."

"Uh oh."

"You familiar with them?"

"Oh yeah. They love immigrants. Used to hang around my first job here. It's like they could smell me, you know? That fresh-off-the-boat perfume." Steve snorts. "I almost joined them. Just for the company."

"It must have been so lonely," I say, hoping he'll keep talking, keep remembering out loud. I need someone else's pain to take the lead. "Moving here, starting over."

"Pier 21 wasn't fancy like it is today." Steve returns to the stove. He's roasting chicken, and the kitchen smells like a kitchen should. Thyme and oregano and maybe even olives. "Ever been to Halifax?"

"No."

"Jesus, really?"

"I've been to Paris, though."

"Who hasn't?"

"I don't know. Lots of people. What's your point, Steve?"

"Nothing. Except that I've seen more of your country than you."

Steve puts his hands in oven mitts, his own, the latex kind from infomercials, and pulls out the chicken.

"I used to be one of them," I say. "A Jehovah's Witness."

"No shit?"

"My mother is a Witness so I went to meetings when I was a kid. I was even baptized. I was twelve, which is technically too young, but she was worried I was losing interest and, you know, having thoughts and ideas of my own."

Steve laughs. "How dare you?"

"So she pulled some strings."

"And your dad? Is he one, too?"

"Oh no. The opposite. He was a scientist."

"Was?"

"He's dead. Cancer."

"*Malaka*," he says, "Sorry."

"It's okay. It happened a while ago. But thanks."

Steve picks at the bird with his fingers, separating the wings from its body. It looks like I feel.

"Steve," I say, "is there a Mrs. . . . Steve?"

He pulls the rest of the meat off the bones and drops it on a plate.

"Was," he says.

"Was?"

"As in past. No longer present. And English is your first language?"

Steve pushes the plate to me. The heat, the scent, the promise of something good and wholesome, it's almost enough.

"I'm just touchy about her." He pulls a napkin from his pocket and tucks it into his collar. "Because she was too good for me."

I reach for a fork but Steve stops me. "Eat with your fingers. Tastes better."

I tug my wedding ring over my knuckle and slide it next to my plate. It sits beneath the pot light. I'm relieved there's no diamond to mock me with its sparkle.

"What was her name?" I ask.

"Accalia."

The chicken is buttery; the thyme reminds me of summer. "Do you mind if I ask what she was like?"

Steve pulls a leg off the bird, holding it with his fingers like a cob of corn. He turns it round and round, as though he is the spit, his eyes the flame. "She was the pride of the town type, you know?" He studies the gristle by the joint. "Beautiful, smart, kind. And her food. *O theé mou.* That woman could cook better than any of those fancy chefs on the television. And she was a real woman, too." He drops the leg to the table, his fingers mapping Accalia's body in the air. "Like a Coke bottle, all right? Not like the kind you see in the magazines. Fake and orange and skinny blonde. No, Accalia had that classic Greek beauty, okay? Black hair so thick and strong you could tie a boat to it. And these cantaloupe breasts. I tell you, they sat so high they almost touched her chin. Incredible. All that weight to carry around, yet she stood so tall, like a dancer. Those huge melons way up in the sky." Steve's hands hang in the air. His palms cupped, empty.

"I'm sorry," I say.

"For what?"

"That she passed away."

"Accalia?" He picks up my plate, scrapes the bone and fat into the sink. "Oh no. Accalia's waiting for me to go first."

The door buzzes. Steve and I look at each other expectantly.

"Maybe it's Henry?" I say.

"Maybe."

"Do you think so? Really? I mean, you saw him. You were here. Did he look upset?"

It buzzes again.

"Maybe you should answer that?"

"Of course," I say. "Of course."

I smooth my hair behind my ears and push the button. "Henry?"

"You keep asking for Henry," says the voice, breathy as a librarian's, the kind of voice you lean in to. "He must be the husband."

I sink into the wall.

"Who is it?" Steve asks.

"My mother."

"You going to let her in?"

"No."

"You have to."

"I don't have to do anything. But you? You have to go."

He looks up to the ceiling. "Can I get my knife first?"

Pushing Steve to the door is like pushing a refrigerator. I leave greasy chicken stains on the back of his shirt.

Door shut, I try to collect myself. The buzzer rings out, then stops. It's so quiet I can hear the bulge moving around the blade. I catch it shifting, the knife moving with it. It won't hold much longer. The pressure will force it out, and all the gunk inside will release like a geyser.

I stand on a chair and reach for the handle, pull fast, drawing out the blade like a samurai. I cover my head, expecting a deluge of liquid to dump itself on me, but the bulge just groans and then burps, leaking out only a few flakes, just a taste of snow. I move quickly, a surgeon in control of the ER. I jump up. Down. Locate duct tape. Sever piece with teeth. Cover hole. It sticks! Another life saved!

A knock at my door.

"Avery?" My mother. "Avery, let me inside."

"How did you get in the building?" I yell through the wood.

"A nice Greek man opened the door."

Swearing, I search for something to impale Steve with. The knife will do nicely. His own knife. It's almost too perfect.

"Can you please just let me in?"

"No."

"Avery!"

"Margaret!"

"It's important," she says. "It's about your uncle Bryan."

I am filthy and nasty and dirty and soiled and disgusting. And she knows it, she's come to face it, to take the blame for her part in it.

I put my hand on the knob, leave fingerprints coated with grease and the skin of dead fowl. *Filthy. Nasty.*

I swing open the door.

Margaret. And a suitcase.

24

Margaret's eyes run over me; they look dead so I know she can see me. *Filthy and nasty and dirty.* I want her to say it. *And soiled.* I want her to recognize me for what I am because of her.

Her lips slacken. "You look ... thin."

That's it? *That's it?*

"And more like your father than me." Her eyes narrow. "But I suppose that's fitting."

"What do you want?" I ask.

"Since you're always asking for him, I'm assuming Henry isn't here?" She looks around. "And that he hasn't been for some time?"

I cross my arms. "None of your business." It feels good to have something she wants.

She huffs. "May I have my purse back, please?"

"I don't have it," I tell her.

I do have it. I hid her purse in the closet beneath a stack of Henry's unworn clothing. Track pants, a ski racing suit, bicycle shorts with tags still on. Henry kept it all squirrelled away like survival provisions, in case he caught a virus that mutated him into an outdoorsman.

"Of course you do," Margaret says. "I threw it up here the other day ... in a regrettable moment of weakness."

I make a point not to break eye contact. I commit to looking at her relentlessly. "I don't have your purse, Margaret."

"This isn't funny; I need it back. I had some cash in my suitcase, but I'm running low."

My face is hot with lies. "What can I say? You must have missed your target."

Her eyes shift sideways. Her hands to hips. "Well, isn't that the strangest thing?"

"It is," I say. My body smoking against the doorframe.

She peers over my shoulder and into the apartment. "May I?"

I step aside, I owe her at least that. She touches the television for heat, the bookshelf for dust, sweeps her foot across the floor for dirt. The state of me via the state of my home.

"It's modern," she says. "But rather barren, don't you think?"

"I like barren."

"No, you like coziness and colour."

Goddammit I do.

"Can't you at least hang a picture?" she says. "How about that spot right there?" She points to the wall where the futon used to sit, to the empty space above it. She maps out the spot with her fingers, a lozenge shape she intends to be a rectangle. "What was that group of painters your dad liked? There were seven of them."

"The Group of Seven," I say, hoping my acerbic tone connects like a kick.

She snaps her fingers. "That's them! One of their pictures would look lovely right there."

I snap my fingers back at her, only with a zesty attitude, like the teenagers who smoke in the Burger Shack parking lot. "You wanted to talk to me about Bryan?"

"Yes, Bryan," she says. "He's doing well these days—"

"That's too bad."

"He's trying to stitch his life back together—"

"After he tore mine—"

Margaret gives me the hand, the one mothers invented and troubled teens co-opted. "He's making an effort," she says. "He's in Narcotics Anonymous."

"In prison," I add. "He's in Narcotics Anonymous *in prison*."

"He's trying to better himself."

I laugh.

"He needs to make reparations. And he wants to see you."

The heat returns. The flames that bursts in my skin over my lie to Margaret. My irreparable shame. "And did he tell you why?" I choke out, the smoke inside me thick. "Why me?"

She looks around me. At the smoke sizzling out of my ears, my smoldering hair. But she won't look at me. "Whatever it was, Avery, if you would just—"

"*Whatever it was?*" I say.

Margaret's posture sinks, her breath halts. She recoils into herself like a child expecting a slap.

I flip on the Weather Network. Calvin Straight, his cheeks like a blowfish, is demonstrating how a weather balloon works. *"It sends back information on atmospheric pressure, temperature, humidity and wind speed."*

"If you could open your heart up to forgiveness," Margaret says, "I think—"

"It uses a telemetry device called a radiosonde."

"—I think you could at least understand one another."

"That's raid-ee-oh-sohnde. Sonde *is German"*—he giggles —*"for* probe."

Margaret grabs the remote. She banishes Calvin Straight into blackness.

"I'm trying to talk to you," she says.

"You left us," I tell her. "Dad was dying of cancer, I was thirteen, and you left us."

She clutches at her chest. Tries to make me believe she has a heart. "I've made mistakes," she says. "But I don't deserve to be treated like this."

"Oh, I'm sorry—is this not the welcome you wanted?" I say.

I'm high on anger, my head a weather balloon expanding, ready to blow. "Shall I roll out the red carpet for you?"

She looks at my rug, pinches a clump of my hair. "That would be an improvement."

I moan.

"This apartment," she says. "It's a little ... sad."

Tear at my hair.

"It's just my opinion, Avery. I'm entitled to that, aren't I?"

Stomp my feet until Fish Sticks bangs on his ceiling.

Margaret presses down on my shoulders, her old trick. "Stop that," she says.

And I do.

"'For we all stumble many times,'" she recites. "'If anyone does not stumble in word, he is a perfect man, able to bridle also his whole body. James 3:2.'"

I brush her fingers off me like dandruff. "Do you even know what that means?"

"It means you need to come with me to see your uncle Bryan."

"I'm pretty sure it doesn't mean that."

"It means forgiveness and—"

"You clearly said 'James' not Bryan."

She wrings her hands. "You're trying to rattle me, but I'm on a mission."

"From god? You are such a narcissist, Margaret."

"I've got a visit with him coming up at the facility."

"At *the prison*."

"Avery, a willingness to forgive others regardless of how they offend us is a Christian requirement."

"I'm not a Christian, Margaret."

She looks around the apartment. "Yes, I can tell."

What is she looking at?

"Just think about it, Avery. Sleep on it."

"I don't need to sleep on anything."

"Well I do—I'm exhausted," she says. "And since my purse is mysteriously gone, and I don't have much money—"

I groan.

"Just until I visit Bryan. You won't even know I'm here."

I groan again; it's becoming my new language. The calculation makes me a loser either way. If I give Margaret her purse back, she wins. If she stays with me, she wins.

"Maybe there is a god," I say, looking up to the ceiling, to the bulge.

"Oh there is most certainly a God," Margaret says. "His name is Jehovah. He is merciful and kind. And he wants you to forgive."

The bulge slithers into my bedroom. I follow it.

I slide the doors shut and the bulge explodes, sending a cascade of snow roaring down. It collapses on top of me just like my father warned me it would, so heavy and suffocating. I hear Dad shouting instructions. Relax! Take short breaths! But I panic, my heavy breaths forcing more air out than I suck in, my body poisoning itself with carbon dioxide. I drive my fist into the snow, punch a hole through the top of it. There's a soccer ball–sized gap in the ceiling where the bulge had been, and the feet of Cowboy, his red socks moving left right left, line dancing over glass.

Days without Henry: 1

25

The snow, the hole, Cowboy's socks, all of it is gone when I regain consciousness. I check my body, feeling around for injury and frostbite but find neither. It's 3:00 a.m. so I inch my way into the living room. She has no bed or futon, of course, so Margaret is doing her best on the chair. Legs drape over an arm, head lolls against the back. Heavy breathing and small cries, the wrestling sounds of her sleep. The weather is back on; she must have wanted company. The channel is a reliable choice for a Jehovah's Witness. No nudity or foul language. The programming one hundred percent proof of god's might.

"Signing off for the Weather Network, I'm Calvin Straight." He pulls his shoulders back, cocks his head. *"Giving the weather strai—"*

I snap off the television.

In the silence that follows, the dim strumming of a guitar. I walk into the bathroom and close the door, my fingers reaching to turn the lock that isn't there. Shampoo perfumes hang in the air: an Irish spring near a freshly paved road.

I would do anything for love.

The song floats through the gap between the ceiling and the shower wall. I climb into the tub, press my forehead to the tile and sing along even though I have no right. My voice breaks when it needs to be strong, brash when it should be soft.

The music pauses. A knock on the wall. "Hello?"

"Oh sorry," I say. "I hoped you couldn't hear me."

"I can hear everything because of that damn gap in the damn wall," Billy Pfeiffer says. His speaking voice is raspy, as though he needs to clear his throat. "I swear, one of these days I'm just going to tear it down and start from scratch."

"I love that song you play," I tell him.

Silence. Then. "Really?"

"You play it very well."

"Yeah? Thanks."

"Why do you play in your bathroom?"

"The acoustics."

"Right. Of course." I scratch the tile with my fingernail. The white of the ceramic is misleading because a thick caking of soap scum comes off, flaking itself down and settling on the bare skin of my arm. White on white and endless. "Are you still there?" I ask.

"Yeah."

"Oh. Good. So, um, how was your day?"

"Fine?"

"Good, good. Mine was fine, too."

"Uh huh."

"Actually, not that fine," I admit.

"No?"

"This day, or the days before that."

An object on my neighbour's side comes to rest on a hard surface. Like a bottle plunked down on a bathtub. I scrape my nail along the tile again, this time reaching the caulking that surrounds the soap dish, where the white scum is thickest.

"Do you have days like that?" I ask. "Not fine?"

"Uh . . ."

"I know you do."

"And how would you know that?"

"Because I hear things through the wall, too."

"Oh yeah? Like what?"

"Sad things. Angry things. Things that make me wonder about you."

Silence. Then. "I wonder about you, too," he says.

"You do not," I tell him.

"No, I do. Because it's so quiet on your side. It's like no one really lives there."

I scrape off a new chunk of white. It works its way under my nail, giving the appearance of a French manicure. I try to dig it out with another nail but it only spreads the problem around.

"My husband moved out," I say.

"Sorry to hear that."

"Thank you," I say. "But I have bigger problems now."

I scrape the tile again and more of the scum falls off. It's satisfying, this kind of cleansing, so I scrape and scrape until my legs are covered in flakes. I picture Calvin's forecast of this weather system. *Avery's tub is getting hammered hard by the white stuff, folks, so shower with caution. I'm Calvin Straight. Giving the weather straight to you.* I scrape once more and the tile falls off. All the walls in the world are held together by white. How incredibly lonely.

"What kind of problems?" Billy Pfeiffer asks.

"Weather problems."

"Oh," he says. "I can't fix that."

"No one can."

He strums a chord on his guitar. "Maybe a weatherman."

26

The news media deemed "The Falling Glass Problem" a crisis. It began three years ago when a tempered pane popped out of its mullion, careened down the west side of a fifty-three-storey condominium and killed a publicist and her assistant. Since then, seven more incidents. Three deaths and four near-misses.

The City blames the developers. The developers blame the engineers. The engineers blame shoddy glass manufactured in China. We've never heard back from China.

When the condos first began to attack, thousands of people were stricken by terrible cricks in the neck from all that looking up. The crisis was a boon for chiropractors. The day after an incident, the lobbies of the accused buildings would be scattered with flyers for discounted spinal adjustment services. Psychologists also got in on the action, publishing on Crystallacrophobia, the fear of being hit by glass from great heights. Self-help groups popped up, hugely popular with the poorly insured. Each night across the city, nervous pedestrians shared their nightmares aloud, painting horrific pictures of Zeus-like buildings growing arms and launching windows and balcony glass down to the streets like lightning. Even I went to a support meeting or two. Like I did at the Jehovah's Witness Recovery Group, I would sit quietly in the circle and listen to the anxiety, the proposals, the rumours. A constant stream of neck and shoulder rubs broke up the nervous chatter. One person would start the chain, at my meetings it was always a fat woman in a Trinidad and Tobago T-shirt, and it would continue on from there — massagee would become massager, like the fulfillment of a silent pact.

Because of "The Falling Glass Problem," I avoid going downtown as much as I can, but TV weatherman Calvin Straight doesn't have that luxury. He works in a building directly across from one of the worst offenders, a condo erected on top of a cinema, restaurant and parking complex. Just last week it launched one of its windowpanes on a charity canvasser. Lopped her head clean off.

I need to talk to Calvin Straight, so I'm downtown, in a safeish spot beneath his office tower's poured concrete canopy.

People come and go. Television producer types in jeans and blazers. Cameramen in cargo shorts. The few who wear suits I recognize from the local news. Their faces are thick with makeup, various shades of beige foundation pressed into their cracks and crevices. The foundation shifts as their mouths do, asking me for a cigarette I don't have.

I do a double take. Calvin Straight? The weatherman? He doesn't move like the other on-camera people do, commanding space around them. He's taller than me, but not by much. He wouldn't have to duck into anywhere: the shower, the closet, cabs. His feet wouldn't hang over the bed. His shoulders cave inward and his skin has a natural sheen, as though he recently scrubbed off his Revlon. What really catches my eye, though, is the bicycle helmet perched atop his head, the strap hanging too loose to keep his skull together, if it came to that.

"You're the weatherman," I say.

He turns toward me. His eyes, the sleepy, heavy-lidded kind, squint as they take me in. "Meteorologist, actually."

"Right, sorry. I'm Avery. I'm a fan."

He shakes my hand. "Hi, Avery. Calvin Straight. But I guess you know that. One question before we have a chat, if that's what you'd like. Is it?"

"Um, sure."

"Did you track me here? Like were you standing here waiting for me to come out? Or is this a coincidental run-in?"

"Run in," I lie.

"Oh that's too bad," he says, "Although I suppose I'll get some of those sooner or later, right? The super-fan stalker types?"

"Um . . ."

"Now about that chat. The weather, I suppose, right? It's kind of tragic that I'm always going on about the one topic that's synonymous with awkward small talk, isn't it? I mean, I don't mind, obviously, but I wonder if people like you . . . Do you really want to talk about cumulous clouds and precipitation? Or do you want to hear about the blogs I'm reading or what I'm binge-watching? My favourite cat memes, perhaps? Whatever you like. Your wish is my command."

"I'd like to talk about weather."

"Oh thank goodness."

"And I actually have a very specific question for you."

"I'm riveted."

"Is there such a thing as a weather system that's so small it only covers, say, a few square feet?"

"You mean like a microclimate?"

"Oh my god, yes!"

"Not quite the reaction I'd expected, but okay."

"But that's it!" I yelp. "That's exactly it!"

"Well, it isn't *exactly*. A microclimate is a zone where the climate is different from others nearby. But an entire weather *system* that's micro? No. There's no such thing."

"But isn't that just tautological?" I said.

"Maybe, if I knew what tautological meant."

"Like you're saying the same thing twice. Microclimate, micro weather system. They're the same thing, aren't they?"

"Hold on a minute. So you know a big word like *tautological* but you missed my point entirely?"

"These microclimates, what brings them on?"

"Well, they're usually near water or in areas affected by very strong, pointed sources of heat. So they can be very small. Even a garden, technically, is a microclimate."

"So they can be caused by people."

"They're caused by wind, heat and water. But yes, people can create those conditions. Turn on a hose and irrigate, build condos everywhere and create wind tunnels. Okay, so I've got to go now. Loads of cat memes to watch." Calvin walks backwards, bumping into the bike rack, then rights his course. I follow. "It was nice talking to you. Keep watching the Weather Network. I appreciate your viewership, et cetera, et cetera."

"But is it possible that these sorts of microclimates just pop up?" I ask.

"It's not *im*possible," he says.

"Really? Like out of thin air?"

"First of all, I hate that expression," he says, wagging his finger at me. "Air is not *thin*, all right? Air is 78.09 percent nitrogen and 20.95 percent oxygen and the rest—"

"Is argon," I say.

Calvin walks back to me. He remaps his steps exactly and trundles into the bike rack. Topples a hipster cruiser with a banana seat. "You *are* a super-fan! I knew it! I—"

"No, sorry. My father was a scientist, so I kind of absorbed these sorts of facts."

Calvin rubs bike tire scuff from his pants. "Then your father would have told you that while micro-systems aren't officially a thing, weather anomalies do happen from time to time."

"And could these micro-systems or climates, these anomalies—"

My hands are in the air. I'm talking with my hands too much.

"—could they happen indoors?"

He laughs. "If you're experiencing that then you need to talk to a psychiatrist, not a meteorologist."

"I'm not crazy."

"So a medical doctor then. Whatever floats your boat in a moat."

"But—"

"Taut-o-log-i-cal. Great word. I'm going to try and use that. Now, if you'll excuse me, I've got a long walk ahead of me." He hurries east, staying as close to the building as he can, as though the sidewalk is a ledge he could tumble from.

"But didn't you bike?" I holler.

"You mean because of my helmet? No, no. I wear this because of all the falling glass. Can't be too careful!"

"There's a self-help group for that."

"Oh, I know. I love the massages."

27

Except for myself and a woman of indeterminate age picking at a family of sores, the waiting room is empty. It usually is, though, because the doctors at this walk-in clinic aren't particularly good. They are all men, first of all, and each one has a unique defect that calls their competency into question. One has a lazy eye, another reeks of whiskey, and the third has wandering hands. Pretty much all the working parts are rotten so I only come here when I'm too desperate to wait in line at a better facility. And, also, they prescribe drugs like they're handing out lollipops.

"Avery Gauthier?"

I scramble out of my chair like I always do, forever surprised when it's my turn. This doctor is new, so new her name hasn't been added to the front door of the clinic. She is plain and flat-chested and wears Birkenstocks with socks, the exact classification of female who could survive this place. She squeezes antibacterial gel on her hands and then shakes mine. "I'm Dr. McMartin. What brings you in?"

I hop on the table, my jeans tearing the paper. "There's this weatherman —"

"I'm sorry?"

"— and he suggested I see a doctor. He was joking, but the more I thought about it . . ."

She checks her watch. "What exactly is this regarding?"

"I think there may be something wrong with my head. My brain, I mean."

She sits down at her computer — it's covered in a clear protective film — and types. "Oh really? How so?"

"I'm seeing things that aren't there. That I'm pretty sure are not there."

Despite the plastic, her fingers work fast. "What kinds of things? Violent things?"

"No."

"Are you hearing voices? Voices telling you to do things?"

"No, nothing like that. It's, well, it's a bit hard to explain."

She crosses her legs. Her left Birkenstock dangles from her foot. "Try me."

"I'm seeing weather," I say. "Inclement weather. Snow mostly."

The Birkenstock falls to the floor. She leaves the sandal and scuttles over to me, the wheels of her stool rolling over the German-crafted leather and cork. "Where are you seeing this snow?"

"Outside, in the park and on the street."

"And this worries you because . . ."

"Because it's July and because the weatherman doesn't mention it and because no one else sees it."

She drags herself closer, placing her cold hand on my arm. She wraps a blood pressure cuff around it and squeezes.

"I also see it inside," I say. "Inside churches. And inside my apartment."

She keeps her eyes on the rising mercury. "Interesting."

"Do you think I could have brain damage?"

She releases the valve and the Velcro. "Have you fallen recently?"

"I have! Holy shit, I actually have! I fainted or something and hit my head!"

She pulls a penlight from her pocket. Aims it at my pupils. "When was that?"

"A few days ago."

"Well, your eyes seem normal." She checks my reflexes, my limbs bouncing up to her command. "Having any neurological symptoms? Tingling, numbness in your limbs? Pain?"

"No. No physical pain."

She checks my lymph nodes, her hands on my neck, armpits and breasts. "But you're having other kinds of pain?"

"No. I don't know. I'm not sure why I said that."

She rolls back to her keyboard. "How's work?"

I slap my head with my palm. "Shit!"

"What?"

"I missed a deadline!"

"So work is stressful." She types up my incompetence, adding it to the permanent record. "And you're married, I see. How's that going?"

I look where she looks — at my ring. It's still on my finger, a little looser than last week, but hanging on. And when this doctor stops wasting my time with these bullshit questions and gets my bruised brain in an MRI or a CT, when she stops playing Dr. House and Dr. Frasier Crane and actually figures out what's wrong with me, Henry will want to come back to me. He'll feel so bad about leaving, in fact, that he'll upgrade this ring to a new setting. "How about two stupid diamond bees kissing?" he'll ask. And we'll laugh and laugh.

"So your marriage?" the doctor says.

"It's perfect," I smile. "He's perfect. We're the perfect married couple."

She's typing. "Uh huh."

What the hell is she typing?

"You think I'm crazy, don't you?"

"We don't use that word. But no, I don't think you are. You might be a little bit stressed out, depressed maybe."

"Depressed? Okay, I'll take that. So can you just give me something?"

"I don't think you need drugs. I do think you may benefit from a counsellor, however."

"I'm in a support group, sort of. Does that count?"

"It does. Certainly. What kind of support group?"

"I'd rather not talk about it."

She slides her Birkenstock back on. "That may be part of your problem."

"The support group?"

"The not talking."

"It really isn't," I say.

"Suppressed stress or depression can exhibit themselves in all kinds of ways. They can take a real physical toll. From hair loss all the way up to cancer, and they can wreak havoc on hormones and the menstrual cycle. By the way, how are your periods?"

"My periods are irrelevant since you clearly think I'm going crazy."

She rifles through her desk and pulls out a pamphlet. *Depression & Anxiety & You.* Hands it to me like a Jehovah's Witness on the street. "Listen, just because you *feel* quote unquote crazy, doesn't mean you are. These things happen to perfectly sane people. Sometimes the wires in the brain just get crossed."

"Wires?" I say. "You went to, what, eight years of medical school and you're telling me it's wires?"

"I'm not diagnosing you—"

"But that's why I'm here."

"—I'm just trying to tell you that it could be all kinds of things other than a full-blown, chronic mental illness. What you say you're seeing could even be a delayed reaction to some kind of trauma."

"I never said anything about trauma."

"I'm just giving you an example."

"But I'd really like some drugs, if you don't mind."

"Of course," she says, pulling out her prescription pad. "What would you like? Morphine, methadone, oxycodone? How about some Quaaludes?"

"Quaaludes, please."

"I was being facetious."

"So was I."

Dr. McMartin regards me silently.

"What drugs can you actually give me?" I ask.

"I'm not going to give you any."

"I thought you doctors were giving out drugs all over the place these days."

"Not this one."

"Then I'd like an appointment with one of the other doctors, please. Preferably the one with the drinking problem."

She crosses her arms. "Why don't you just keep going to that support group of yours? Come back and see me in a month."

I leave the exam room without a prescription, which is fine, because what I see in the waiting room is enough of a trip. In the seat where the woman and her sores had been now sits young, sweet, broken Kristie. The fallen Jehovah's Witness in her Frankenstein parka.

28

"Kristie?"

"Hey!" Her hair is messy and wild, skin blotchy, eyes red as if she's been crying, or rubbing or shampooing them. "How are you? Sick I guess, right? Kind of a stupid question, really, since you're like at the doctor."

"Yeah," I say. "I've got the flu or something."

"Yeah, me too. Must be the flu." She crosses and uncrosses her legs and bounces her knees in between. "You know what? I actually just lied to you. I don't have the flu."

"Um, okay."

"Can we go to like the Starbucks down the street or something?"

"Sure," I say. "But don't you have to—"

"Nah. It doesn't matter. These doctors can't help me either."

Kristie scans the Starbucks as if sweeping for cameras or spies smuggling microfiche in lipstick. She uncrosses her legs, crosses them, bounces in her seat.

"What can I get you?" she asks me. "It's my treat. A misto? Caramel macchiato? Iced coffee? Mocha? White mocha? Mocha Valencia? Java chip frappuccino? Espresso con panna? Vanilla crème frappuccino? No, wait, let me guess: You're a tall, sugar-free, non-fat, half-caf, vanilla latte kind of girl."

"Do you work here?" I ask, impressed and disturbed.

"I wish! It's always been my dream to be a barista."

I laugh and Kristie looks at me, confused.

"Oh, you're serious."

"It looks like so much fun," she says. "All these exotic drinks and machines. And like cool young people with Band-Aids over their nose rings."

"Why don't you apply?"

"My parents would never allow it. Too many bad influences." She allows herself the luxury of a frown for a moment and then forces the corners of her mouth upright. They wiggle back and forth, fighting against her, and then release, springing into a smile. The muscle memory of a good Christian. "So what'll it be?" she says.

"A hot chocolate would be good," I say.

"Ooh. I'll have that too."

We used to drink hot chocolate in the chemo ward. Every time the volunteer with the beverage cart would round the corner, my dad would wave her down. It was a good job for her because she was incredibly old; she needed that cart to keep her upright and moving. I imagined she had one just like it at home, only it was full of newspapers and cats. It seemed so backwards, I thought then, this old sagging woman working where this sturdy strong man lay dying. My dad would always ask for three packets of hot chocolate even though there were just two of us. He'd empty one and a half in each cup, the dust of cocoa and sugar and corn syrup solids drifting up into the quadruple-filtered hospital air. We had to pour the boiling water ourselves — the volunteer's hands were curled by a disease she called Dupytren's — but my father didn't mind. He would inhale the chocolate steam as the water flowed out of the kettle. "If there was a God," he'd say, "he'd make this chemo taste like hot chocolate instead of metal."

"Change my order!" I call out to Kristie. "I'll take anything other than hot chocolate!" But it's too late. She's already carrying our drinks back to the table. Her movements are fast and fidgety and her hands are shaking.

"Cheers," she says, getting whipped cream on her coat.

"You got some—"

"I'm pregnant," she says. "And I'm going to have an abortion."

I squawk, and Kristie leaps up. "You?" she says. "Really? I thought you'd be different, Avery. I thought—"

I touch her arm. "No, no. Please. You surprised me, that's all. It was a surprised squawk, not a judgmental squawk."

She sits back down. "Good, because, like, as if I don't already know that what I'm doing is a sin."

"According to whom?"

"What?"

"Do *you*—Kristie—think premarital sex and abortion is a sin? Do you believe that yourself? Or are you just repeating what you've been told?"

She thinks about it. "I don't know the difference."

I smile. "That's the most honest thing I've ever heard."

Kristie makes a face, and it reminds me that she's still just a sixteen-year-old kid. "They talk about stuff like that at support group," she says. "Like what's actually real versus what the Watchtower tells us is real."

"Is the group helping you?" I ask her.

"Those guys? No way. They just tell me to, like, hug myself. Junk like that. And then gossip about me later when they think I can't hear."

"That sounds about right," I say.

"They talk about you too."

"Really?"

"They don't trust you," she says. "Because you came back after being gone for so long. And because you don't share. Some of them think you're a spy."

"What?" I say. "That's totally insane."

"I know that," she says. "I told them you're too sad to be a spy."

I lean back in my chair, try to get a grip on her. "You're pretty observant."

"Yeah, my sisters tell me that all the time." Kristie plays with her lid. She scratches a heart into it with a fingernail.

"How many sisters do you have?"

"Two," says Kristie, rubbing her stomach and the baby inside of it. "It sucks because they don't talk to me much since . . . Anyways, they slide notes under my bedroom door when they're feeling brave. I keep them in a shoebox in my closet."

Kristie's hands tremble. Or maybe the baby? Can a baby kick at this stage?

"It'll be okay," I tell her. "You'll be okay."

"Okay like you?" Kristie says, her mood shifting. "Okay like seeing invisible snow? Or coats? Am I wearing it now?"

"How could you—"

"The doctor left the door wide open. But it doesn't matter; it was obvious anyways. You're having a mental breakdown, Avery. I mean, hello!"

I look down at my drink. The foam has disappeared almost completely, but I've lost my appetite for what's underneath. Kristie rises from her seat and walks to the door, her hot chocolate untouched—same as mine. Snow falls as she steps outside, flakes the size of quarters. They don't melt when they land on the sidewalk so I figure the temperature has dropped. A gust of wind confirms my suspicion, but Kristie doesn't react. She lets go of the door and walks out into the cold, leaving her coat behind.

Two seniors eyeball me. They're kind of bitchy about it.

"You think I should go after her, don't you?" I say to them. "But it's not like I'm her mother. It's not my responsibility to take care of her. I mean, look at me; I can't even take care of myself."

They stare at the chair that Kristie's left empty. "Are you almost done with this table?" one of them asks.

I take a sip of my drink without blowing on it first. A welt blooms on my tongue. "Thorry, no," I say, as they huff and stomp off.

I'm not Kristie's mother, or anyone's. And I don't want to be. Getting fat, tearing my body in two pushing the damn thing out, then raising it for nineteen years? And for what? So it could steal my purse? Swear at me? Make me sleep in a chair? And anyways, a baby couldn't happen now. It's too late; I'm ruined in that way. Aren't I? Even if I *could* have a baby, a baby with Henry, Current Henry, it would be a mistake. He'd see it as a desperate attempt to hold on to him and I would resent him for forcing his religion on our child. No, when Henry comes back and we have sex and I get pregnant, I will get rid of the baby. Unless . . . unless Current Henry changes back into Old Henry and we raise our son together, teaching him to love birthday cake, *Star Wars*, competitive sports, Santa Claus and blood transfusions.

What's in this hot chocolate?

I reach across the table for Kristie's coat. It's coated in waxy polyurethane, and reflective tape runs along the torso, back and sleeves. Stiff as cardboard and resilient. I bend it and it springs right back. I slip into the arms stuffed to the seams with thick artificial filler, polyester, instead of feathers. I feel through the pockets for a cellphone or ID, some sort of tool that will help me return the coat to Kristie. All I find is a Kevlar patch in the chest pocket, the kind used in bulletproof vests.

"Damn," I say.

This coat is ready for war.

29

Steve is in his broom closet. He's sitting in his raggedy arm-chair, the fabric torn, the stuffing spilling out of the seat and the back. He isn't reading a book or a magazine or even napping. He's staring at the wall.

I knock on the doorframe. He doesn't bother to turn his head.

"Can I help you?" he asks, his tone formal.

It's not exactly an invitation, but Kristie's coat has my back and it makes me feel brave. "You let my mother in the building."

"Which you should have done yourself."

"My mother is a bitch."

He turns and points his finger at me. There's grease on it. Car, not kitchen. "You're an ungrateful daughter, Avory," he says.

"You don't know her! She could be a psycho! She could have killed me!"

"Oh give me a break." He pulls the chair's lever. It swings his legs horizontal. "You're fine."

A tingle courses through my veins. It's probably the excite-ment of anger and the resulting adrenaline, but the energy feels tactical, as though my blood is being given orders from a com-mand post I dare not question. I step on Steve's footrest, grind it back into the body of the chair. Steve's mouth gapes.

"I'm actually very upset," I say. "It's a security breach is what this is. I'm going to have to call the owner of the building and report the incident. It's got to be against some kind of code of conduct to let a non-resident inside without permission."

Steve's top denture loosens, his faux gums separating from whatever's left in a wet clunk. I give a small shriek and he stuffs his teeth back into position. "Coffee?" he asks, groaning himself out of his chair and toward his hotplate. He grasps for a shiny copper pot with a long handle. It looks magical, like a net for catching fairies. He measures out what he needs. Two cups of ice water. Two teaspoons of sugar. One heaping teaspoon of coffee. "You need it coarse, like it's been ground by an animal's teeth." No filter. "Filters are for little girls." He stirs the coffee until the grounds dissolve and dark, brown foam rises above the lip of the pot. Thick, undrinkable swamp mud. "Drink," he says, pouring it into a mug as ringed as a tree.

Syrupy, yet bitter. Grainy as sand. I feel my face grimace.

"So?" he says. "Best coffee in the world, right?"

I smile. "Best coffee in the world." The grounds fill the gaps between my teeth. They make Steve laugh. They make me laugh too.

I sit in his recliner. "Sorry I threatened you, Steve."

He pulls the lever, settles me in. "I'm sorry I let your mother in."

Steve pours himself a cup. The coffee, thicker now, oozes from the pot. "Accalia used to say I wanted a mother, not a wife. And she was right. Even for leaving me like she did. One moment: cooking at the stove. The next: gone."

"Did you ever forgive her for leaving?" I ask.

"Are you kidding? It was my fault." He swirls the coffee and stares into his mug, reading his fortune in the grounds gypsy-style. "Which is too bad for me, because I'm the hardest person to forgive."

Margaret's on all fours with a hand broom and pan. She's working the bristles into the greedy fibres of my damn rug. One corner is perfectly clean. Three to go.

My mind flashes to Henry cleaning the same rug only *1, nearly 2, days without Henry* ago. "What do you people think this is?" I say. "A magic carpet?"

"It's just filthy," my mother says.

"Get up," I pull her into a standing position. "You don't have to clean."

"I cleaned your bathroom, too. A man tried to talk to me through the wall."

"Yeah, we do that."

"Is he Henry?"

I laugh.

"I didn't think so," she says. "Your neighbour's voice doesn't sound like it belongs to the man in the photo."

"What photo?"

"Your wedding photo."

Goddamn it!

Language, please!

No! She's already in my head!

"I think it's wonderful that you're married," she says. "I'm only sad I couldn't be there for the big day."

"You weren't there for any days."

"I was there for twelve years of your life. I gave you values and morals."

"You gave me misery."

"You were always good with the drama, Avery." She sighs. "Are you an actress? I always thought you'd end up on the stage."

"I'm a research assistant for a vanity legal publishing company."

She recoils and tries to recover. "Well, I'm sure that's very interesting." She squirms back down to the rug, starts on corner number two. "Now tell me about this Henry of yours. How did you meet?"

I kneel down beside her. Two schoolgirls sharing secrets at a slumber party. "A pterodactyl had just swooped down and stolen his hat. I chased him through the fields of lava and—"

Margaret frowns. "Avery—"

I start braiding her hair. "A long time ago in a galaxy far, far away—"

"Avery!"

"Margaret!"

"Just . . . tell me *something*. Something basic. How old is he?"

"Thirty-one."

"Oh? An older man?"

"Please. He's only six years older."

"A lot can happen to a man in six years."

"Stop it, Margaret."

"I'm just saying that—"

"He doesn't control me, if that's what you're getting at."

"That's not at all what—"

"Because he doesn't control me, okay?"

She clears her throat. "What are his parents like?"

"I don't know."

"You don't know?"

"He doesn't talk about them. Just like I don't talk about mine."

"Well, what does Henry do for work then?"

"He's god's editor."

My mother purses her lips blue.

"What?" I say.

"You're trying to shock me."

I point my fingers at her and make a zapping noise. My body shakes with sarcastic electricity. "Henry's the new editor-in-chief of *Awake!* magazine—"

Margaret's eyebrows jump halfway up her head.

"—and, according to your religion, *Awake!* is the product of quote unquote divine guidance. Ipso facto, Henry is god's editor."

"Just wait one minute now." She points her fingers at me. "You're telling me that your husband . . . is a Jehovah's Witness?"

"Currently," I say, "he is under that impression."

"And not only that, but he's the editor-in-chief of *Awake!*—"

"At the moment."

"—in Wallkill, New York?"

"He may or may not be in that general area—"

"Yes or no, Avery?"

"Yes!" I yell. "Does that make you feel vindicated, Margaret? Huh? Does that make you happy?"

But she doesn't smile. She does the opposite; she sucks in her cheeks like she's tasting sour. "It's just so . . . full circle."

"No, it isn't," I say. "It's just a temporary glitch in the Matrix."

Margaret returns to the rug. Her sweeping makes a scraping sound. She's going to leave a scab. "Well, it's very impressive that Henry has made it to Wallkill. That Bethel is part of the World Headquarters."

Beth. Hell. Wall. Kill. Head. Quarter. It's as violent as it sounds. I see heavy machinery spewing blood and Bibles; Henry standing in the middle of it, his arms raised in victory.

"Did you know they print 200,000 magazines an hour in that facility?" Margaret says.

"It's not a facility," I say. "It's a fucking slaughterhouse."

"Avery! Language! Please!"

"Did you say that out loud?" I ask her.

"Pardon?"

"Never mind."

Margaret must be full of static because bits of my hair and dust are stuck to her, the only parts of me she doesn't repel. "And how is your marriage going?" she asks.

"What kind of a question is that?"

"Well, he's in Wallkill and you're here, so I'm just wondering how . . ."

"How what, Margaret? How our sex life is?"

Dirty filthy disgusting.

"Avery, I didn't say that."

"But that's what you're thinking, right? That I'm not giving him enough? That I'm not fulfilling my wifely duties?"

Nasty.

"I'm just trying to understand why—"

"Well, for your information, I let Henry do me from behind."

"Avery!"

"I let him tie me up."

"I know what you're doing."

"On Fridays his friends stop by and watch."

"You're trying to shock me—"

"Sometimes they have a go too."

"—but it isn't going to work!"

The door buzzes and I'm grateful for the interruption, be it Girl Guide, politician, charity canvasser, or axe murderer. I open the door and it's Gloria: a bona fide combo of all four. "Hi hun, sorry to bug you." She smells like coconut rum. "But I was thinking about our talk the other day and I—"

"Hello, Gloria."

"Margie? Is that you? You look awful. What happened to your hair? It's all stringy? And you're as skinny as a beanpole!"

"Well, time marches on," Margaret sighs. "For both of us. There's no denying that."

Gloria turns to me. "Why didn't you tell me she was back?" Her eyes as bright and big as the fronts of flashlights.

"Bryan asked me to come," Margaret says. "He wants to see Avery, and he thought I might be able to arrange a visit."

Gloria flits about the room like a stunned bird. "I'm taking care of that, Margie."

"Well, I suppose he thought that I, *her mother*, would be able to help."

"And what a mother you are." Gloria perches herself on the coffee table. "I was there for her when her father died, when her uncle was in prison. It was just Avery and me after you abandoned her. *I* raised her."

"And you did a wonderful job."

"Fuck you, Margie."

"Excuse me?"

Gloria looks to me for support, but I am useless, my mouth a non-functional cavernous O. So Gloria does what Gloria does best. She attacks, striking my mother's chest, her fingers stiff as a beak. "I said. Fuck. You. Margie." My mother backs up but Gloria pounces.

I try to get in between, steering Gloria away, using my forearm defensively, but she won't be moved. She punches my mother in the eye and lunges at her neck. It takes all of my strength to pull my mother and Gloria apart.

30

Gloria's living room is a landfill. Overflowing ashtrays, empty pizza boxes, bottles and cans of booze buzzing with wasps. The white leather couch looks yellow, as though the cigarette stains from the ceiling laid down for a rest and never made it back up.

"The maid's been sick," Gloria says. She paces the room, picking up the trash and laying it down somewhere else. Her kind of problem-solving.

"That bitch," she mutters. "Just turns up after all these years? And now what? She wants to be your mother again? I was your mother, Avery! It was me!"

"Just sit down, Gloria. Your blood pressure's through the roof."

"I was a good mom, wasn't I, hun?"

"You did the best you could."

"What the fuck is that supposed to mean?"

"Do you really want to get into this now?"

"Why not? I've got nothing to be ashamed of. You're the one who stopped talking to me. Never called me, not once since you moved out of the house and left for university. Shame on you, Avery! After everything I did!"

"Like ruin my life, you mean?"

Gloria takes my words like a punch. She stumbles back into a pile of *Cosmopolitan* magazines. October 2009, August 2008, December 2010, March 2009, June 2012 spill across the floor. "Do you think I wanted another kid? Your dad died and your idiot mother was AWOL and we got stuck with you. I was barely able to take care of myself. And with your uncle in and out of prison? Honey, what could I do?"

"That's the thing, Gloria. When it was just you and me, it was okay. But when Bryan would come home it's like you shut down. I need to understand what you were thinking."

Gloria picks up the magazines. She tries to arrange them chronologically. But the months, the years — she can't seem to make sense of it.

"I thought the elders were taking care of all that," she says.

"They blamed me, Gloria, and you know it."

"They told me Jehovah forgave him. I thought—"

"They didn't report it to the police, they didn't even disfellowship him."

"I know, but—"

"I should have gone to the police myself. I never should have—"

"It wasn't Bryan's fault! He was on so many drugs! He thought you were me!"

"You're still using that excuse?"

"It's the truth!"

"I can't believe I let you talk me out of it," I say. "I should have pressed charges."

"Go ahead then! What's stopping you?"

I run for the door, and Gloria grabs onto my ankle. She's on the floor, her outfit having a go with the rug. I see her varicose veins, thick blue rivers winding up her calves. "Don't, Avery. Please! I'm begging you! He's all I've got." Gloria cries and her mascara loses all control, sliding down her face, pulling a fake eyelash along with it. I lower myself next to her, pull a velvet pillow from the couch and slide it under her head.

"I did my best for you," she cries. "It wasn't enough? Fine, but it was my best."

"I know, Gloria. I know."

She fights to keep her eyes open but they sink closed. White foam gathers at the edges of her lips, her precursor to vomit I know too well. I wiggle my hands underneath her hips and turn her on her side. It's a miracle that she's lived this long, that she hasn't yet drowned in her own boozy sick.

"It happened to me, too," she mumbles. "And she blamed me, my mother. Told me I made my father do it. 'When you were born everything changed,' she said. 'You coming out of me and into the world changed him.'"

I sit with Gloria and look out the window. The snowflakes hang like curtains instead of falling, perfectly framing the Szechuan restaurant across the street. Gloria's breathing evens out and the gurgling stops; it's safe to leave her now. I stand, walk past my uncle's living room and turn down the hall. My old bedroom, so pink you'd assume the girl who lived here liked the colour. Empty bottles of beer and whiskey clutter my dresser and windowsill. Garbage bags in the middle of the room turned grey with dust and good intentions. I try not to look at the bed. It takes up almost the entire room, and yet it's so small, only a twin. A half-empty bottle of Jim Beam is sleeping it off on my pillow. I twist the cap free and drink. I curl up on the floor, the neck of the bottle gripped in my hand. No level of exhaustion is enough to get me back inside that bed.

My head lolls on my neck. Under the bed — dust and bottles and a *Teen Beat*. Above it — a poster of a painting, the only goodness this room has to offer. It's simple enough, a depiction of a bit of forest in Northern Ontario. Azure, mauve, salmon, olive and cornflower blue, painted on thick as peanut butter. The foreground is a shamble of fir trees weighted down by snow. They are still green, though, the life of them fighting through the cold. There is so much vigour in these branches that if I brush the snow off they'll spring back up, launching loose needles a hundred feet into the sky. *Snow* by Lawren Harris. My father gave it to me on my tenth birthday. We used to flip through Group of Seven art books in the summer when we were trapped inside with the air conditioning, when my brain had lost some of its plump and freshness to the television, which the art was supposed to correct. We always lingered the longest on this picture, Dad and I.

I roll up from the floor and stand on the mattress. The alcohol unsteadies me. I'm on waves, I'm in wind, I'm walking on a sea instead of a twin-sized bed. I settle myself and my eyes level with the print, the *Snow*. I slip my fingers beneath the poster and peel it back. The hole. The size of a beach ball. It's exactly where I left it.

It's not a real hole; it's a drawing of a hole, the kind a prisoner would etch in his cell. I was embarrassingly old, nearly fourteen, when I drew it. I was hopeful back then, thought all I needed to escape was a hand-drawn wormhole and a crude understanding of perspective. A light, beam-focused and white, shines into my eye. It's coming from the wall, from the hole that is only a picture. I close my eyes, it will blind me if I don't, and I reach toward the light. My lids are shut but the light still penetrates—I see pink and rosy when I should see black. I reach my arm into the hole and where there should be crayon, messy shading above a circle, there is an empty void. I touch it with my finger. Instead of wall, it feels like nothing—the most peculiar determinate of realness there can be. I put my whole arm into it and a gentle suction of warm air, like a vacuum on low, swirls through my clothes. It smells like pine and mold and earth. I crawl inside the hole, my knees sinking by an inch into warm Jello. The air moves in fast sweeping circles; I try to back out but the force of it is too strong. I put my hands into the walls of the hole and try to get a grip, but a roaring void sucks me away.

It's black now. I'm beyond the light.

Upside down, spinning, sideways. The hole expels me. To the outside. A wintery forest, familiar, alien. I stand beneath two enormous trees, their weighty branches reaching to my arms and my shoulders. The branches are heavy with snow, but it's not soft and forgiving and made of millions of crystals. It's wet like paint, sloppy and viscous.

I'm inside the painting.

I pinch the pine needles between my fingers, release, and let the branches fly. The snow springs up into the air, moving as one mass, one clump. It hovers for a moment then returns, orderly, to the branch, like a movie in reverse, as though it never left. I allow myself the luxury of a tantrum. Stomp in the snow, abuse it with my footprints. The lines of my ribbed socks impress and then disappear — my footprints refilling with snow as though an underground faucet is turned on. I look up to the sky but there isn't one. Above me is smooth, flat wood, the underside of a picture frame.

My phone rings.

"You have a call from a federal prison from —"

"Don't ignore me, kid! I need you!"

The vacuum starts up again, the hole tugging me back. I cling to a branch, but it offers no grip against the suction. The paint is wet and slimy. *Dirty and filthy and nasty.*

The door creaks. There is light and there is Uncle Bryan. I'm in my bed but it's not my bed and he's drunk and sour. His hands are so big. "Stop him," the robot voice says. "Why are you just lying there, pretending to be asleep?" I want to scream for Gloria but nothing's coming out. "Kick him," the robot chants. "Save yourself." If I could just reach the hole, I could crawl through and be gone forever, escape to another dimension like a beam of light. If I could just get outside to the snow, I know I could be safe. My father taught me how to be safe.

It's too late. This isn't the first time.

Dirty and filthy and nasty.

"Are you still there?"

No one will ever love you now.

Days without Henry: 2

31

I have a window seat, but it's no consolation. The woman beside me is eating a fish sandwich, not tuna or salmon, but something more exotic and potent. The scales are still on whatever the poor beast is that she tucked between two pieces of pumpernickel, and its red oils ooze onto my shoes and the armrest between us, which I so dearly want to make use of. I curl up against the window instead, my hands as pillows.

The movie the bus driver has chosen stars Keanu Reeves — lover, fighter, scientist — and the attention of all of my fellow passengers is rapt. I have no headphones, though; there wasn't time to pack headphones, to pack anything for that matter. I ran out of Gloria's house, to the bus, to the subway, to the Greyhound bus station, to the ticket window, to this bus, to this seat next to this fish-oozing woman too fast. I look up at Keanu's angular, high-contrast face, at his mouth pushing out some words, and I wonder what I'm missing.

A little girl sits in front of me. Tied to her wrist is a pink balloon, which is supposed to keep her entertained, so she's using it to beat her brother over the head. The sound is infuriating, a dull thwump followed by static. Her brother is troublingly quiet. I poke her arm through the gap in the seats. "It's called a cumulative effect," I tell her. "Do you want your little brother to turn out stupid?" She looks at me with scorn and so I know she's used to a hard life shuttling from one parent to another. Burnt bus station coffee, stale cigarettes from strangers. She gives me the finger — it's very small — and continues to pummel her brother with the balloon.

The nurses gave my father a balloon in the chemo ward on his very last day. It was lemon yellow with a happy face stamped on the middle, made with that metallic stuff that wrinkles down the sides. My father walked behind me as we shuffled into the hospital; me hampered by my enormous backpack, him by the cancer, or the treatment for it, not that the difference mattered. He never looked sick to me until around that time, when the treatments wound down. His cancer was easier to camouflage than others because his symptoms could hide behind excuses of indigestion, corn, beans and the bathroom door. But now, five months into treatment, his legs were flaking, the skin looking both tight and loose at the same time. I could see it when his grotesquely bloated ankle peeked out from underneath his pants because he was one of those men who enjoyed sitting cross-legged.

When his cycle was complete and his tubes detached, the nurses led him over to the victory bell, the one that everyone lucky enough to finish treatment alive and with hands got to ring. *Ding ding. Ding ding.* The other patients applauded and cried tears of joy. That would soon be me, they hoped, while their cheerleaders hoped even harder. But my dad didn't smile. He looked unsure of what to do next without drugs, nurses or a tube in his arm—just a stupid bell ringing in his ears for the rest of the day and that lemon-yellow balloon flapping from his wrist.

I wake up and the bus is empty, the absence of the little girl and her balloon more disturbing than their presence. I rub my eyes and inch my way to the door, careful in case a bus-jacking has taken place while I was asleep. Like the one from the news. Near Portage la Prairie, I think it was. That poor farm boy. Decapitated by a schizophrenic.

I step off the bus and I'm in Wallkill. Or at least nearby enough. A warehouse in the parking lot says Wallkill Valley

Self Storage. The driver is leaning against the luggage side of the bus, his impossibly round belly protruding like a pregnant woman's. He's taking in the industrial scenery and eating French fries out of an unrecognizable paper bag. The fact that this town is either too small or insignificant for a McDonald's makes me shudder.

"Why didn't you wake me up?" I ask him.

He shrugs and inhales another fry. "I didn't even know you were there. Everyone always gets off in Manhattan." He wipes the grease from his chin with his bus company T-shirt and gives me a breathtaking view of his hairy gut.

"But I paid for a ticket to Wallkill," I say. "The bus does officially stop here."

He looks at me with disdain. His left forearm is badly sunburned, his Betty Boop tattoo a shameful shade of crimson. "What's a person like you come to the Kill for?" he asks.

"Watchtower Farms."

"Oh yeah? Why were you on my bus then? Why didn't you come on one of your people's *charters?*" He says the word as though it's meant for kings and queens. "God knows there's more than enough of those damn things."

I fix my hands on my hips. "My people?"

"Yeah. Your Joho people."

"I'm not a Jehovah's Witness."

"Just a tourist, then, huh? Here to see the religious freak show? You know there's more to this town than that fucking place. We have a golf course. A motocross. A spa. Two prisons."

"You live here?"

"Been here long before the Johos. Bastards think they run this town." He takes a sip from his two-gallon cup.

"I really need to get to that farm," I say.

"Yeah? And why is that?"

I eye what's left of his food. I haven't eaten anything solid and proper in two days, not since Steve's chicken. "They took something of mine, the Johos," I say, my mouth salivating. "And I'd like it back."

The driver squints and offers me what's left at the bottom of the paper bag. A palmful of crispy, half-burnt potato bits.

"They take something," he says, "or someone?"

He watches me chew and swallow.

"They took everything," I say.

He sighs and spits and climbs onto his bus.

It has its own water tower, "Watchtower Farms and Printery" stenciled in letters fifteen feet high. But from my vantage point outside the gated entrance, the place looks more like an industrial park plunked in the centre of a botanical arctic garden. Wide open expanses carpeted in white. Trees everywhere — pine, maple, and heartbreaking weeping willows, their branches depressed more than usual by the weight of the snow. Dozens of what could be graves but are probably flowerbeds. Witnesses, a hundred of them, gathered in small groups, reading and snacking, staring at the sky. Bridges to nowhere arching out of the ground and diving back into it again. Gazebos positioned so that no matter which direction you turn — north, east, west or south — you will find yourself looking at one. It must have been paradise back in the days of summer, a true Garden of Eden.

I thank the driver and step off the bus, trudging past three young women picnicking on white bread sandwiches, their long skirts fanning out on their checkered blanket. They're oblivious to the snow that swirls round them, smiling blankly like they have no cares in their heads, no sense, no worries, no brain.

"Hey!" the driver yells. "They won't let you in if you're not on a tour!"

I turn to face him. "Then I'll go on a tour."

"Good luck, girlie," he chuckles, Betty Boop hanging out the window as he peels out to the highway.

I pass a pond carved into the permafrost, its angel fountain sculpture frozen in midstream. I hurry past it toward the main building. A large sign hangs overhead. "Welcome, Visitors." I duck, needlessly, and hurry into the building. There's a hum of chatter, and a dozen Witnesses standing in a line. Mothers and babies. Whining middle-school-aged kids. An elderly woman in a wheelchair. Teenagers who actually want to be here. Men talking in voices as deep as rolling thunder. A family, I guess, since they float from group to group in easy conversation. And since they're all black. And since they all have the same body type — tall, obese. Their fashion sense is genetic, too. Dresses, suits, ties, fanny packs and the whitest of white sneakers. Nametags applied directly over hearts. Tote bags slung over shoulders, "*Read* Awake! *5 cents per copy!*" stamped on the canvas in general store calligraphy. The wheelchair woman passes out, drool pooling on her delicately embroidered sweater. I reach for her tote and pull it from her osteoarthritic shoulder, hiding the spot over my heart where my nametag should be.

"Welcome welcome welcome!" A white man in a suit. Broad shoulders. A football player's neck. "My name is Geoffrey. I'll be your guide through the Wallkill Bethel. I'm so glad you could join us!"

He leads us through an expansive communal living room. A furniture store's worth of floral sofas, lace pillow shams, and loveseats. It manages to look anything but cozy. A woman in a crocheted vest bounces on her toes. "We're here, Sandra! Can you believe it?" Sandra holds her down to the earth.

"If you'll notice the fine wood panelling," says Geoffrey, "and the air conditioning ducting that is among the most efficient in the world."

We walk into a formal room, like a dining room without a table, filled with paintings of families dressed neat and tidy for church but frolicking in nature. Witnesses not on the tour wait in long, organized lineups for mysterious administrative services, holding folders and files. They wave at us and smile, and we wave at them and smile.

"This is the museum of early printing presses," says Geoffrey. He points to Watchtower books and posters protected inside of temperature-controlled cases, a multimedia display on ancient Bible production. "Please note the detailed plans and maps outlining the Watchtower's impressive expansion plans for Wallkill and the surrounding area." Sandra and some others stop to have their photos taken with a sepia-toned cardboard cutout of a child, a sign hanging from his neck proclaiming "Read the Watchtower! Explains Theocratic Government!" Geoffrey points out some more wood panelling, lines us up and steers us left.

"And now, brothers and sisters," Geoffrey says. "What you no doubt have all been waiting for. The heart of the Watchtower organization: the printing presses!"

With the flare and pomp of Willy Wonka, he swings open the double-wide doors. Instead of rivers of chocolate and Oompa Loompas, reams of paper stretch as far as the eye can see and a dozen Latino men hoist pallets of shrink-wrapped Bibles on forklifts. The wheelchair woman gasps in wonder and then hacks. A teenager shouts "Cool!" and means it. The woman next to Sandra is flat-out shrieking with joy. Am I the only one who's disappointed?

"Ours is the largest in-plant printing operation in the United States," Geoffrey announces. "Aside from, ahem, the federal government's."

The equipment is massive and, quite strangely, every cog is clearly labelled: chill rollers, folder, inline endsheet feeder, paster, Corona C12/46" perfect binder, splitting saw, Merit S three-knife trimmers and CTP prepress. The plant is spotless. The smooth concrete floors swept clean, the machinery rust-free. The air smells of green apples.

"Now follow me. Please stay within the yellow lines, which have been painted on for your safety. And please, brothers and sisters, do not touch the machinery."

There is clutter, though. The plant is polluted with signs, all of them written in a typographical style more often seen in pre-schools than industrial warehouses. Lemon and violet bubble lettering directing us to rooms where all manner of activities take place: Graphics, Bindery, Carton Sorting, Bar Coding, Shipping. Other signs are more arrogant. Over 21,443,257 *Awake!* Magazines Printed In The Year 2009! 4000 Standard Bibles Or 5000 Pocket Bibles Printed Per Day! $200,000 Saved Per Year By Recycling Trimmings! 300 Gallons Of Ink In Each Barrel! I sort through the visual detritus until I find the sign I came here for: Editorial.

I back away from the group and as they turn one corner, I turn another. I walk into the office marked Copy Editing. An old man is bent over a stack of pages so hot off the presses they literally burn his fingertips.

"Fudge," he whimpers.

"Hello," I say.

His head snaps upwards, his injured finger dropping out from between his soothing lips. "Did you lose your tour group?"

"I'm looking for Henry Marshall. I think he works in this department."

"Brother Henry! The new editorial director! Yes, of course! We're so excited to have him! He's going to be a shining star here. The next generation of disciples to bring the Word of Jehovah to the world."

"Fabulous just super and wondrous praise Jehovah," I say. "Can you tell me where he is?"

The man turns through his pages, cooler now. A spread with a ghostly illustration of a wrinkled couple, their younger selves faded in the background. "Can Old Age Be Reversed?" the headline asks.

"Why Henry's in Canada, of course."

"Canada?" I yelp. "You mean he's not here?"

"He hasn't started work yet."

"Do you know where I can find him?"

"In Canada."

"Yes, thank you," I say. "But where?"

"I don't know my Canadian cities very well, I'm afraid," he says. "Is Vancouver one of them?"

I tear his pages away, my hands ready to rip them in two if it comes to that.

"Hold on now, what are you—"

"I came all the way here to this . . . this . . ."

"Bethel and printing facility."

"Bethel and printing facility, thank you. I sat on that bus with that stinking fish woman for ten hours—"

"Please put the *Awake!* down, young lady."

"—and you're telling me Henry isn't even here?"

The man wipes sweat from his bald head. He leaves a Gorbachev smudge of ink behind and my faith in him recovers. I expect post-Soviet-style solutions, Perestroikan reforms. The man shrugs and I tremble with hope. "He's in Canada," is all he says.

"Yes!" I shout. "Thank you for that specific information!"

"Please, we'll figure all this out for you," he says. "If you just hand me those proofs."

I flip through the pages roughly. "Bible Prophecies Provide Clear Signs of Impending Disaster: Will You Act On Them?"

"The End of the World: How and When Will It Happen?" "A Visit to Liechtenstein: What Attracts Tourists to This Micro State?"

"You publish this shit," I say, "and you think *I'm* crazy?"

"I don't think you're crazy," he says. "I think you had an unpleasant bus ride and a disappointment."

I laugh.

"It's not funny, miss. That's the Word of Jehovah you're holding in your hands and if you—"

"If I what?" I say, ripping a page, just a sliver.

He gasps. "If you tear it in hate and anger, I don't know what will happen."

"Will I go to hell?" I ask. "Is hell even real for you people?"

"Ecclesiastes 3:19, 20."

"I. Don't. Speak. Brainwash. Any. More."

"'Hell is nothing more than a common grave of mankind,'" he says, praying. He's praying because of me. Because he's afraid of me. "'Hell is the house of meeting for everyone living.'"

The tour group dances around the corner in a flurry of chatter, every Witness flaunting a souvenir of some kind or another: "Proud to be a Jehovah's Witness" T-shirts, and mugs that read "Live the Word, Love the Word, Be the Word." Sandra wears an apron silkscreened "Paradise Earth." Geoffrey sports a "Jehovah's Fitness: Running and Jumping Around for God" T-shirt. He's jogging in place, making the woman in the wheelchair laugh herself into a coughing fit.

I toss the proofs back to Gorbachev. "I'm definitely in hell."

Days without Henry: 3

32

They don't notice me when I walk inside, my mother and Steve. They're layering filo pastry into a pan, the sheets as translucent as ghosts. They're focused on their work, as though the pastry might swoop up and vanish if they look away. So I don't have to be too precious about it when I jam my souvenir tote bag into the closet with Margaret's purse and Kristie's jacket. My growing collection of stolen things.

"Your face looks terrible," I say, stepping into the kitchen.

Margaret's eye is purple as jelly. A small welt, outlined in dried blood, marks her right cheek. It's shaped like bees' wings.

"I think it makes you look tough," Steve says, flexing his wrinkled, flabby muscles. "No one better mess with Margie. Margie: Warrior Princess."

My mother giggles. "You're so silly."

"Looks like Gloria got you with a left hook," I say. "Hit you with that bee ring of hers."

"I'd rather not talk about it," my mother says. She turns to Steve, who demonstrates how to paint the filo layers with butter. She's too gentle so Steve puts his hand on hers, applying more pressure.

"The dough is stronger than it looks, Margie."

"Did you know you should always clarify the butter first?" she says to me. "That's the secret to a golden crust."

"You're such a good student," Steve says.

"I have an excellent teacher."

"So are you two baking buddies now?" I say. A bowl of pistachios, green as limes, sits on the counter. I dig into it and roll the nuts around in my palms like dice. "Because, Margie, I'm pretty sure you're not allowed to consort with a worldly vessel of Satan."

They look at me blankly.

"It's just baklava, Avory. Relax."

"You were gone for nearly two days," Margaret says. "I didn't have a key, I couldn't leave. I had no idea when you'd be back."

Steve sprinkles nuts on the pastry like a gardener spreads seeds. "I came to cook — our deal, remember? — and she was here."

My mother hovers over his shoulder. "I was in my robe and he just waltzed in."

"She ran to the kitchen so fast I couldn't even —"

"I pulled out a knife, Avery! I couldn't believe —"

"I thought I was going to die a bloody —"

"I wasn't going to stab you."

"What's with you Gauthier women and knives?"

My mother bumps Steve's hip with hers and giggles again. Steve smiles. A gold incisor I've never noticed gleams like treasure.

"He brought me an air mattress." She points to a box by my television. A happy family in a campsite. All the comforts of home.

"The poor woman can't sleep in a chair, Avory."

"And he made me a key."

"Excuse me?" I say. "You made her a what?"

"A key to your apartment."

"And now he's teaching me some recipes."

"It's as simple as that, Avory." He winks at Margaret. She winks back.

"You've got to be joking," I say. "Are you two flirting?"

"Don't be silly, Avery."

"We aren't? Oh my aching heart!" Steve clutches at his chest. My mother howls.

I can't handle this on an empty stomach, so I reach for more nuts. Steve slaps my hand with a spoon.

"He took care of me," my mother says. "He put ice on my eye, cleaned me up. You have quite a super, here." She drapes a hand towel on his back, his mild hunch keeping it in place. "He's a super super."

Steve reaches his arms out and flies around the table.

My mother doubles over with laughter.

Steve descends; he's out of breath. "She was. Very. Upset. That you. Disappeared."

"So was I," I tell him, "when she abandoned me."

"Don't talk about your mother that way."

"Oh please. Gloria was more of a mother to me than she ever was."

Margaret gasps and speed-walks to the bathroom, closing the door with a squeak. The taps are running at full force, which means she's crying. Her routine was the same after a fight with my dad. She'd flee to the bathroom and run the water for hours. I used to think she'd drown in there. I'd sit outside the door sometimes and listen for her quiet sobs. It was the only way I could know if she was still breathing.

"Why are you being such a . . . a . . ."

"A what, Steve?"

"What's the word?"

"A jerk? A brat?"

"Yes! Brat! You're being one of those."

"Because she's the enemy."

"She isn't. She did a bad thing—"

"A bad thing? What exactly did she tell you?"

"That she left you and your father."

"Who was dying. Did she tell you that part?"

"She knew he was sick. She didn't know he was dying."

Steve reaches for a chair, bending and groaning, his spine battling two forces: gravity and calcification. I peel the cape off his back and his true identity is wholly revealed—a tired, old man.

"I thought you were on my side," I say to him.

"There are two sides to every story, Avory, just like there are two sides to people: the good side and the bad. There's a lot of bad in your mother's story, but it's not so simple."

"What the hell do you mean?"

He squints at me and I wonder just how much he can see. "Just talk to her, okay?"

"I've tried to talk to her. She won't—"

"No, you don't *talk*. You shout and accuse." Steve drapes the cape on my back. Pats it into place. "Talk to her like she wants, in her way. Maybe then you'll learn something. Like how to work the system so the system works for you." He winks.

"You mean I should be some sort of double agent?"

"We had those in the war," he says. "The most beautiful women were best at it. They'd fuck an Italian commander two different ways, if you get my drift. You could do it. You have it in you." Steve looks me up and down. "Just maybe some lipstick and a dress. Could you wash your hair?"

I run my fingers through it. They get stuck in a tangle. When was the last time I brushed it? Washed and conditioned it? Plucked out the eager greys?

Steve knocks on the bathroom door. "Margie?" She opens it and Steve pulls her by the hand. "Let's give Avory some time alone with her thoughts," he says. "And with the baklava."

33

According to the scale, I've dropped four pounds — one for every day Henry's been gone. But I'm in my bathtub, I'm naked, and I can't see the loss on my body. My thighs are still dimpled like the chin of a movie star, my knees still fleshy around the caps. I assume the pounds have fallen from the spots out of sight: from my brain, my lungs, my heart.

I lost weight when my father was sick, too. My father, though? He gained, at least at first. When he stood stirring at the stove, I would stare at his strange new stomach hanging over his belt, wishing for a belch to release the pressure. When he'd take his long afternoon naps, I'd pinch his bloated cheeks to wake him, his skin thick and clammy as dough. His extra weight was difficult for me to make sense of because in the movies cancer made people skinny; it didn't make them crave Parmigiano-Reggiano and noodles and deep-fried basil that crunched and crackled. But in his last months, my dad was a starved fat man. He put on forty pounds during his course of treatment. He said it was the steroids, but I had my doubts. He was so used to ingesting drugs that I think food became one, too. Whatever it was, I was grateful because it was his hunger that tricked me into believing he wasn't dying. I saw that Julia Roberts movie, the one with the rich guy with blood cancer. And the one with Michael Keaton and Nicole Kidman. And, oh god, the one with Mandy Moore. So I knew. I knew that no one with any serious kind of cancer could crave penne arrabbiata in the middle of the night.

I can't look at my body for long because it's the most ruined part of me. So I turn to the bathtub's ledge, to where my buffet is presented before me. I gulp back the Christmas vodka and gnaw off a monster's portion of baklava. I really focus on gaining my weight back. Henry has the futon, CDs and books, but he cannot have my four pounds. I take one more bite and submerge my head beneath the water and soapy foam. I think about staying down here forever, under the cover of a white that is warm for once.

I would do anything for love.

It's an echo in the water I can feel through the wall and in between the sudsy wrinkles in my skin. How can sound travel, I wonder, but I'm stuck here.

My head bobs back to the surface and takes in a deep breath, strangely grateful to be alive. It seems disembodied from the rest of me completely, with ideas separate from my legs, stomach, arms and breasts still drowned beneath the water.

"Hello?" the head calls out.

"Hi," my neighbour says.

"What are you doing?"

"I'm sitting in my bathtub playing guitar," he says.

I would do anything for love.

I pull the plug from the drain and watch the water ebb from my body like a tidal flow. I am filthy with soap. I look at my wedding ring. It's slippery on my finger and slides off with no effort at all. I dangle it over the drain, a circle at the mercy of another circle.

"Can I ask you something?" I say.

"Sure."

"What kind of a man are you?"

Silence.

"Do you do what you want no matter how much it hurts someone else? Someone you love?"

"No."

"Yes you do."

"I do not."

"Do you know what kind of man I think you are?" I say.

"Please, enlighten me."

"I think you're the kind of man who beats up his girlfriend when he gets drunk and sad because his life didn't turn out the way he wanted it to."

"Oh you do, do you?"

"I can hear it through the walls."

"Then why don't you call the police?"

Silence. Mine this time.

"I'll tell you why: because you know it's just as much your fault. You chicks fuck up as much as us and then, when you want to, you punch us and scratch and kick and throw our shit at the walls. And what can we do? Hit you? As hard as you hit us? Nah. We just have to leave. Because we're not allowed to fight back. No matter how hard you women beat us down, all we can do is walk away."

I set my ring next to the drain and spin it clockwise. It travels in predictable circles but then hits an imperfection in the tub and wobbles into the drain. I scramble for it, but it's unnecessary. The ring is sitting comfortably in a nest of my hair, the route to the sewers and the lake blockaded by my relentless shedding. I pluck it out and stuff it back on my finger but it won't go. I'm too bloated. From heat, from vodka, from baklava.

My four pounds have come home. That means Henry must be next.

Days without Henry: 4

34

Like many Jehovah's Witnesses, my mother went through a paranoid phase that made her suspicious of lawyers and wills and especially her secular husband, so when I was quite young, she took it upon herself to begin the process of re-assigning ownership of every single object she possessed. When she would leave us to run errands, my dad and I would turn her morbid inventory into a treasure hunt, ransacking the house like pirates, searching for my name dangling down on a label, the old-fashioned kind that get affixed to Christmas presents from snips of red string. The two of us would run wild through the house, turning stuff over that had bottoms and turning stuff round that had backs. *Mutiny!* we'd howl as we'd hurry up and down the stairs, our hands hoisting invisible swords high in the air. Most of the items were destined for the Witnesses. Her things would be sold by the Watchtower when she died, that was her plan, the money put toward a mission in Somalia or Eritrea or Indonesia — the more entrenched in Islam or civil war or famine the better. I always started with the biggest items: couches, tables, chairs. I took turns lying underneath each one and batting the tags like a cat, the name Jehovah swinging back and forth. Then off I'd race again, my little fingers feeling their way through the dusty closets, drawers and chests scattered throughout the upstairs rooms. My fingers tugged and pulled their way through items so expensive-looking they belonged on royalty, not my mother: delicate diamond bracelets, gold rings, drop earrings of pearl and amethyst, ruby and opal. She had boxes and boxes, so many that I assumed we were rich, even though my father swore at the bills when they came clanging through the slot in our front door. Out of everything, my mother's plum Prada dress was the object I most wanted for myself. Every chance I'd get I'd take it off the hanger and drape it over my body. I had plans to wear it on a hot date with Wesley Crusher. He'd fly to Earth on the Starship Enterprise, kiss my hand and compliment me on my beauty. Like fruit, he'd say, pretty enough to eat. Then we'd shoot off into the stars, Wesley pointing out the Milky Way and the wormhole that could take me any place and time I wanted to go.

I pull the dress from my closet and slip into it. I tug the zipper up my back. I've got it halfway, but I can't make it the rest, not on my own, not without Henry. I reach and squeal and groan and struggle. I swear. At myself, at Henry, at the designer, at all designers everywhere — the effeminate sons of industrialists. Heartless and bitter! Angry at their mothers for being cold, but taking revenge on my zipper? My dress? Me?

Margaret knocks and slides the bedroom door open. "What on earth is going on?"

I point at the zipper. "My dress, please."

"You mean *my* dress," she says. "I wondered what happened to it."

"You didn't come back for me," I say, "so I didn't think you'd come back for the dress."

She zips me up and brushes off a certain kind of lint — the fibres only mothers can see on the dresses of daughters. Like a whistle only dogs can hear. "You're giving this prayer meeting a chance," she says, turning me around, "so I suppose I can give you this dress."

She looks like I remember her, before she changed into a sad sack of bones. The skin between her eyes isn't furrowed from worry; her hair isn't limp; her clothing isn't hanging off her. She looks refreshed and lit up. She wears a high-collared dress of silk and her hair is curled and pinned into romantic waves. Her body doesn't look sickly thin, but lithe as a dancer's. She is elegant and graceful, serene — the kind of woman who gets sketched by artists in cafés along the Seine.

"Only . . . it's a little racy for the occasion," she says, her eyes rating me like censors.

"What are you talking about?" I slip on my black heels. "You used to wear this dress to Kingdom Hall all the time."

"With a sweater. And a scarf. Sometimes both."

"Well, now I wear it with these." I push my breasts together, testing them out. "Sometimes both."

Margaret sighs. "I know you think you're shocking me, Avery, with these antics of yours. But I'm a Jehovah's Witness; I'm not Amish."

I stifle a laugh, and so does Margaret. Her smile comes easier than I hoped it would, than she deserves.

"I want to thank you," she says. "For hosting this prayer meeting with me. It's a beautiful gesture." She hugs me and I think maybe, *maybe* we can actually start over. Only I don't feel her flesh at all, not even the fabric of her dress. I feel electricity humming at the frenzied pace of television static.

The intercom buzzes, and I release her. Her electricity stays with me until the knock at the door. Through the peephole, Akono is much less intimidating. The fish-eye lens gives him a vulnerable look, like he's shorter and squatter and far away. Plus I can see him, but he can't see me. Oh the power; I could get used to it. I could stand here for the rest of my life and be bigger and all-seeing and knowing. But Margaret won't have it. She shoos me off, sitting me down roughly at my own table. "Don't make the man wait!"

My power gone now, I retreat into my familiar comfort zones of panic and regret. I'm an idiot for listening to Steve and for inviting Akono into the apartment, for making an effort for my mother, no matter how feigned, no matter I'm manipulating her to get Henry back. Is that what I'm doing? Really? Because Steve told me to work the system. But Margaret is just a person, not a system. And the Watchtower is as unworkable as a busted clock. I'm not a double agent — I'm a twenty-five-year-old research assistant at a vanity legal publishing house.

"Oh my god," I say. "I missed my deadline!"

"Language, Avery, please."

I'm a soon-to-be-unemployed twenty-five-year-old research assistant at a vanity legal publishing house who listened to the advice of a superintendent, took a bath and put on a dress, and I think that I will what? Tear down the walls of injustice? Convince Henry to come back to me through my mother and Akono? These are people, not portals! This is a plum-coloured dress, not a gun!

"Oh my god oh my god."

"Avery!"

I don't have the powers of persuasion. I don't have anything. I am a sucker and a loser, and I need to get out. So I evaluate my escape plans. Plan A. My teeth are grinding, which could be of service. Grind enough and they'll pulverize their way through my jaw and eventually down through the floor. Plan B. The window. I can jump through it like the birds that crash into the mirrored glass of the Kingdom Hall. I'll be stunned at first, but then I'll continue, somehow, and fly far away. I twist my body so I'm facing the window. The birds. There are so many. Canada geese, blue jays, even a hummingbird at my neighbour's feeder, all kinds of migratory species that should have been somewhere else than in this horrible nightmare snow. Hundreds of them.

My mother opens the door. "Welcome!" It's too late.

Akono smiles with every single tooth, his mouth a blister pack of peppermint gum. A woman curls out from behind him.

Cecily. Of throaty laugh. Of red bow and straight perfect black hair. The porcelain doll.

Akono is wearing a full suit, a pressed beige jacket and pants, and a crisp white shirt, his collar stiff as a milk carton. "Don't you and your daughter look lovely," he says to Margaret. "What's the occasion?"

"Why you, of course," she says, nearly curtseying.

He turns. Looks at my chest, and then me.

Filthy and nasty and disgusting.

"And you, Avery?"

Of all my mistakes lately, this dress is my worst. I am not a sexy double agent; I am *filthy and nasty* and I must not be seen. My body agrees and so gets to work. My shoulders hunch, my spine crumbles, my breasts hide their curves behind fabric, shadow and whatever hair they can reach.

Akono lowers one eyebrow, raises the other. "I was surprised to get the call from your mother," he says to me. "I didn't think you would want a prayer meeting, what with everything going on in your personal life."

I clear my throat of wavers and cracks. "I'm trying to make an effort. For Henry."

Cecily turns to me. "And how about for you?"

"*Henry* is for me."

"But what about your personal spiritual needs?" she says.

"Henry is everything I need."

Cecily squints, evaluates me further.

I feel a rough fabric against me so I turn in my chair. My father's parka. Its lime-with-the-lights-off arms are wrapped around me. The rest of it hangs from the back of the chair. So casual, so cool, like a coat sloughed off at the end of a long ski day. Not a dead man's second skin risen from the grave. I sit up straight and access the part of my brain that stores curative TED

Talks. I pull back my shoulders. Raise my arms above my head. My testosterone and cortisol levels rise, my confidence soars above Cecily and that stupid red bow in her stupid beautiful hair. I am a Y! A tree! A more powerful, better me!

"What on earth are you doing?" my mother asks.

"It's called a Power Pose," I say. "Do you live under a rock?"

"Now, now, ladies," says Akono.

My mother pulls my hands down. "Avery, please. Don't be weird."

Akono loops his arm through my mother's. "As you said on the phone, you've been a Witness since—"

"Since I was born. My original Kingdom Hall was in Ottawa. Today, I'm a member of the Walker Road Kingdom Hall in Richmond, BC."

I balk. "You live on the West Coast?"

"I do."

"Why didn't you tell me—"

"And you, Avery? You went to Kingdom Hall in Ottawa as well?" Akono asks. He's under the impression that a line of questioning will calm the storm. "Until you were thirteen or so?"

"Yes, she did," my mother answers. "I did my best to keep her on track. But her father was more of an influence on her, unfortunately. And he didn't agree with the teachings of Jehovah."

"My father," I hiss, "agreed with reason, common sense and compassion."

"As do we," says Akono. "And we're here together in that same spirit, are we not?"

My mother nods. "Open minds, open hearts."

"Now let's make the most of our Bible study time, shall we?"

They join me at the kitchen table.

Cecily across from me. Akono across from my mother. My mother smiles and claps her hands. I have never seen her so happy. "This is so nice! Avery, isn't this nice?" I stretch my leg out to see if it will reach Cecily. One swift drop of my heel and her porcelain foot could shatter. But I reach nothing. She's admiring the kitchen table, running her hand across its durable natural material. "Is this a Björkudden?" she asks, and I pretend I don't hear. Akono deals out copies of *Awake!* like cards. The cover is the most ridiculous one yet. A man in a wheelchair holds a pink carnation near his wife's nose. He smiles huge; she has her arm around his shoulder and smiles back. He's disabled or malformed, got a leg blown off or two, and she is perfectly happy about it. *Attitude!* The headline shouts. *It Makes a Difference!*

"Let's get started, shall we?" Akono flips to his page and reads. "'What is the Battle of Armageddon? Armageddon is directly tied to God's most valiant quality: His love of justice. From on high, He has watched the world, witnessed every single act of injustice that mankind has performed throughout the history of time. He is displeased, and justly so, and He is taking action by appointing His Son to wage a war to do away with the wicked system here on earth and the wicked humans who have perpetuated it.'"

When I was a child, every Sunday and Wednesday night were devoted to Armageddon. My mother's Kingdom Hall was in a half-abandoned part of downtown Ottawa, as far from the suburbs as it was from the Parliament buildings and the other places visiting dignitaries would see. A red brick low-rise with slits for windows, nowhere near as showy as the hall here with its storeys of bewitching glass. It sat across from rows of slumped houses and Capital Dominion Radiator. The way the elders would rant and sweat about Armageddon made it seem as though it was right around the corner, so close I could feel the hot flames lick my neck. It was confusing for me back then, my mother and all these loud adults warning me that the end of the world was coming, and my soft-spoken father telling me it wasn't. When I'd overhear the news, though—AIDs, genocide in Rwanda, the Oklahoma City bombings—I believed the elders. Plus, their version of the afterlife was more compelling than my father's: an eternity in paradise if I was special enough, versus nothing at all.

"'Over the centuries,'" reads Akono, his voice much louder than it needs to be, "'billions of people have wondered in fear about Armageddon—what shape it will take, who will be spared—and many more still have wondered exactly when Armageddon will come.'"

The arms of my father's parka stiffen around my waist. They thrust the words out of me like they're performing the Heimlich. "Nineteen fourteen!"

Margaret, Cecily, Akono. All eyes on me.

I untangle myself from the Gore-Tex. "The Watchtower said the world was supposed to end in 1914."

"Excellent memory, Avery," says Akono.

"Aren't you embarrassed?" I ask.

"Avery!" says Margaret.

Akono waves me off. "Of course I'm not embarrassed. Why would I be?"

"Because it's 2013—"

My mother shoots up from her chair. "Avery! Stop this at once."

"—and I'm not dead. And you're definitely not in heaven."

"The year is insignificant, Avery," Akono says. "Turn on the news, read a paper, a history book, look around!" His Adam's apple stretches his neck skin as he speaks. It bobs up and down with his deep, sing-song inflections. "In the 20th century alone, over one hundred million people have been killed in wars, more than four times as many as in the previous four hundred years put together. And then there's the increase in crime, major earth-quakes and disease. The Spanish flu killed two hundred million people! God foretold all of that." He stands and moves to the window, turning the pages.

"Your god certainly foretells a lot," I say, "but he doesn't exactly help in a crisis, does he?"

"She just wants to interrupt," my mother says, smiling in shame. "We're getting nowhere."

Akono purses his lips, makes a smacking sound. "I have an idea," he says. "Let's split up." His eyes are on my chest again. This time, though, I don't squirm. This time, the parka's nearby.

"I agree," I say. "My mother knows all this stuff anyway. She's been a Witness for fifty-five years."

"Fifty-three!"

"Are you sure, Brother Akono? It's highly unusual—"

"I know, Cecily, but it's best. I think Avery and I will do better alone, with a more directed study. Fair?"

"Fair," my mother says.

Cecily shrugs.

"Why don't you take Margaret into the bedroom and Avery and I will stay here at the table?"

My mother and Cecily walk off and I long for The Force so I can will the coffee table into their path, tripping them into a pile of limbs and bruises and hair bows. But that doesn't happen. The coffee table stays put, and they make it inside my bedroom. Cecily slides the doors together, a thud and a bounce as wood meets wood, and then me, my non-powers of levitation, Dad's parka and the Björkudden—all four of us are alone with Akono.

"'What would the world be like if God did not bring about Armageddon?'" he reads. "'Would not terrorism, violence, fear and hate continue to plague the human race? Of course!'" Akono leans against the kitchen counter, crossing his legs. He licks his finger unhurriedly, indulging in the taste of his own salty skin, and turns the page. "'The battle of Armageddon is the greatest gift that God could ever give to us! It is not to be feared; it is to be welcomed, for it is mankind's only hope.'"

I stand and push my boobs out, jut my hip, pout my lips. Akono misses every signal, which means I'm a failure as a double agent. I'll never be called on by someone else's country to steal secrets. Never own a tampon gun or lipstick taser.

"'For the righteous followers of Jehovah,'" he continues, "'Armageddon will signal a happy beginning; it will be the start of an eternity lived on an earth of perfect design, remolded by the hands of God Himself. When it comes, Armageddon shall bring about' — Avery, what are you doing?"

I tug the magazine from him. "Is this what you really want to talk about, Akono?"

"What would you prefer?"

"I want to talk about where Henry is."

Akono smiles. "Let's talk about where Henry *was*."

"He was here. With me, his wife. Until you brainwashed him and took him away."

He leans in closer. He smells like musky cologne. Like the 1980s. "No, I mean where he was when he met you."

"In a meeting to help people like us recover from people like you."

"Yes, yes, I know all about those meetings," he says. "Lots of coffee and pastries and projecting problems and blame onto the Watchtower."

"If that helps you sleep at night, Akono."

"So you met at this meeting, and you shared your hardships, your stories of woe. And then what? You fell in love?"

"Yes, as a matter of fact, we did."

"Or that's what you wanted Henry to think."

"Excuse me?"

"So you could trap him in a cold marriage."

"He told you that?"

"He didn't have to. I know women like you, Avery. You strut around in dresses like that, making promises you have no intention of keeping. Henry thought you were an honest woman. But you lied. With your body. With your eyes. You trapped him. And when a man is trapped, he will gnaw off his own leg to escape."

"So will I," I say.

He pulls the magazine away from me. I've shredded it. My hands are stained with ink.

"No, you won't," he says. "You're not that type."

I'm wearing my father's coat. It must have slithered down from the chair and across the floor, climbed my legs and reached up to my back. I can see the trail it's left. A line of silken feathers billowing in the air conditioning.

"Why did you come to me that night in the park?" I ask him.

"Because I happened to see you there."

I could scream at him, at his non-answers. "Fuck off, Akono. You know what I mean. How did you know who I was?"

"Calm down, Avery. It's not a grand conspiracy. I'm a Jehovah's Witness, not a Scientologist."

I grab him by his lapels. The ink from my fingers is on him now. "How did you know my name?"

Akono sighs and pulls out his phone.

Henry's Facebook page.

"Henry and Avery." A close-up. A dock, a river, a sunset.

We crashed a Jehovah's Witness summer camp last July. It was like our dinosaur creation myth, Henry's tattoo, maybe even our entire marriage — another box to tick on our list of rebellions against the Watchtower. The camp was on the outskirts of Wakefield, a narrow Quebec town tucked beside a swirling river and train tracks. I swear to god it was called Camp Winkles. Henry's parents sent him to Winkles every summer of his childhood. Tell me more about your parents, I'd said, but he had shushed me, said not now, it's starting. Henry pulled me behind a rack of canoes just as a young man, nineteen years old if even that, stepped onto the dock. Hunched shoulders, sweaty neck. On his forehead a volcanic pimple. His suit a standard rental. His young bride followed him, struggling in her shoes. Layers of mosquito-netting chiffon. Strapless but not fitted and in a state of being perpetually tugged up. Blush overcompensating for the white that washed her out. Matrimonial ringlets curled too tight. This happens every summer, whispered Henry, like the migration of the wildebeest. The couples who met at Winkles would come back to this dock to have their wedding photos taken. Smile for the camera. Don't smile. Stare into his/her eyes. Think about the future, all the possibilities, babies!, the wonders that God has in store! They wrapped their arms around each other, the man trying not to squeeze the woman's ass but succumbing to the urge. They walked across the dock in the slow motion that a photo requires, their feet making that lonely hollow sound that a dock makes after the sun starts to set and the bathing suits are hanging dry. Henry told me to wait for it . . . wait for it . . . for the part when the man would turn back into a boy and push his bride into the water. The boy tried but failed, because, I told Henry, *brides* — once that status is official — can't ever turn back into girls. They'll spend the rest of their lives stopping themselves an inch from the lake, stabilizing their footing, disciplining their men with a look, placing their unnatural curls back into their unnatural places and tugging at their strapless dresses. Smiling. Not smiling. Thinking seriously about the future. Then I thought seriously about mine, about Henry's, about ours together. That's when he took that photo.

Akono turns off the tap, which I don't remember turning on. A glass is overflowing.

"I understand you're going through a hard time," Akono says. "But Jehovah can save you if you let Him."

I march to the bedroom and spread the doors open. My mother and Cecily are sitting on the bed, each studying their own Bible. My mother follows along with her finger like it's a recipe. "It's time for you to go," I tell Cecily.

"Avery, please," says Margaret. "We're having such a nice time."

Akono gathers his things and walks to the door. "Avery is right. I think we've done all we can here today."

Margaret stuffs her feet into her shoes. "Well, I'll at least walk you back to the hall." She opens the door and all three slip out.

My phone rings. I don't pick up. I run to the window and watch them cross the street together. My mother. Akono. And that porcelain doll. A drunk driver would crash her into a million pieces.

My phone rings again. I don't pick up.

Rings and rings and rings.

"STOP THE FUCK CALLING ME, YOU FUCKING PRISON ROBOT —"

"Avery?"

"— YOU UNCLE FROM HELL."

"V, calm down, okay? It's me."

My head is light. I can't breathe.

"It's Henry."

35

Everything I know about art I learned from my father. He wasn't the most creative man but he understood colour and light, how paintings could speak while staying quiet. He taught me about art the way he taught me about science. The rational behind an emotionally driven process. He appreciated the work of the Group of Seven most, loved the artists of this most exclusive collective for their discipline and unbending respect for the Canadian wilderness. For me, though, the paintings of Carmichael, Harris, Jackson and the rest of them speak of a pathological apathy for mankind. Portraits from these artists are rare and those that are painted don't evoke even close to as much feeling as the landscapes. It's this disconnect that I can relate to. Why peer into the dark soul of man when you can swaddle yourself in the arms of a tree? The original *Snow* by Lawren Harris hangs in the Art Gallery of Ontario on Dundas Street. Harris was perhaps the most disconnected of the bunch. He was born rich so didn't have to suffer the social responsibilities of the workplace, agonized through a nervous breakdown when he tried to follow rank in the army, and his most famous portrait, of which there weren't many, was of Dr. Salem Bland, a Methodist theologian whose name defines him wholly. Eventually, Harris stopped signing his own work. The painter removed from the painting. You can't get much more disconnected than that.

When I feel grey in mood, feel myself forgetting my father's face, his presence, I go to the gallery and stand in front of *Snow*. Henry used to join me now and then, especially on Wednesday nights when admission was free and the crowds were teeming with perfume and chatter, with the various shades that skin comes in — all of it turning the gallery into its own work of art. The gallery is mostly empty now. There's no special exhibition so the tourists have instead chosen hotel pools and Ripley's Aquarium and Yorkdale Mall. Security guards are picking at their nails and phones, and the regulars who've seen it all drift in and out like vapour.

To get to Henry I have to pass through the Galleria Italia, a wood-beamed wing that resembles the hull of a ship, only upside down and dominated by twenty-foot-tall windows. It was funded by wealthy Italian Canadians whose lives had turned out well in Toronto, and who donated the wing as their thank you. It's meant for sculptures, for pieces that can stand up to the sun, and for quiet reflection. So I was surprised when I walked inside the Galleria and was greeted by the screams of an espresso machine. "Turned into a café last month," the barista tells me. All but one of the sculptures has been removed. Bronze and thin and as sharp as a needle, it rises so high, stretches up to the roof as though it could pierce the hull and sink the whole ship. The barista uses its marble base as the self-service stand for milk and sugar.

I exit the Galleria and pass through the modern art wing. The ceilings are tallest here because there are too many people trying to be artists today so you have to make BIG art to get noticed. I stand in front of one such large-scale piece: an enormously long metal-framed bed twisted into a kind of rollercoaster. Seven Wednesdays ago Henry and I argued about it. I said it was the saddest thing I'd ever seen, the embodiment of long-running pain and confusion. The artist was struggling with her sexuality, her fertility, her abuse. "Relax, sweetie," Henry told me, pulling me into his arms. "It's a child's dream bed. Pure fun." I buried my face in his T-shirt and whispered the absolute truth — that no important art in the history of the world was ever inspired by fun.

I wind down the staircase, my hand skimming the smooth railing as wide as a slide. I want to hoist my body up on it and take my chances, but an elderly security guard has her eyes on me. She's nervous, as though I might actually go for it. I feel sorry for her, in her thick orthopedic shoes, having to worry about people like me in what should be her retirement years, so I walk sedately down instead. As further penance, when I reach the first floor, I amble through the collections of model ships and Inuit art, nodding and touching my chin, pretending I care.

Only now I do care. Because Henry. Henry is here. In the Canadian Collection standing in front of *Snow* by Lawren Harris. His body so tall he has to look down at the painting instead of straight ahead. He's grown an inch since I last saw him one two three four five days ago. I am small and insignificant next to him, like the Murray Favro no one ever sees, blocked by tourists angling for the Picasso.

"Henry." I lunge. I wrap my arms around him, but I don't feel him at all. I'm enveloping an invisible bubble that's enveloping Henry.

"How are you?" he asks.

"You look good," is what I say. "You got a haircut. Did you dye it too? It looks richer. Like dark chocolate instead of milk."

"V—"

"I miss you," I say, my voice struggling. "I miss you so much. I went all the way to Wallkill to find you but you weren't there."

"I know," he says, and I feel his chest rise against me. "They told me. And V, you cannot do that. Promise me you won't do that again."

"I won't need to," I say, "because you're here. You're staying here with me."

Henry looks at the floor, the last place anyone in an art gallery would ever think to look. "I'm leaving tomorrow." He pries me from him, my fingers like claws. There must be chunks of Henry underneath my nails.

"No, Henry—" I reach for him and he backs away. The security guard is coming. I can hear her ID pass slap-slapping against her belt.

"I needed to tell you goodbye," Henry says. "Properly."

The guard rounds the corner. Her shoes squeak, her walkie-talkie chatters and sneezes.

"What are you talking about, 'properly'?" I say.

"You weren't thinking clearly when I left," Henry says.

"I was too. I saw you leave. I saw you fly out the window like . . ."

"Like what, V?"

I wrap my hands around my own throat. "Like nothing. Forget it."

"See? You didn't absorb the reality of what was happening. You were behind some veil, using whatever coping mechanism you use."

"So you're leaving me again?" I cry. "And you bring me here to do it? In front of my favourite painting? Why, Henry? To ruin it for me?"

"I thought you'd be calm here," he says. "It's your special place."

"Not anymore it isn't, thanks to you."

"You're right." He scratches behind his ear. Haircut left-overs and product residue are probably irritating his skin. "I'm an idiot. I just didn't want you to make a scene and I thought—"

I laugh. "*This* is where scenes are made!"

The guard mumbles into her walkie-talkie. "Possible four-oh-nine" or "glass-o-wine." I can't quite make it out.

"Sorry," Henry says to her. He turns to me with the word still on his lips, the word he only says and means to other people. "I have to go now, V."

I reach for his hand. It's soft, like he's been moisturizing, and I can't help but wonder for who. "If I have sex with you," I say, "will you stay?"

Henry smiles, but it's a pity smile, the kind people reserve for a homeless man with a funny sign. Spread Some Cheese On This Broke Cracker. Too Ugly To Prostitute. Henry walks past the security guard who looks up, way up at him. Because Henry is twenty feet tall now. He doesn't look back at me as he lumbers away. The hallway narrows — it's an ideal example of linear perspective — and Henry's getting smaller and smaller, but he's not fooling anyone. He's still a giant, and his head grazes every ceiling as he goes. Chandeliers ring with their special music. Dust is stirred from ornate moldings. The painted clouds in the children's gallery are tickled by his hair. In his wake, Henry leaves a mess. The floors are covered in chandelier glass and dust and sky.

I can't look at him for one more second, my eyes and my heart are too strained. I turn to the painting. Focus, Avery! On the yellow behind the trees at the forest's edge. When I was a kid I'd pretend it was the light from a UFO, but now I see it for what it really is: the sun setting, taking all that's warm and bright to the other side of the earth. The canvas makes a hollow rattling sound, like a ring shaking in a shoebox. The light from the back of the forest doubles, then triples, growing in intensity, pulsing. The heat of it is summer. I step closer to the painting, over the line on the floor I'm not supposed to cross.

"Four-oh-nine," the guard says, louder now, clearer. Slap slap slap. Her pass against her belt. She's coming for me.

Something wet hits the floor, but I don't look down; I stare straight ahead into the painting and watch it change. Snow slides from the fir trees, the branches spring up, the green of them overtaking the canvas. The wet sound grows louder, closer. I have to look. Snow drips down the canvas and flows over the lip of the baroque frame. My shoes are soaked, the floor a fast-spreading puddle. The heat spreads too, then the light. The beam, golden and blue like a flame, breaks free of the canvas and fills the gallery.

"Four-oh-nine! Four-oh-nine!"

A beeping. An alarm? It's loud and incessant, but tasteful. Not for a fire, but for an incident. For me.

"Four-ohhh-nine!" The security guard is running but she can't catch me. She's too old for this job. She knows it; human resources knows it; the gallery director knows it. And now heads are going to roll.

Not mine though, because I'm running. Away from Henry. Away from the security guard and the Canadian Collection and through the Red Salon. A hundred paintings in this room, hung too close together, shoving for space and attention. Their colours slide from their canvasses, reaching for my shoes. All of it will be gone, flooded into the sewers, into the lake that surrounds this city. The Renoir, the David Milne, the van Gogh on loan from the MOMA, all of their colours filling the cracks in the floors, slipping after me, after the canvas — *Snow* by Lawren Harris, its gilded frame rubbing against my pumping legs.

36

A park. Piss-burned grass. Vegan restaurants. Streetcar tracks. Asian storefronts. International phone cards. Ginseng root. Bubble tea. Massage. Massage! Massage!!! The painting is too heavy. Lungs, too heavy. Blackness. Light. Black. I can't see. I can't move my legs anymore. Air. I can't. The harder I breathe the less oxygen comes. Hyper. Vent. Ilation.

I collapse in an alley behind the Ontario College of Art and Design. It's one of the most spectacular buildings in the city, a black-and-white checkered "tabletop superstructure" the length of two football fields and balanced on ten fifty-foot rainbow stilts. It looks like a headless dairy cow at the gay pride parade. I'm wheezing. On a smoker's bench conceived and welded by a third-year honour student. *Tsunami*, it's called. The plaque describes it as an "interpretation of waves on land: the ebbing and flowing of life." The smooth stainless steel and the sloping angles make it impossible for me to lie in one spot without sliding off and then readjusting. My lower back aches: the inverted arch of the wave it leans against is putting painful pressure on my sacrum and vertebrae, L2 through 5. The painting rests, face down, against my jumping chest.

"Avery?"

It's a figure I recognize but don't know, a young woman and a cigarette. It takes her a few attempts before she can get the lighter to work in the wind, and in her struggle, I piece together her identity. Marnie. The only other person alive who knows the true demands of vanity legal publishing.

"Avery Gauthier? Is that you?"

The only person alive who speaks in underlines.

Marnie looks so different here, outside in the sun and free of the structure of corporate clothes. She wears a short skirt with another skirt, longer and see-through, over top of it. "It's called a hi-low," she tells me, when I compliment it. Her blonde hair is cropped and asymmetrical, and she's added a pink stripe to it that matches her nails.

"Are you just in the neighbourhood?" I say as my body slips away from the bench. I shift my hips and re-cross my legs, thrusting my heel into the ground like a tent peg.

"I'm actually a student here now," Marnie says. "When I left my job, I followed my passion: art. Which I guess is your passion too." She gestures at the frame I'm hugging to my body. "Wanna see?" Marnie pulls a sketchpad out of her purse. Flips through a charcoal series of fat abstract women sitting on a pink rococo antique sofa. They're perched on the arms, backs, legs of it—everywhere except the cushions. "I'm really into the act of sitting. The rebellion of it. The ways in which we aren't supposed to sit."

"Very cool," I say. "Sort of feminist, right?"

Her smile vanishes. "No." She puts the sketchpad away. "But I don't care if you don't get it, if my professor doesn't get it, if my moth . . . I don't care. Because I've found the real me here. Sitting at a desk all day was rotting my brain. Writing about other peoples' achievements? I mean come on. It was a daily reminder of my own failure, my own cowardice to go out there and achieve something myself. I was turning into every other asshole at that company." Her skin is flushed and her eyes huge. It's a good look on her, the kind that makes men want to kiss wild women. "Sorry, I didn't mean to rant," she says. "I guess I still have some unresolved anger with that place. But it wasn't all bad, right? I mean, I'm here now, aren't I? It inspired me to do better for myself, didn't it?"

I nod and her smile returns, as though my head is the switch.

"How is the job going, by the way?" she asks.

"Not good," I say.

"Oh?"

"I haven't really been doing it lately."

"Oh."

"I'm definitely going to get fired."

"Probably for the best," she says. "That job is awful. Remember my anxiety attacks and narcolepsy? Have you been having any similar issues?"

I sit up. Steady the painting between my thighs and chin. "Maybe."

"Really? Like what?"

"I'm having some strange, um, side effects."

"What exactly?"

I look up at the sky for signs of snow. I see only the base of the tabletop superstructure. A huddle of pink squares among the black and white, like enormous udders. Police sirens moan and bounce off the building and the nearby condos. Dogs howl in solidarity. "Shit," I say, "they're coming for me."

Marnie recoils and sucks on her cigarette. "You think people are after you."

"Never mind," I say.

"You're feeling paranoid? Having delusions?"

"I have to go." I slide my body off the bench. Hoist *Snow* under my arm.

"You can tell me, Avery."

The alley is narrow and she blocks me.

"You don't understand," I say. "They're going to lock me up."

"I told you about my issues, didn't I?"

"Yeah, you told me you were fucking crazy," I say. "And don't you regret it?"

"Well, I do now," she says, her eyes glowing and wet. "Now that you're throwing it back in my face."

The sirens are closer now, I think, maybe. The Doppler effect confuses everything. I push past Marnie, run by the bubble tea place, the massage parlours and phone card posters, and down into the subway. She's thudding behind me.

"I was trying to help you," she says. "To warn you so you wouldn't go into the job unprepared like I did."

She slides her transit pass when I slide mine. We race down the stairs just in time to catch the subway going south. The doors close on her, but Marnie fights against them, shoves them open, delays the train by five irretrievable seconds. She drops on to the seat to my left. "But boredom and disliking your job aren't going to lead to a breakdown," she says. "I thought that's what happened in my case, but really, the job was just the match that set the fire." She pulls her sketchpad out. "I'd been soaking in gasoline for years."

What would the consequences be if I blew up on the subway? For a few days, grief would envelope the city, wreaths and flowers rotting at the entrance to St. Patrick Station, candlelit vigils in the downtown, and an upswing in hugging between strangers. Eventually, the media would excavate my photo from Facebook, swarm to my apartment building and knock on the door of Billy Pfeiffer. She seemed nice, he'd tell them, a good person to live next to. She liked music and she took long showers. She did talk through the wall now and then, though. By the public, my actions would be considered random and senseless, the most terrifying kind of all. What a fearful mystery I would become. A young woman with white skin, no apparent political leanings or manifesto, no hijabs in her closet.

And no bomb—that would be the biggest surprise of all. The police would be stumped. How did she blow up the subway if she had no explosives strapped to her body? What spread the fire when she had no fertilizer stash in her apartment, and no Google searches for pentaerythrite tetranitrate, trinitrotoluene or potassium nitrate traced on her computer? The RCMP would be called in. They'd arrive on their stallions, clomping down the stairs and into the subway tunnel, the reek of burnt metal and flesh overwhelming even the stink of the horses. After examining the scene and turning up nothing, the officers would leap from atop their saddles and look into their horses' sad brown eyes. It was the Witnesses, they'd whisper. It must have been the Witnesses.

I can't see what Marnie is drawing, but I can hear it. Her hand moves furiously, the charcoal scraping against the heavy paper like a match on sandpaper.

"What exactly are you saying?" I ask her.

"I'm saying that I was deeply troubled when I had my breakdown." Marnie drags a line and then another. "And I think you're deeply troubled too."

She tears off the page and hands me her sketch. A portrait of me, there's no denying it, no matter how badly I don't want to lay claim to the miserable figure. My shoulders slump, bending me nearly in half. My lips like two chapped worms. Cheeks hollow with shadow, nose crooked in the slanted light. My eyes black as the burnt, petrified wood that she scratched across the paper—a thick X drawn over top, quartering me through the centre of my chest—cancelling me out.

37

Sirens. Their whirring and whining is all I hear as I scramble into my apartment. Maybe they're not for me at all? This city is full of criminals. Our mayor — body of bowling ball, brain of third-string junior high quarterback — wants us to believe the gangs are in the north end, near York University where the subways don't run, but gangs drive cars and people downtown buy drugs too. Even the mayor does drugs, crack cocaine to be specific. He lied about it at first, like he lied about reading while driving, drinking while driving, labour strikes, subways in Scarborough, but there wasn't much point. Lying was an ineffective strategy, in fact. Drugs made him more popular. "He's just like us!" was the general battle cry. And it's true. Walk into any lobby, stairwell, PTA meeting parking lot, community pool, and sniff the air, examine the ground. The evidence is there: we're a city on drugs. Drugs and falling glass and mad women stealing national treasures from galleries. I don't even remember grabbing the painting off the wall. The light, the rivers of colour, Henry, it was an impossible mess. I couldn't see through it to my hands reaching for the painting and pulling. So how can I be held responsible?

I cradle the painting to the floor. My arms feel weightless, like wings riding the wind. You'd never think it to look at it, it's only the size of a pizza box, but *Snow* is incredibly heavy. Is it the paint? Just how many layers did Lawren Harris stroke across this canvas? What's underneath *Snow*? I want to X-ray the painting and exfoliate the strata with chemicals. A self-portrait? A list of enemies? An actual boreal forest? The full weight of the sun? I thought the heaviness was from the gilded frame, but I dug my nail into it while I was lying on that wave bench and it sliced like a coffee cup. The frame is not carved bronze or wood, but foam core spray-painted gold. I know all about it, the faux techniques, from TV. Glazing and sponging and crackling, transforming wood into marble and drywall into suede. And because Henry forced me to transform too — from person to wife to estranged wife to art thief. But I'll show Henry. I'll make a life out of it. I might even be good at professional thieving. After all, the painting is here now, and safer in my closet than in a gallery too concerned with workplace equity to protect it.

Margaret is at the sink washing dishes, humming the theme song from *The Andy Griffith Show*, a show I have never seen, not once, and yet I know the song completely. The tap running and her humming are commotion enough, so I open the closet door and fumble with my pile of stolen things: Margaret's purse, Kristie's coat, Watchtower tote bag, and now one of the great masterworks of the twentieth century. I wrap the painting in a plastic bag, the receipt for celery seed and pantyliners still inside, and slide it beneath Henry's Body Glove wetsuit. Its logo, a black hand on yellow, a sign from the gods for STOP!

"I can't stop," I whisper. "It's too late."

The taps squeal off and Margaret turns. "Avery, there you are."

I shut the closet door. I wish I had a key.

"Why have you been avoiding me?"

"I haven't," I say. "Work is just crazy right now."

"You work?"

"Of course I work. And I need to check in." I walk over to my computer and sit down. Marnie's sketch carves at my hip, so I pull it out of my pocket, bury it under a file folder. A trail of speech bubbles pops up in my Messenger window when I wiggle the mouse. I brace for what I know is coming.

Boss: *Avry? Hullo?*

Boss: *Anser me. Now.*

Boss: *Were are you?*

Boss: *You missed yore dedline!*

My Boss. A fifty-five-year-old Wharton executive MBA who cannot spell. His avatar is Mr. Burns, his nose a fishhook, his yellow fingers tented in evil anticipation.

Boss: *Don't avoid me!*

Boss: ...

Boss: *Thats it.*

Boss: *Your fired.*

Shit shit shit. I type faster than I think.

Avery: *Please don't. I'm sorry!*

Boss: *Im serius.*

Avery: *Can we talk about this on the phone?*

Boss: *No point. You arent working.*

Avery: *I missed a few deadlines, yes, and I'm sorry.*

Avery: *I'll make it up to you, I promise.*

Avery: *You won't even have to pay me this week.*

Boss: ...

Boss: *hellllll*

Boss: ....

Boss: *Ok but its your last chanx*

He's right—it is my last chanx. If I don't make everything right, starting now, the rest of my life will unravel. I'll probably end up like Marnie, sharing my traumas with near-strangers, smoking in alleys, drawing pictures of dimpled asses. I click off Messenger and click into Google. I type in "Jehov"—oops, hit caps lock—"AH'S WITNESS RECOVERY GROUP." There's a meeting tonight; there's a meeting every night.

"I have to go out," I tell Margaret. "I have a meeting."

"What kind of meeting?"

"A meeting for people like me who've been psychologically scarred by people like you."

"Oh please," she scoffs. "You're fine."

I laugh. "I am not fine."

"What's wrong with you then, Avery? Tell me. I want to know." She sits down at the table, cradles her chin in her palm. I can see every vein and bone on the back of her hand. Hollow and dried up like the branches of dead trees.

"Never mind," I say. "Nothing is wrong with me."

"See? You're fine."

I tug at my hair. "Oh my god, you —"

She slaps her hand on the table. "It's a lowercase 'g' to you, isn't it?"

"Pardon?"

"If you wrote this conversation down, the letter g in God would be lowercase. Yes or no?"

"You're not making sense."

"Because God is nothing to you but a turn of phrase, a swear word." She stands and opens the closet. I hold my breath as she rummages through the hangers. "You turning against our religion is one thing. I can deal with that. I've *dealt* with that. But against God altogether?" She pulls out a cardigan.

I exhale. "So you want me to say *god* like it's a proper noun?"

"Yes. And I want to go to one of these meetings of yours."

"You can't come. Cannot."

"I damaged you, apparently," she says. "So I'd like to help fix you."

38

I lose her by running, but it's hard to shake someone on a straight path with no trees to duck behind, no cloaking fog, just a few newspaper boxes and raccoon-proof garbage cans. I look back and see Margaret in the distance, at least three minutes behind me at the pace she's going. I make it to the community centre, but a man dodges ahead. He struggles with the door, pushing instead of pulling. He's wearing a bicycle helmet.

"Calvin?" I say. "Calvin Straight?"

"Well fuck a duck." Calvin puts his hands on the hips he doesn't have. "So you *are* stalking me."

"Just a coincidence, I'm afraid. I live at the far end of the street."

"Oh."

"Sorry."

"That's okay. I just . . . I don't know. It would be nice to feel appreciated. The other weathermen, meteorologists rather, they tell these stories about groupies they call Climate Cun—"

"I should really get inside," I say.

"What are you here for? Yoga?"

"Yep," I lie. "You?"

"The crystallacrophobia support group. You know, fear of being hit by glass from—"

"I thought that was a downtown group."

Calvin removes his helmet. His hair looks surprised. "Used to be, but then some shattered glass pellets fell on one of our group leaders. From that new condo on King with the slides inside the lobby? And the adults-only sandbox on the roof? The guy was wearing his helmet, so he's okay — a little shaken and stirred, if you know what I mean, but . . . Anyways, we meet uptown now, which is actually much safer. Shorter buildings, more convenient parking for first responders." He smiles at me. "Listen, why don't you ditch the hippies and come with me? You can't get a better shoulder rub in the city. There's a woman in there with hands the size of badminton rackets. Swear to God."

I turn and see that Margaret is making good time, even in those kitten heels of hers. I have a minute, if that, before she's on top of me.

"Okay," I say. "I'll come."

"Really?"

"Just go!"

We hurry down the hallway, Calvin jumping and punching every third foam ceiling tile. "If you're lucky you might see a de-helmeting tonight," he says. "There's some real wackos in here, trust me. Some of them wear their helmets *inside*. Oh hey Jerry."

Calvin steps into room 109 and I follow, slamming the door behind me by mistake. A woman yelps, her hands covering her ears. "You're making the glass shake in the frame!"

I apologize and Calvin backs me up. "Chill, Janet," he says to her. "It's a new door to her. She doesn't yet know its ways." He winks at me and pats his hand on the chair next to his. I sit and cross my legs, my corduroy catching on his, locking us together. A new feeling happens beneath my surface, like an old engine running inside of me, gears grinding, oil glugging. It's a feeling I want gone, so I pull my leg away and focus on the group. Except for helmets on top of the more nervous-looking heads, this support group circle looks just like mine. Sounds like it too. Fear in search of sympathy, companionship, hope.

"My boss keeps threatening to fire me if I don't come in. But a window just fell out of my office building. Flattened another publicist. So my boss can go fuck himself."

"One word: tunnels."

"And think of it. The fucking media is always going on about nickel sulfide in the glass and defects, right? The nature of the glass itself. But they never mention the nature of the fucking condo developers."

"I don't just mean for shopping and subways, like what we have now. I'm talking tunnels we can live in. Permanently."

"And these windows are supposed to be, like, super windows. Self-cleaning, nanotechnology, all that shit. They treat the glass with this sealant that's invisible to the human eye. It's triggered by UV rays, then the film breaks down the dirt and blah blah blah you've got a clean window. So they can make fucking super windows? But they can't figure out how to stop them from falling out?"

"The government just pushed a new law through, guys. Construction companies have to use heat-strengthened laminated glass, the kind used in windshields. So we should be safe, right?"

"I can only drink out of plastic cups now."

"Shouldn't we? Guys?"

"I wet the bed again last night."

"I mean, the government must know what they're doing. Right? Guys?"

Calvin doesn't say a word. Instead he focuses his attention on me. I am hot, my whole body burning. Can he measure me with his eyes? Does he know I'm a million degrees? I need to cool down or I'll melt in my chair. I wish for a solution and it comes in the form of the giant, freezing cold hands of Marsha, a carpenter from Etobicoke. Heaven, on my fevered shoulders.

"Well, that was disappointing," Calvin says as we step outside into the night. The air is warm and it smells like the hot dogs being sold across the street. The vendor is busy warding off the attention of a Jehovah's Witness. I squint. Akono. He's holding a sausage in one hand and a roll of *Awake!* magazines in the other.

Calvin stretches his head from side to side. Makes a crunching sound that I'll hear in my nightmares. "Not a single de-helmeting and Marsha was totally off her game. My neck, Christ, it's still killing me. Did you get anything out of it at all?"

"No," I say. "But then again, I'm not afraid of falling glass anymore."

"Really? I mean, you probably should be. But, I guess . . . Congratulations?"

"Thanks."

Calvin touches my hand, just a pat, but there's no fly on it and no fuzz; men only touch for one reason.

"How did you get over it? The fear?"

"That's a big question, Calvin."

Dimples I didn't know he had tuck into his cheeks. I smile back. I don't even try not to.

"Listen, I think you're kind of a cool person," Calvin says. "And I have this huge case of ginger ale at home."

Ginger ale?

"Canada Dry sent it to me for, you know, being on TV. Or maybe they expect me to like mention it during a broadcast? Or on Facebook? I really have no idea. Anyways, what I'm trying to say is do you want to come over to my place? Nothing untoward—"

Untoward?

"will happen. I just, I think I'd like to talk to you some more."

Akono backs off the hot dog vendor and crosses the street. To my side of the street. He sees me. Sees Calvin. Waves.

"I know you're married," Calvin says.

Are his fingers really still on my hand?

"But with a ring like that I can't help but wonder *how* married."

I shove my hand into my pocket.

"Like what kind of guy gives a woman like you a crummy ring like that, and no engagement ring either? I mean I know diamonds are just part of the De Beers cartel and actually are quite worthless but... Anyways, I just think we could hang out, maybe have a couple ginger ales and, you know, chat. That's all. Really."

I feel the engine inside of me. It's rusty, the gears are scraping. It needs oil. In through my belly button it would pour, and maybe then I'd be ready. But I'm not.

"Maybe another time," I say.

Calvin puts his helmet on. Tufts of hair stick out desperately, like prisoners' fingers through bars. "Sure," he nods. "Another time." He walks away, steps like a man with springs in his toes.

Akono sidles up to me, takes a bite of his sausage. "Who's that?" he asks in between chews.

"The weatherman," I say.

"Does Henry know you talk to weathermen?"

"Henry doesn't care what I do."

"You're still his wife," Akono says. "At least for another day or two until the annulment is filed. And he would be very jealous if he thought there was a weatherman in the picture."

I point to Akono's chin. There's nothing there, not a drop of mustard, but Akono doesn't know that. He wipes at it with a napkin.

"Well, there *is* a weatherman and I'm going to his house," I say. "To have sex with him if I feel like it."

Akono chokes and coughs up a chunk of sausage. Pigeons dive-bomb and scramble.

I chase after Calvin's head bouncing down the sidewalk, until that new feeling slows me down. It's churning inside of me, my organs grinding and screeching. There must be smoke coming out of my ears. I turn. Akono's chin is still smeared with invisible mustard. "You tell Henry!" I yell. "You tell him I'm moving on!"

Just saying it out loud, even though it's a lie, I feel like a witch who's cast a spell. I want to reel the incantation back in, but it's too late. I look up to the sky and it's pouring out snow, the coloured kind, my favourite from my father's files. Snow borne of cold and painted by algae. *Chlamydomonas* for green, *Chlamydomonas nivalis* for pink, red and orange. It piles up in seconds and turns every step I take into hard labour. Calvin though? He walks as though it's a sunny summer day, his helmet the only sign of emotional misfortune. Calvin stops at Mount Pleasant Cemetery; thirty paces back, so do I. It's just us on this long and lonely expanse of Yonge Street. Calvin and me, the subway speeding past aboveground, and whatever ghosts slip out of the dirt and through the cemetery fence. Calvin stands still, taking in a gargoyle perched atop a tall obelisk. It's a dragon, claws curled around the stone, wings spread and coated with the coloured snow, condemned to stare down death forever. I look away and across the miles of rolling hills and tombstones behind it. The snow is endless. It stings my eyes. Pink, green and orange for miles, like the whole world has been tagged with graffiti.

Calvin moves on and so do I. He walks, and I lumber, all the way to Forest Hill, a wealthy neighbourhood with four Starbucks, two spinning studios and eight hair salons, but no other services. Every other storefront is empty, out of business, as though the rich have no need for vegetables, pharmaceuticals or gasoline. We turn onto a dead-end street and to a large house, a mansion from the early days of the city that's been quartered into apartments. Calvin unlocks the front door and steps inside. I watch all the windows and wait. A light flickers on in the basement. It's Calvin's kitchen. He sits at his table and pulls his helmet off. The engine inside of me churns and purrs. Makes me want to run my fingers through Calvin's flattened hair. I creep closer, to a bush a few feet from his window, and watch as he cracks open a can of ginger ale. He must be enjoying it because he takes long sips and says *ah* even though there is no one there to hear it. He scratches at his nose and shifts in his chair. I'm not sure what I'm waiting for, but it's not happening. It's just Calvin, staring at the refrigerator, downing can after can of Canada Dry.

A splashing sound. I stand very still. There it is again. I notice the edge of a backyard pool. It's attached to the pretentiously modern home next door, the kind that's a tribute to squares. I approach the fence and peek through the slats. The swimmer is wearing a red-and-black polka dot bikini, goggles and bathing cap. She's backstroking through deep, orange snow, at least nine feet of it.

She swims like a pro, her arms slapping down close to her sides, her feet kicking up pounds of snow without losing speed. When she reaches the end of the pool, she flips her body around, takes a breath and disappears. Eight, nine, ten seconds. Eleven. I panic. Thirteen. Her head pokes through. Clots of orange, like spoonfuls of shaved ice from a carnival, rest on the crown of her bathing cap. She is so close I hear her breathing, see the muscles in her shoulders release and relax, the ones strong enough to pull her through the heavy snow. She hoists herself out. Her legs, sinewy and long, flex gracefully as she steps onto the diving board. The board is frosted with ice and I worry for her safety. She doesn't slip, though, and when she gazes down at the pool, so do I. This time, though, it's not snow that fills it. It's ice. Nine feet deep. Solid. Orange. The swimmer takes a grand bouncing step, jumps high in the air and points her toes. I scream, but she lets her body plummet anyway, crashing through the ice, leaving an entry wound on the surface. I hold my breath: eight, nine, ten. Nothing. Thirteen. I picture her trapped inside. A fly in amber.

I scale the fence, hurtling toward the pool. I see wisps of her under the ice, red and tan, but they aren't moving. I press my hands against it. It's solid so I step onto it, lie down on my stomach, drag my body to the hole and reach my arm into the abyss. "Hello?" I yell. "Are you okay?"

Twenty-nine seconds.

The swimmer bursts through, sending tangerine shards flying into the air. She breathes deeply as she stares me down. "Who. The fuck. Are you?"

Before I can answer, my body sinks, engulfed by water. It's liquid and warm. I can't breathe and I can't surface.

My father. He stands as straight and as tall as he would on the earth, his lime-with-the-lights-off parka puffed by the water. He's so handsome, his face just as it was before he got sick. Clear green eyes, thick strawberry-blonde hair I could tug when it wouldn't come out in clumps, that charmingly crooked smile. He reaches down and plucks a feather off my shoulder. I let it dance in the water.

An arm pulls at me and I struggle against it. I want to stay here where it's warm, where my father is. But the arm is insistent. It reaches me back into the air I need, and yet breathing is impossible.

"Who the fuck are you?" the swimmer says.

I dive back down. My father's gone, but the feather isn't. It's still dancing in the undercurrent.

The arm again. "And what the fuck are you doing in my pool?"

I cling to the pool's edge, suck in air thick as syrup. "I thought. I thought. You were. In trouble."

"Well, as you can see, I'm fine."

"But how are you?" I cry.

"What are you, deaf? I just told you I'm fine."

"I mean, how is it possible to be fine?"

Days without Henry: 4+1

39

The swimmer, the pool, my father — it's too much. Final nail, final straw, final everything. Maybe Henry was right. Maybe I am using unhealthy coping mechanisms. "This has got to change. Right now," I say. "I'm a normal person going through a normal breakup." Normal. I look outside. It's summer as it should be. My mother isn't inside my apartment. All is as it should be.

Normal. Starting now.

Watch *Battlestar Galactica*, season two, episode two: Valley of Darkness. Shave legs. Do fifteen sit-ups and seven push-ups. Overpluck eyebrows. Write bio for

WEISS, RALPH: LEGAL COUNSEL
FORD GYMS

Mr. Weiss joined Ford Gyms as legal counsel in 1997 following eight years of private practice in Toronto, during which time he specialized in commercial real estate and mortgage enforcement. He also provides assistance in areas such as acquisitions, due diligence, and sticking his thumb up his ass.

Leave the house and walk into summer. Drag my shoes against the pavement soft with cigarette butts, not snow, and supple rubberized crack filler. The sun, there it is, just a bit of it hiding behind a cloud that's hiding behind Burger Shack. Buy a shitty Bic lighter and a pack of cigarettes at the Daisy Mart. Smoke three in a row. Slowly. Inhaaaaale. Suppress gag, suppress cough. Send plume of grey smoke straight into the dazzling blue sky.

Normal.

Go grocery shopping and instead of cereal, buy ingredients intended to combine to form an actual meal! The chickpeas are dry and as hard as stones, though, and land with a crack on the counter. Should be soaked overnight as per Steve's instructions. "No" is my conclusion. Instead will speed things up by adding a little modernity, some twenty-first century innovation, into the ancient recipe. "Progress!" I chant. "And progress is normal! Striving for efficiency is superlatively normal!" Pour the beans into a shallow bowl, spoon some water over top and slide the experiment into the microwave. Stand in front of the machine, bathe in the radiation and pick at cuticles. The timer counts down. Forty-nine, fifty seconds. Tiny explosions rattle and pop. Open the door. Steam or smoke spills out like dry ice. Wave it away and peer in. The beans have detonated, leaving the walls of the microwave spattered with beige flesh. Scrape it off with a spatula and plop the mess into a pot. Hunt through my grocery bag for fresh rosemary, olive oil and a grenade of lemon juice. Pluck the rosemary from its stem. Roll the scent of Christmas and Thanksgiving stuffing between my fingers. Guess at secret ingredient, the one that Steve wouldn't give away. Sage? Tablespoon it in and let it simmer. Wonder, which is a thing that normal people do, about Steve and about the two of us as friends. Steve and Avery. Avery and Steve. Scrawl our names on the grocery store receipt and surround them with curls of heat. Creepy. Scratch it out. Replace my name with Accalia. Wonder about her: where Accalia is now, why she really left, if she still loves Steve or was ever in love with him, how that love ebbed and flowed. The pain of love unrequited. It's not real pain, they say, but Steve and I know better — that the pain of nothing is far worse than the pain of something. Like after an amputation. Phantom pain. I feel it now. Have felt it since Henry went away 4 + 1.5 days ago. A throb. A heartbeat. In the empty space to my left. A bag of ice would be soothing. Hang it in the air by my hip where Henry should be.

Carry the rivithia to the basement, hands protected from the heat of the metal by potholders but my face still victim to the steam. Steve's broom closet? Empty. Walk down the hall to his apartment. Place the pot down. It sizzles, releases the scent of burnt industrial carpet fibres and mold. Lean against the door. Sobbing? Male, definitely, which makes the scenario more unsettling and alien.

Makes it Not Normal. Because I haven't lived the kind of life that's flush with the crying of men.

"Steve?" I say. "You okay?"

Sniffling. A nose blown.

"Steve?"

"I'm fine."

"You don't sound fine."

The sandpaper shuffling of feet. He must be wearing slippers.

"What's the matter?"

A long sniffle.

"What's that smell?" he asks.

I hoist the pot to the peephole. "Rivithia."

"You cooked?"

"I'm trying to be normal."

Laughter. Coughing. Hand thumping against chest.

"Are you in pain?" I ask him. "Is it that place by your side where Accalia used to be? Does it ache? Because my side hurts, too. It's the left side, the side of the bed Henry used to sleep on."

Silence.

"I'm trying to be normal, Steve. I'm trying my best. But I don't know how without Henry."

A whimper.

"Steve?"

"Please go, Avory."

I turn from the door.

"Leave the soup," he says.

40

The hunger. It's back. I haven't felt it since Henry left and now it's here and rumbling up a fuss. Steve has all of my soup, but it doesn't matter; the hunger doesn't want soup anyway. Doesn't need to be nourished or fed, just filled. So I head to the Daisy Mart. The door chimes and I'm in, safe and secure in the Lotto Max junk food Disneyland. I grab one litre of Limited Edition Häagen-Dazs Sticky Toffee Pudding from the freezer. The lid is frosted over, the insides likely burned by the cold. It's my fault; I've kept it waiting too long. "I'm sorry," I say, "but I'm here now." Then Cheetos, Cap'n Crunch, chocolate milk, Nibs, licorice allsorts, peanut M&M'S, mini Mars bars, mini eggs, a triple discounted Easter bunny with busted ears and droopy candy-coated eyes. I could stay here forever, with the Kool-Aid Man and the

Pillsbury Doughboy, but the cashier is swearing and scratching his Instant Bingo! with an inhospitable ferocity, so Cap'n Crunch and I remove ourselves from the premises to the outdoors and the picture window of the Taekwondo Academy. Mats on floors. Mirrors on walls. Grown men tackling kids wearing pajamas.

"Perverts."

My mother is nowhere to be seen when I step inside the apartment, so I lay my treasures on the coffee table, tear into the packages. With every bite and swallow, I feel my stomach expand, thighs tingle, ass twitch — the food growing my body centimetres farther into the universe than it was yesterday. Then a glorious pulsing peace takes over. The euphoric hypnotic haze of sugar and fat. Now this, *this* is heaven. There's no hidden kingdom in the sky, no invisible pocket floating amidst the ether. My stomach is the place for those 144,000 Witnesses, the chosen ones with immortal life and spirit bodies. They're all hunched here next to my Cheetos, swimming happily in the acid and bile and Orange #40.

I lie down in my kingdom of wrappers, boxes, bins and crumbs, my head resting in the Häagen-Dazs tub like a crown. A scent wafts in that isn't chocolate. Bloodied roses. A rusted fence around an English garden.

"So you miss Henry, I take it?" Margaret's face looms over me, blocking out the ceiling. "I mean, my goodness, Avery. The *entire* Easter bunny?"

I belch and its volume and duration come as a surprise to us both. My stomach whinnies like a horse.

Margaret pinches her nose. "Was that necessary?" Her voice is nasal.

I spread my arms through the wrappers like snow. Up down, up down. I'm a beautiful garbage angel. The plastic crunches and tears, scratches my skin where it's softest.

"'Your camp must be holy,'" Margaret recites, "'so Jehovah does not see anything indecent in you and turn away from accompanying you.'"

"Chillax, Margie," I say, my arms flapping. "When god comes to smite down me and all the rest of us non-believers 'uncleanliness of all sorts will disappear forever.'"

She feigns a heart attack. "You remember the psalms?"

"You did force me to go to Kingdom Hall for like twelve years."

"Yes, but I just assumed you annexed that part of your heart."

I pick up the Cheetos bag and shake the dust into my mouth. Orange #40 blushes my skin.

"I suppose binge-eating isn't so bad," she says, "given the options." Margaret rolls up her sleeve. Purplish scars stripe her arm like the tail of a tiger. I want to look away but I'm compelled to count them. Ten, eleven, twelve. Thirteen is raised and reddish, scabby, much fresher than the rest. "One for every year I was away from you," she says.

I pull her sleeve down. I want her to suffer, but only psychically. I never wanted her to bleed.

"I worried I'd passed my bad habit on to you," she says.

"You didn't pass anything on to me. I'm nothing like you."

"You don't even really know me."

"I know enough."

Margaret rummages through the wrappers and finds a wish M&M: two peanuts stuck together sharing the same glossy shell. "I was hoping you'd get to hear my side of things at that community centre meeting last night." She pops it in her mouth. "But you weren't there."

"And you weren't supposed to be either," I say.

"I told my side of the story to Kristie—"

"Kristie?" I rake my hands through the pile, collecting every last wrapper and crumb. It's suddenly very important that Margaret never find anything good ever again.

"She has such an open heart," says Margaret. "And I can't get over how much you two look alike."

"What the hell—"

"Language, Avery."

"—are you talking about?"

Margaret locks her hands to her hips. She's wearing jeans. She's never worn jeans. Never ever. "You could be sisters," she says.

I crawl to my desk, pull out Marnie's sketch from under the file. My face is smudged now, black marking up my cheeks, chin and forehead. *Dirty and filthy.* It's uncanny. "See? Kristie and I look nothing alike."

Margaret takes the paper. Her features twist. "This is a drawing. In charcoal."

"But the colouring is the same."

"You have strawberry-blonde hair, Avery. The same as Kristie."

"Are you blind, Margaret? It's black." I point to the drawing. "Just like this."

"And you have green eyes. Your father's green eyes."

"No, they're black and sooty and filthy—"

"Look at yourself."

Margaret forces my head to turn toward the window. "Look!"

But she can't make me open my eyes.

"Is this why Henry left without you?" she says.

I shuffle myself as close to the TV as I can get.

"Are you having problems, Avery? Psychological—"

I turn it on. The Space Network. *The Wrath of Khan.*

Margaret's neck is angry. Peripherally I can see the gradients progress—blush to rose to crimson. "This old game?" she says. "Like you and your father used to play? Fine, then." She plunks down next to me, reaches into her bag and pulls out knitting needles and a project in progress. It's long enough to be a scarf but far too wide.

"You may not believe this," she says, "but your father, even though he wasn't a Jehovah's Witness, he believed in God. The way he used to talk about the trees and the animals, about the snow? He had more faith than any Witness I know."

Captain Spock is dead and "Amazing Grace" cries from Scotty's bagpipes. No one on the crew, not Sulu or McCoy or Uhura, can bring themselves to look at the coffin, and their stiff, inhibited posture makes my own back ache. Kirk's shoulders square as corners.

"It was a harder thing to reconcile in the city," Margaret says, "that joy, that wonder. So it just faded, and your dad grew angry and distant—always watching those movies and shows instead of talking to me, running off with his skis to the Gatineau Hills. And running off with you, turning you against me. And maybe it was all my fault. I shouldn't have married someone outside of my faith. I shouldn't have had a child with him. I shouldn't have convinced him to take that job in Ottawa. But I did, and each of those choices led to the next and the next and the next. And now we're here."

Spock's coffin shoots out into space and soars by a star bright as the sun, landing on planet Genesis. The impact's not shown, but I know the landing is gentle because there is Spock's coffin, all cozy in the tall grasses and foliage, with ferns swaying overhead in the light and the cool mist. And then the soothing voice of Spock himself, the dead Vulcan who is not dead at all, thrums over the classical score.

Margaret drops her knitting and reaches for the remote. I have it too tight, though; it's a part of my hand, a sixth finger. She pulls the plug from the wall and the screen goes black. I jump up and so does she. She swipes Henry's trophy from the shelf, #1 *Husband,* and threatens the screen with it.

"Don't make me do it," she says.

I've shown her my weaknesses; it's my own fault. "What do you want, Margaret?" I yell.

"I want you to talk to me instead of the television," she says.

I take the trophy back. I wipe her fingerprints from it because Henry will notice. He sees all the smudges.

"And I want you to visit Bryan in prison."

"That is not going to happen," I tell her.

"What if I give you something?" she says. "Like a trade."

"You have nothing I want, Margaret."

"I know where Henry is."

"So do I. In Wallkill."

"No, he's *going* there. But he's not there yet. They say he's having second thoughts about the job. That he's stalling. Because of love."

I grip the trophy. "#1" stamps into my palm, changing my fortune. "Who's 'they'? Who told you this?"

"If you see Bryan, I'll tell you where you can find Henry."

"Was it Akono?"

Margaret returns to her knitting. She can never look me in the eye when she lies and omits. Growing up, almost all of my conversations with her took place in the car. "I'm making one of those carpets that runs up the stairs," she says, knitting one, purling one. "A — what's it called? Oh darn —"

"A stair runner?"

"Yes, that's it!" she says. "I'm making it for you."

"But I don't have stairs."

"Maybe someday."

"If Jehovah deems me worthy?"

"Avery, Jehovah's love is unconditional." She rolls out what she's done so far. The wool is a deep burgundy. It will bleed when washed, will ruin everything it touches. "Just like a mother's."

41

Akono is working. His lips and tongue enunciate silent words. Sleeves rolled up, suit jacket drapes a chair. He sits on the stage, legs splayed, eyes closed, hands moving in grand gestures as though summoning lightning. It would be an intimidating omnipotent scene — but for his pants. They're short and give me a glimpse of his everyman socks: one black, one navy.

"Laundry day?" I say.

Akono's eyes snap open. "I wasn't expecting an audience."

"I can see that." I match his Zeus-like gestures with my own.

"I'm rehearsing for tonight's worship —"

"And it's very theatrical, Akono. Very Cirque du Soleil."

I step up to the stage, choosing to stand behind the pulpit, the very one that Akono proselytized from so effectively that Henry is now his. I lean over, my elbows in the grooves made by Akono's. Something touches my leg. A leather strap. I follow it to the end of a pair of binoculars. The weight feels good around my neck, but when I look through the glass at Akono, at his mouth, he's too close to see clearly. "What can I do for you?" he says, his lips-tongue-teeth a blur.

"You can tell me where Henry is."

"Aha. So you heard about our little bump in the road."

"Bump?" I say. "Henry's changing his mind. He wants me back."

Akono crosses his arms. They look so skinny in the world outside his suit. "May I tell you a story, Avery?"

"If it's about where Henry is."

"It is."

"Then I'm all ears. And all-seeing, all-knowing eyes." I fiddle with the adjustment ring on the binoculars. Akono is much clearer now and when he opens his mouth to speak it looks as though I'll be swallowed whole.

"It all started with a knock on a door," he says. "The woman was in her bathrobe. She was short, a thick accent. Megan gave her the standard, 'I want to share with you the good news about the coming paradise on earth.' The woman invited her in and Megan was very excited. Maybe this woman would actually listen, she thought."

"And Megan would be—"

"I'll get to that," Akono tells me. "Megan sat on the couch and the woman offered her a hot chocolate. She accepted, of course. It was winter and she'd been walking around all day. So the woman went into the kitchen and returned with a mug. Megan took a sip; it burned her throat. She asked what it was and the woman smiled as though she had good news to share and said, 'Cocoa mixed with antifreeze.'"

I raise my hand. "Is that like a seasonal thing at Starbucks?"

Akono smiles. "Do you *want* to know where Henry is?" he says. "Or do you *need* to know?"

I lower my arm.

"Megan got to the hospital in time so she was fine physically. But mentally and emotionally? That woman had tried to kill her. And for what? For doing as Jesus has done? For trying to show her reason? For reaching her heart? Megan had a hard time coming to grips with this hatred. She wanted to know why. She started to read the propaganda against the Watchtower on the Internet: hypocrisy and false prophecies, Bible tampering, stories of families breaking apart, intimidation. Crazy things. But Megan believed them. She confided in her husband. Said she was having doubts, was confused. She told him she didn't think she could forget everything she'd read and continue on as if nothing had changed: as if she herself hadn't been changed."

"And let me guess," I say. "That husband was you."

Akono straightens his tie.

"And you left her?"

"I did," he says. "Just like Henry left you."

"Only it's not the same. Because Henry wants me back—"

"You're missing the point."

"—and if I can just get to him, he'll know that he belongs with me, not with you, not with those freaks in Wallkill."

Akono stands, his confidence restored by the act of making himself vertical, by the concealment of those humiliating socks. "My wife lost her faith, yes, but that's not why I left her. It wasn't the religion; we could have stayed together despite that. It was her. She changed. She became argumentative, questioning and—"

"And you couldn't control her."

"And I stopped loving her."

His words like a punch. "But Henry loves me," I say, balling my fists, stiffening my stance.

"Does he?" says Akono. "Does he even know you? Who is Avery Gauthier to Henry?"

"I, I—"

Am the pterodactyl chaser who scaled the volcano.

"Am—"

The tattoo fading from Henry's arm.

"The—"

Useless piece of garbage who slept on the couch on our honeymoon who never let her husband see her naked *filthy and nasty and dirty and soiled.*

Akono touches my hand.

I recoil, it's all I know how to do, and my back hits the wall. I lean as far into it as I can, hoping another me from another time has been through this nightmare already; has come back from the future and prepared a hole to an alternate dimension for my escape. I look for marker or crayon or the faint line of a pencil. But there's nothing. Only salmon-rose paint and Akono breathing on my neck.

"Do you remember that first time we met?" he says. "In the park, in the middle of the night? The heavens circling over our heads?"

"Get. Away. From. Me."

"Henry isn't the man you want him to be," he says. "You've probably known that for a long time, though, haven't you? Is that why you wouldn't have sex with him? Because deep down you knew you couldn't trust him?"

My phone rings. My hands are shaking so it juggles; I nearly drop it.

"It's Henry," I say, sticking the phone in his face like a badge. "And if you don't back off, I'll tell him everything."

"Go ahead," Akono says.

"He'll kick your ass!"

"In fact, let's put Henry on speaker." He takes the phone from me.

"You have a call from a federal prison from—"

"HAVE SOME COMPASSION, KID!"

"Press one to accept the call."

"That's a 613 number." Akono hangs up. "Henry's area code is 718." He slides the phone into my pocket. His fingers. My hip. *Soiled and disgusting.*

"What's wrong with you?" I say.

"What's wrong with *Henry*? How could he leave a woman like you?"

"You don't even know—"

Akono silences me with his finger on my lips. He makes me taste it. Carpet and newsprint. "I know what I see," he says. "I know you're beautiful. And lonely. And I know I'm lonely, too." He moves closer. It's Akono, I know that, but all I see is my uncle Bryan. Bryan standing by my doorway trying to look handsome instead of drunk. Bryan sucking in his stomach and then forgetting, sucking in, forgetting. "I know you stare at the Kingdom Hall every night from your window."

My hands shake. I raise the binoculars to my eyes, and to my apartment across the street. I can see everything inside in perfect relief: the blankness, the television the only source of light, the shadow of my mother thrown against the wall, the wall the futon used to lean against before Henry took it, took everything.

"Are you hoping I see you when you stare out like that?" Akono says. "Because I do. Every single night I do."

I adjust the rings and see snow—it's pouring out of the sky as though a giant ripped a zipper or a plane finally tore a hole up there. The smothering weight of it, the relentless whiteness, the snow is assaulting the city. Pedestrians and bikers and drivers, they're all drowning, only they don't know it. That's how powerful denial can be.

"Where are you going?" Akono moves toward me.

I raise the binoculars over his head. They're so heavy; I could crush his skull. He pulls them from me, and I pull back. It's childish, this back and forth, but the stakes are so high.

I shove them at him, let him win that battle, and run to the end of the hallway. Akono is on me, his hand pulling my sleeve, when I push through the first doors I see. The room opens itself up: a carbon copy of the one I just escaped. Dozens of Witnesses — men, women, children — turn toward us, all smiles, as if we're sunshine crashing into the room instead of chaos.

"Well, hello!" calls the elder. "What a most welcome surprise!"

I turn to Akono. "Tell me where Henry is," I whisper.

"Everyone, this is Brother Akono Balewa! The youngest Toronto elder in the Watchtower's history!"

The crowd breaks into polite applause.

I lean in to Akono. Make him taste my breath. "Tell me where Henry is or I'll scream."

Akono lets me go. "Just calm down. There's no reason to —"

"Where is he?" I say.

"I'm trying to protect you."

"Tell me."

"Just trust me; you need to move on."

"Move on to what? To you?" I laugh.

He shakes his head and appeals to the ceiling. His Adam's apple bulges his throat like a rat in a snake.

"You're a con man," I say. "You're a fucking door-to-door salesman."

"Henry's in Brooklyn," he says, spits it out like venom. "The Bossert Hotel. Room 808."

Days without Henry: 4 + 2

42

Montague Street, Brooklyn Heights. Where trees grow from the sidewalks and fire escapes bisect like lace. A laundromat shares a front entrance with a liquor store. Teresa's Restaurant, stacks of pallets, Peerless Shoe Repair, Thai Kitchen, windowless delivery vans. Things are happening here and the Bossert Hotel is at the centre of it, a landmark building in an area with many to boast about. It's tall and white with towering roman columns bookending the front door. Rusty air conditioners stick out all over, but the effect is glamorous, like dozens of runway models smoking cigarettes out windows. The extravagant lobby welcomes me so warmly I almost forget who owns it: the Watchtower Bible and Tract Society. The hotel is theirs, part of their compensation package to the members of the church, in a way. Be a good Witness and you too can stay at the Bossert. Three days. For free. In New York.

When I was seven, I stayed here with my mother, the one winter she was able to pry me away from my father and the Gatineau Hills. We went shopping in Manhattan, and ate spaghetti that the waiter described as "nouveau rustic." She took me to the Watchtower's headquarters, too, to see my uncle Bryan. It was never just Bryan to my mother, though. The woman couldn't say his name without adding a worrisome prefix to it. Oh Bryan. Sigh Bryan. Poor Bryan. Dear dear Bryan. Poor dear Bryan seemed to be doing just fine when I saw him. He was wearing a tie and was surrounded by papers and stamps that made him look important. But to my mother, he was a cause for deep concern. His body was too thin, my mother said as she hugged him. I felt it too, his hipbone rubbing against my leg when he groaned and picked me up. It wasn't a warm gesture at all. We'd only met once or twice. My uncle was nothing to me back then but a man I knew through the mournful gazes of my mother. And now here he was, hoisting me up because he thought he should, pecking my cheek and then releasing me to the floor like a suitcase. "You want to see what your uncle Bryan does all day, kid?"

Rip.

Twenty-five envelopes slit open. "It's an industrial blade, sharp as a sword," Bryan said. He chucked the decapitated strips and pulled the letters out one by one, dating everything, except checks, money orders, legal documents. His handwriting looks like mine, I told my mother, his eights and threes shaky and taking the longest. He blushed and added symbols to each paper: C for cash, K for check, D for draft or cashiers' check, B for bank money order, O for post-office money order, S for stamps, X for express money order. Bryan confused them half a dozen times but I knew better than to point it out. Complaint letters were the most interesting, he said. But he was forbidden to read more than what was necessary for redirection to the proper department.

His desk was positioned next to a photocopier. "Most people think it's degrading to sit here," he said. "Like it's a punishment." But he liked the Xerox. It was warm and he loved the sound of paper being pushed around, the way the machine hummed when it took a moment to sleep. "When no one's around," he whispered to me, "I take a sleep, too." Bryan didn't have a phone because he didn't need one. "The Watchtower believes that letters deserve more attention than telephone calls, that they're more respectful," he said. "They're definitely more efficient. I can handle two or three letters in the time it takes to handle one call." My mother promised to keep that in mind.

Rip.

Bryan took us on a tour of the permanent file room and into a special section: Disfellowshipped and Disassociated Persons. Hundreds of thousands of tidy caramel-coloured folders in hundreds of metal shelves were organized alphabetically, with labels pasted to each one. S-79a — Disfellowshipping, orange folder. S-79b — Disassociation, tan. "You do not want to end up here, kid," Bryan said. Then he ducked behind the shelves and I chased him until he wanted to be found. "Boo!" He picked me up, his hands grazing me where they shouldn't, until my mother rounded the corner.

By the time Bryan hugged me goodbye, with two symmetrical and hollow pats on the back, it was night and the building's sign was at its very best. WATCHTOWER. Fifteen feet tall, shining down on the East River and the Brooklyn Bridge, turning the cars and the water red as blood.

I was excited when we got home. The lights of the big city, the fancy pasta, even my exotic uncle. My father was upset, though, and he yelled at my mother. She ran to the bathroom and turned the taps on. He tried to win me back with a ski day in the Gatineau Hills. "It's not God that your mother and the rest of them are all about," he said. "It's just ordinary men. Men in short-sleeved dress shirts in Brooklyn telling their followers what the Bible means as it suits them. They haven't got anything to do with God, aside from trying to be Him themselves. If you want to know God, Ave, you keep coming up to the Gatineau Hills with me. These trails are as close to heaven as we're going to get."

But did I ever get to make up my own mind?

I drop my bag and then myself into one of the Bossert's many lobby armchairs, a wingback with exaggerated, deep tufting that leaves my spine feeling strangely unsupported.

The fabric is luxurious silk, but it's old and worn, and the seams are vulnerable. If I just pull on this thread, the whole chair will collapse.

I knock on the door. Room 808. "Room service," I yell. Check it off my list of things I've always wanted to say.

Henry answers; he isn't wearing his glasses so he's squinting, his eyes like slits. "What are you doing here?" he says.

I want to hold him, squeeze him hard enough that I can feel his bones creak. I'm afraid I'll crush him to death, though, so I cross my arms instead, behind my back like a French waiter. "I heard you were having second thoughts," I say. "I heard you want to come back home. Back to me."

I move past him and into the room. It's basic, like any other room in any other hotel, except for the art, that's the only give-away — a painting of the murder of Jesus Christ, his body lifeless on a stake instead of a cross.

"I don't know who told you that, V, but I'm not coming back to you."

"But you still love me, I know you do."

He's still standing by the door. He closes it, but not all the way. Leaves it open an inch. "Do you even love me, V?" A gust of icy wind. "We were married for a year, and you never touched me."

"What are you talking about?" I say. "I touch you all the time!" I circle my arms around him. Henry puts his hand on my lower back and my organs jump, my kidneys and the bases of my lungs feel healthier than they have since he left 4 + 2.5 days ago. I can breathe again, my blood is clean and chemically balanced.

"That's not what I mean, V, and you know it. You cling to me, you hold on for dear life. But you won't touch me like a wife is supposed to touch her husband." He takes his hand off me and my body stiffens with cold. "I've never even seen you naked."

"I can change," I plead. "I can work on that."

"It's too late, V; I filed the annulment paperwork. There's a few steps to go, but as far as the law is concerned, as far as God is concerned, we were never married."

"Henry, don't—"

He throws his hands up over his head. He's so tall they hit the ceiling. "Why are you here? Why are you making me do this again?"

"I'm not making you do anything."

"Do you know how hard it was to leave, V? It almost killed me."

I look down at my shoes. They're standing in shallow puddles, souvenirs from the snow outside that I didn't notice until now. "It did kill me," I say, quietly.

Henry slams his hand against the door. It shuts.

"It feels like I'm dead, Henry. Like I'm in some kind of purgatory watching everyone move around in the normal world, while I'm stuck somewhere else."

"You say these things, V! You *see* these things." He's pacing, running a race around me. "How can I . . . how can *anyone* be with someone like that?"

"What if I get baptized again and rejoin the Watchtower?" I reach for his hand, but he doesn't take it. He rubs his temples instead. "I'll open myself up to all the possibilities of god. Of capital *G* God." I kiss him and his lips give in to mine. "What if I show you the kind of wife I can be." I move his hands up my shirt and lead him over to the bed. He stops abruptly, his socks charging on the carpet, shocking me, jolting me back. *Dirty filthy disgusting.* Bryan's hands moist from his Coors. Knuckles rough from knocking on doors. Fingers stained with ink from *Awake! Wake up! Wake the fuck up, Avery!*

"I didn't want you to find out like this," Henry says, slumping on the bed. It's messy and slept in. And then I see. Both pillows are dented, on one a red ribbon. A black bra under the white sheets, the cups like little mountain ranges covered in a dusting of morning snow. "I'm engaged."

There is one other door, only one. I run to it. I throw it open and there she is. Cecily, the perfect black hair that deserves the red bow, the doll. She's cowering in the shower, a towel draped over her small frame.

"Why didn't you lock the door?" It's all I can think to say.

"It's . . . broken," she says.

I smile. "Of course it is." I turn to Henry, who's still sitting on the bed, still hanging his head limp in his hands, still not coming to the rescue. I reach around the door for the lock that isn't there and turn it until it doesn't click. It's a push-button lock that's been pried out of the handle — the same handyman treatment Henry gave our bathroom at home. He probably brought a screwdriver with him, or borrowed one from the hotel's maintenance man, telling him some story about his silly wife locking herself in the bathroom. Women, he'd have said, you know how they are. I pull my hand away and a metal sliver sticks me.

I reach for Cecily's towel. I don't know why I do it. Maybe I want to see what he's attracted to, if she's worth the loss of me. Or maybe I want to humiliate her as much as she has humiliated me. I whip it off her body and she squeals, hiding behind the shower curtain that's clear and useless. I see everything before she has the chance to cover it. Her breasts are smaller than mine, her legs thinner and shapelier, her stomach flat but not muscular, her hips surprisingly round for a woman so slight. She has only a strip of pubic hair, as narrow as a Band-Aid.

I feel my body wrenching back, like I'm in my hole sucking through time and space. Leaving this horrific alternate universe for the real one where Henry loves me. Another yank. Henry. His hand clamped on my arm so hard he could tear it off.

"'Til death do us part," I cry. "You said that."

"V —"

"You promised me that." I let my body fall against the wall. I feel the stuff inside, the shaking of water pipes, the rumbling of subways.

"I tried to be patient," Henry says, his voice distant with defeat. "I tried, V, to get you to talk to me. But you wouldn't tell me anything; you wouldn't let me connect. I didn't know what to do."

"You. Keep. Trying."

"And what about you? What have you been doing to fix yourself? Anything?"

"You don't have the slightest clue what I've been doing. Not a fucking clue."

"Exactly. You live in your own isolated world, V. There's no room in it for me."

"And then you met *her* and everything was perfect, right?"

"It wasn't like that. It didn't start like —"

"And you thought, 'Wow. She gets me. She understands me spiritually and emotionally. I bet she'd fuck me too.'"

"Tell me, V." His face is haggard. He hasn't shaved or slept. "What would you have done?"

There's no snow outside. The sun shines so brightly it's scrubbing the glass with radiation and light. I reach out, my fingers clawing the window frame; paint crumbles in my hand. I push the window up. Pigeons coo. The white of their shit has splatted the ledge and the air conditioners below.

I climb through the opening and into the outside, the wind, the clouds, the birds, the trees. Henry is shouting. His hand grazes my ankle. The ledge is narrower than it looks, so my shoes hang over. My back against brick, my nails digging into the mortar. The air conditioners look like steps from this perspective, like if I just let go of the wall I could make my way down the side of the building, leapfrogging from box to box.

Cecily is screaming on the phone to someone, the front desk manager or 911.

"Grab my hand!" Henry's arm is stretched out toward my leg.

I shouldn't, but I look down. The people aren't ants, I'm not high enough — only eight storeys — so I can make out their faces. A few point up at me, their mouths stretched into Os, their phones snapping pictures. Others look then pass by as though they hadn't. Some are shouting — at me? Or at each other? Hard to know, the howling wind carries away their voices. It's cold and my skin is thickening with goose bumps. Until it lands. My father's coat. Warmth and protection. I can fly if I want to. Jump, let the wind do with me what it will. But the feathers have other plans. Flocks of eiderdown push their way through the Gore-Tex, their sharp quills piercing the fabric like needles, and the wind sucks them up into the sky. They're fleeing at a remarkable rate, turning the coat into a shell. Brittle and transparent when you hold it up to the sun.

I inch back along the ledge, the concrete crumbling just enough to remind me of fear. I scream and reach for Henry's hand. He pulls me inside and I fall into his arms. The woman he's in love with instead of me is crying on the bed. She's dressed now, in a sweet summer shift that ebbs and flows with the force of her sobs.

"We were in love," I say to him. "We were."

Henry lets me go and swoops down to Cecily. He rocks with her, sharing her body, sharing what her insides are doing to her outsides. "I'm so sorry I'm so sorry," he keeps repeating.

But he's not saying it to me.

43

Airplane, cab from airport, driver's Hindi shouts, the metre, traffic on the highway, local roads because all street lights are green and stop signs don't apply to us. Everything is moving so quickly. I stuff a fifty into the driver's palm and scramble out of the cab. The swimmer's splashing, I can smell the chlorine, and I'm sick with jealousy. She can stay under the water where it's safe and warm; she has learned how to breathe in a new language. She doesn't deserve that kind of happiness, and I decide someone should take it away. But it won't be me. I'm not here to fish; I'm here to hunt.

I creep to Calvin's basement window. He's in the living room, which resembles a small television studio. A sheet in a shade of green much like my father's coat is fixed to the wall and lit with large square lamps, the kind used on movie sets, and a camera balances on a tripod. Calvin stands in front of the sheet and gesticulates awkwardly, his arms flailing in misshapen circles, his hands making karate chops.

I knock against the glass and he turns. He isn't surprised to see me, as though women perch themselves outside his apartment at a comfortably familiar rate. He walks in my direction, a smile breaking out across his face. He stands in front of the window, his "Science is cool" T-shirt too large in the shoulders. Says nothing, only fogs up the glass with a warm exhalation of air. Writes "hi" in the condensation with his finger.

Calvin's living room is tragic. It's century-old fine craftsmanship wall to wall, but Calvin treats the lot like an aisle in Best Buy. Mahogany panelling carved with ornate leaves and ivy hide behind posters for shooter video games. A widescreen television gags the mouth of a fireplace rich with marble and brass, cherubs hand-carved into the cherry. His floor — wide oak planks that yuppies would strangle a farmer for — are concealed by a terrible geometric rug with bold concentric circles, the world's worst rug, the very same as my own.

"Nice carpet," I say.

"Thanks. I got it on a trip to Morocco."

"Is that a fact?"

I peek behind the green sheet, which is actually a plastic tarp, and find a stained glass window and Baroque wall sconces. I mourn the loss of good taste as I let go of the tarp and plunk down on Calvin's leather couch, the kind with those double chins for lumbar support. I watch him watch himself on his enormous computer monitor. It displays a satellite map of Canada, just like on the Weather Network, with numbers and charts superimposed on mountain ranges and great lakes, and weather-related graphics, letters and symbols floating around like spectres.

Calvin struggles to keep up with a cold front sweeping over eastern Ontario. "You're too late," he says, the weather swirling around him. "Just finished off the last of the ginger ale." A can lies on the floor. He boots it, bends it left.

"I'm sorry I missed it," I say.

Calvin busies himself again with the weather. Footage of an old forecast rolls behind him, a raging snowstorm that plagued Toronto eight winters ago. Three feet of snow fell in two hours. Clogged subways and sewers, emptied the city coffers of salt. The military dug us out, and the rest of the country laughed. Pussies, they called us. And we were.

"So does this mean you're my official stalker?" he says. "My number one super-fan?"

"You invited me here."

"Yeah, but I never gave you the address."

A low-pressure system moves in from Thunder Bay, but Calvin misses it entirely, his hand cupping Hudson's Bay like testicles.

"What makes you think you even deserve a stalker?" I ask.

"Why not?"

"You're absolutely terrible. You're the worst TV weatherman I've ever seen."

"Whoa, whoa. Unfair! It's not like I asked to be on TV. I'm a meteorologist, the guy who compiles the data and tells the on-camera people what to say. The producers pushed me into this. Cheap bastards expect us all to multitask now."

"Sorry, I didn't—"

"I'm trying to get better. I set up this stupid green screen in my living room so I could practise, didn't I?"

"Maybe you're practising too hard," I say.

"What does that mean?"

"You need to relax and just, you know, interact."

"But how? Nothing's there. How do you interact with nothing?"

"There is something. It's on the screen."

"But I'm not in front of the screen," he says, shaking the tarp like a windstorm. "I'm in front of this stupid thing."

"Think of the tarp as the screen."

"But it isn't. It's a tarp."

"Ignore the tarp."

"I can't. It's the only thing that's real."

"Use your imagination."

He kneels in front of me, tents his fingers in prayer. A crude lightning bolt tattoo on his middle finger flexes and retracts. "You don't seem to get it," he says. "I don't have an imagination. I use math—model output stats, atmospheric dynamics, parameterization—I don't *have* to imagine anything."

I stand and pull Calvin with me, thrusting his hand under the cold front. I hold his forearm and force it upwards. A controlled motion with no jerks or spams. Professional.

"See?" I say. "You're doing it."

I let go and his arm slacks.

"No, you're doing it," he says.

"Just try."

He looks at the screen and then the tarp, losing track of the cold-pressure system. "I can't," he groans. "It's too discombobulating."

"Yes, you can."

"I'm too analytical. That's why morons do TV weather."

"Just watch me." I turn and face the camera, stretching my smile like a beauty queen. My father's coat must be an exact match to the green screen because when I look back at myself in the monitor there are only the symbols of weather: a red arrow and a large "L" for low-pressure system where my abdomen, stomach and rib cage should be. I cup the "L" in the palm of my hands and make it move to the west. It will be in Winnipeg by Sunday.

"You look like God," Calvin says. "Like you're making the weather, not just forecasting it."

I curve my palm under a blue "C" and carry the cold-air system, push it upwards. A line jagged with triangles floats up to meet me. I shove it into eastern Ontario.

Calvin takes my hand, lacing his fingers through mine, and presses it against the tarp. The skin of my wrist burns under the lights but the pain of it is sweet—infinitely better than the numbness of being in the cold too long, nerve endings frozen, organs shut down. The engine inside of me revs and grinds, and settles into a purr. Calvin pulls me close, his breath hot and gingery. He kisses me. His tongue between my lips and I gasp and push him away.

"Not here," I tell him.

I turn on the shower, scalding hot. I make Calvin stand by the door as I unzip my dad's jacket. It fights me and leaves a strong odour behind on my clothes like smoke, but not cigarettes, something vast and fatal. The scent layers around me as I remove the coat: wood and plastic. A house burnt to ashes, lives ended, destroyed. This coat the only thing that has survived. I shake it off my body, and cover myself with my hands, with the steam. Henry used to watch me undress like this in the bathroom. Every time he heard the water running, he'd open the door a crack and peek through. "Why do you take your clothes off like that?" he'd ask. "Like you're hiding from me?" But I would say nothing, only close the door and hope that was answer enough.

Calvin is looking at me like I deserve: like a predator. "You're wild," he says.

I lift my shirt an inch, then another. Circle my hips. Another inch. Give him a show. Then another. With a final flair, I yank it over my head.

"Is this what you want from me, Henry?" I say.

"Calvin."

"Is this good enough?"

We do it in the shower. We do it everywhere. Mahogany leaves and ivy carve into our backs. Stained glass windows crack and wall sconces quiver. The double-chinned couch scratches a path across the plank floor, across the geometric rug, the world's worst. No, I am the worst. I AM THE WORST. The fireplace cherubs nod and agree. Calvin is on top of me, sweaty and gasping. "So sex for you is a what?" he pants. "A weapon?" I catch a glimpse of myself naked in the monitor as he heaves himself off me — my coat and the weather long gone. *Filthy and nasty and dirty and soiled and disgusting.* The quarter-second time delay is just enough to show me what I've become.

44

Calvin is unconscious with sleep when I leave him for the real world, for the snow, alien, unlike any I've ever known. Flakes thick and heavy as dimes. Every one is exactly alike: pearlescent and crystalline with six large points and six smaller. The edges are sharp, I realize, as I catch one on my tongue. The city is blanketed by white, on what should have been myrtle-green foliage in the park, on every shingled roof that should have been tar black, taking up every piece of sky that should have been sky blue. It sucks on my shoes and makes walking impossible. It's too heavy, I can't fight it. I don't have the energy. My blood tries its best to chug, but the temperature is ten below so my blood gives up, freezing to my veins like a tongue on steel. My shoulders hunch me into a protective shell, the fat on my thighs insulates my bones, and my shivers plug the last of the gaps.

Mount Pleasant Cemetery. I've made it this far. The gate screeches open and I look for a level site that my father would approve of. *Marcus Van Hagen — 1890–1955 — Beloved father of seven. Your reward waits for you in heaven.* I make a pile three times as big as my own body and pack it down firm. Give it some time for the cold air to harden. Pick at the snow sticking to my corduroy pants. Think of the ingredients of the dead grey sky overhead. Nitrogen, oxygen, water vapour, argon, neon, carbon dioxide, methane. Dig a tunnel that slopes up. Use my hands because who has a shovel when you need one? Hollow out a domed cave, and done. It's familiarly warm inside the fort, which is incredible when I think about it. If cold can lead to warm then anything, anything is possible. I release myself into the snow and it gives in to me, melting just enough to accommodate my body.

Then the whole fort caves in.

Can't breathe alone in the dark where is my father! And then light and my father's hand and I'm above my own body. I'm reaching for the light and I'm watching Dad breathe life back into me. Between breaths he swears, which makes me want to laugh but I can't because I'm not breathing and that makes him sad. The light pulls me with the force of a train and I want to relax into the ride. But Dad is crying so I fight back to my body. I cough, gasp, tell him about seeing him from high above, about the light, and he explains it to me like he does everything. "You weren't a ghost. The light wasn't heaven. A lack of oxygen caused brain hypoxia. Ave — it was a hallucination. You hear me? Everything you experienced was inside your head." I nod because I know I should believe him. But, for the first time ever, I don't. And maybe I never should have. My father was a liar, after all, in his own way. Quebecois to the core, with a dash of Algonquin mixed in, but he used to insist he was Italian, with blood "red as pomodoro sauce," he'd say, coursing through his veins. More specifically, he'd claim he came from a long line of champion cross-country skiers borne from the snow of the Italian Alps. He told me these stories when we were skiing our usual trails deep in Quebec's Gatineau Hills, usually while my body, too exhausted to keep going, was balanced on the front of his Salomons. "Hold on, Ave," he'd say, and off we'd take, wind and snow whipping my face before his. "Your dad is one of the greats from Italy!" he'd cheer. "Marco Albarello, Guidina Dal Sasso, Fulvio Valbusa!" And "Silvio Confortola!" — my favourite name of all because it came out of his mouth like a song. "You have a bit of that blood in you somewhere. Maybe one-sixteenth, but still, that counts for something. You're not all your mother, you know."

He lied to me about his cancer, too — didn't tell me it had spread from his colon to his lungs — so I had no idea what was coming until our last time together in the hills. As we skied our route around the lake, I could tell he was more tired than usual even though he was taunting and catcalling me all the way. But after the first mile, I zipped far ahead without even trying. It was an awful angle to watch him from. When I'd pull over near the trees, I'd look back to find him bent, catching his breath, adjusting the takeout bottle of chemo tucked inside his jacket. "I see you looking, Ave. I see you! But don't get any ideas. When I die, I'm taking this coat with me!"

My father's jacket was his third most favourite thing in the world, after snow and me. He'd go on about it every time we hit the trails. He did that day, too, even though he needed to save his breath for breathing. "It's called the Resolute, Ave. It's what they label an industrial parka because it's made for explorers on solo trans-Antarctic expeditions, for scientists like your dad who work in the high Arctic. Double reinforced elbows, coyote fur–lined hood, adjustable bracing wire that reduces wind penetration. And see the thigh-length cut? It's got a storm flap over a two-way locking front zipper and heavy-duty, flexible rib-knit cuffs. It's even got a pair of air-activated biodegradable warmers. They fit perfectly into mesh kidney pouches, Ave. And an ID window on the sleeve in case a polar bear attacks. Or your mother."

My dad wore a neck warmer pulled up over his mouth that day. It was baby blue because it was mine. He didn't own one. Normally, he loved the feeling of that cold air screaming into his throat, lungs, brain. So it was hard to watch him breathe like me, his mouth sucking in the polar fleece, a wet spot stiffening with spit and frost. The cold still gets in, no matter how many walls we raise between us and winter — a truth more certain than death and taxes. "Stop," my dad cried. I braked on a hill, splayed my legs into a V and turned around. My dad. Clinging to the branch of a birch tree. He croaked my name and passed out backwards into the snow, the silver bark sheering off and into the air like confetti. I raced off into the hills for help.

The effects of the cold mixed with the platinum in the drug he was on had caused something called Per — iph — er — al Neur — op — athy, the nurse had explained slowly. It makes your skin sensitive to cold, even the skin in the throat. So when your dad was breathing cold in, it sent a message to his brain that made it feel like his throat was closing. He was never really dying, she added in a tone she thought comforting, it just felt like it. Then she turned to my dad, wagging her finger at him like he was a very bad dog. No more skiing for you, Mr. Gauthier. No more nothing outside this winter, you hear? My father looked at me, but his eyes were watery so I couldn't look back for long. "Think of me as a grand science experiment, Ave. Full of chemicals and reactions and mitochondrial priming. So don't you worry about me, okay? Science has always saved me."

I knew he wasn't going to make it, my father. I must have known, somewhere inside myself, in that place I couldn't go. Just like I must have known it was more than the platinum that stopped him on the hills that day, our last time together on the trails around the lake. I must have known that the cancer had spread to his lungs, despite the deal he'd made with his nurses not to tell. Nothing could save him. Not science, not his coat. Not me.

45

Coffee and vanilla and salted butter and industrial bleach. The scents of Steve baking in his broom closet.

"Since when do you bake cookies?" I ask him.

He pulls a sheet from his toaster oven. Oatmeal raisin.

"You made rivithia," he says, "so I make cookies."

"About that. I heard you crying and —"

He shoves a cookie into my hand, a misshapen lump. "Eat," he says.

I juggle it, blow it cool, take a bite. "I just want to know if you're okay," I say despite my mouth being full.

"Okay enough." He pours a thick coffee, passes it to me. "But your mother is very upset. She wants to talk to you."

"And you think I should?"

"Hey, I'm not big on talking myself," he says. "I was raised to stuff my problems down inside so deep they'll never crawl out. Like it's a diamond mine down there inside me, all that pressure turning problems into *mystiká*."

"*Mystiká?*" I ask.

"Secrets."

He gestures to the coffee, so I take a drink. It flows down my throat like lava.

"Back home," he says, "you would never hear anyone say the word out loud. That's how much you weren't supposed to talk about what you weren't supposed to talk about. Take away the word that describes what hangs over your heart and then what? You turn into a lonely old man with a kitchen in a broom closet."

"Steve, I —"

"I want to explain to you," he says, "about my oven. About why I cook here in the closet or your kitchen."

"You don't have to, Steve, really. It's none of my business."

"But it is, is how I'm starting to see it. Because you, Avory, you are my friend."

A smile reaches across my face. The first in weeks. "You're my friend too, Steve."

"You are too young and ignorant about the world, but somehow, that doesn't matter so much."

"And you're ancient and ornery. Crotchety."

"And I'm fat, too," he adds, pulling a stool out for me. I manage to bump it out of the closet. I have to do a kind of shuffle to get back in, my ass wiggling and the stool scraping its way along the floor.

"See?" he hoots. "You don't even know how to sit in a chair!"

We both laugh.

"I want you to ask me again why I don't cook in my oven at home," he says. "Only this time, I will give you the real answer."

I press my hands to my thighs, make myself sturdy. "Why don't you cook in your oven, friend?"

"Because I'm lonely," he says, imitating my posture. "Because I left my family and my food and my culture and my language. I left it all for a new life in Canada, but it didn't turn out like it was supposed to. Sixty years I've been here in this city with no history, moving from one basement to another. I've lost all feeling, except loneliness."

"I'm lonely, too," I say.

He nods. "I could tell from when I first met you. You didn't look like a whole person. More like three-quarters."

I wipe my nose on my sleeve. "That's how I feel."

"It feels, for me, like being held down by something I can't see. Do you know that feeling?"

I nod. My head is so heavy.

"Like everything in the universe is pressing on me."

"It feels so big, doesn't it?" I say. "Loneliness?"

He stretches his arms and fingers. "Only wider."

I agree. Our arms are not long enough to convey that kind of scale.

"I thought building that fancy kitchen in my apartment would make me happy." He adjusts himself in his chair, crosses one leg over the other, the kind of thing I didn't think he'd be able to do. "But I can't get used to cooking and eating alone — it's not Greek. We cook together: one big, loud, miserable group. I don't have that here in Toronto. Everyone keeps to themselves. At least in my broom closet I can leave the door open. At least there's a chance that someone will walk by and I can see a face that isn't mine looking back at me from my own spoon." He rests his leathery hand on my shoulder. "I don't want you to be lonely, Avory. And I don't want you to be angry with your mother." I feel a tickle when he lifts his palm away, a feather leaving with it. He turns it over in his hand and watches it flutter to the drain in the floor, lost in the soapy dirty water from his mop bucket. "I don't want you to be like me."

"Okay," I say. "I'll talk to Margaret."

"And you'll listen?"

"I'll try."

Steve plucks a cookie from the baking sheet and raises it in the air like a champagne flute. I meet it with mine, a crumble instead of a clink.

46

My closet is open. Track pants, ski racing suit, bicycle shorts with tags still on. Body Glove wetsuit, the black hand on yellow. STOP! But it's too late. Margaret sits in the pile of Henry's leftovers. *Snow* by Lawren Harris in her hands.

"It's so sad," Margaret says, her fingers running over the frame. "The way the snow is tugging on the branches."

I drop to my knees, the bones cushioned by Henry's hunting jacket. "I can explain," I say.

"It's almost morbid," she continues. "All that life struggling under the weight. It's like watching a murder unfold, like the snow is trying to kill the poor tree." She sets the painting on her lap and claps her hands together. "I say we go to Ikea tomorrow and get you something more cheery. Maybe one of those lovely sushi roll paintings they have. We could even stop for sushi on the way home, make it a whole sushi theme!"

"You can quit the act, Margaret," I say. "You know I stole it."

"You? Steal? Like the art bandit they're going on about on the news? No, you would never do that." She pulls her purse out from under Henry's wetsuit. "Oh, right. I should have mentioned. When I found this painting . . ." she holds her purse up by the worn leatherette straps. "Isn't that the strangest thing?"

I would rather be anywhere else. Choking under the weight of the snow, drowning in thick, black Greek coffee.

"If you're going to be so miserable about it, Avery, forget Ikea. Just go ahead and hang this one." She shoves the painting into my arms. "Maybe I'll like it more when it's up on the wall."

"I don't want to hang it."

"Well, if *you* don't want to hang it," she says, "maybe the police will?"

She pulls nails and a hammer from a Home Depot bag. She's had a busy afternoon.

The painting hangs crooked. No matter what angle I inch it to, no matter where I move the nail, it won't settle straight. Fifteen degrees off level is as close as I can get. It makes the living room lonelier, the picture, up there on an empty wall without even a bifold futon to balance it out.

"Are you going to turn me in?" I ask her.

Margaret smiles. I see my teeth in her mouth, the canines just crooked enough to be teased for in school and the pair in the front softly rounded at the bottom. They are so white, all on their own, with no help from a dentist's bleach. Something about our enamel makes them impermeable to acids, to coffee, to cold and other sensitivities. My teeth are the strongest part of me and I got them from her.

"Depends," she says.

"On what?"

"On how fast you can drive us to Kingston."

47

Steve's Smart Car is tiny, a snack for transport trucks, so it doesn't take me long to brush off the snow. I buckle in and key the ignition. The engine revs and so I guess driving is happening. The car smells my fear and kicks backs as I weave to the corner and collect my mother.

"This is so kind of Steve," Margaret says. She crouches ridiculously low and crawls into the front like an animal.

"Have you never sat in a car before?" I ask.

She struggles with the knobs until she finds the radio.

"Still no leads on the AGO art bandit. Sources tell us that crucial surveillance footage was accidentally erased by an intern who mistook the video for a multimedia installation—"

I snap it off.

"Even better," Margaret says. "Now we have to talk."

"Actually, I have to drive," I say. "Remember? Because of the blackmail?"

I push my foot into the sticky gas pedal. Margaret braces herself against the dash.

"Our Father, Jehovah in heaven, please keep us safe on our journey. I pray in Your Son's name. Amen."

"Would you stop that," I say.

"I pray for you too, you know. Every night."

"Whatever makes you feel less guilty, Margaret," I say, changing lanes and then signalling. "Or do you not feel guilt? Do you feel anything?"

She huffs. "Is that really what you think of me?"

I pull on to the highway and merge next to a truck hulking with pigs. Their snorting and Margaret's yapping are two distractions I do not need. I am a subway-taker, a walker, a busser and a cabber, not a driver. Nothing ever feels real to me on the 401. Lights dazzle and flash. Bass thumps the road like an earthquake. Speeds are inhuman. Driving's a video game, not real life. It's hypnotic and I feel myself getting sucked into the vortex of other cars. I forget I'm in charge, that the life of every person on the road is in my hands, and that they trust me not to take it. I look across the four lanes and I see each one convince themselves of me. Contractor in the Ford checks me in his mirror.

You, Avery, you will not swerve. Mom in the Dodge Caravan. *Will not fall asleep at the wheel.* Hipster in a Prius. *Will not text, will not slam on the brake, will not flip over the guardrail and take me with you.* I could make a hundred thousand things go wrong.

"Of course I feel guilt," Margaret says. "It was torture for me, watching your father pull you away, not just from me, but from Jehovah. I know you're not a mother, but you can still imagine, you've always been so good at that. So imagine what it feels like to have your own child be committed to the worst fate there is. Imagine picturing her when Armageddon comes — annihilated along with billions of others. Then picture yourself left walking alone on Paradise Earth without her, carrying the shame of knowing that you didn't save her."

"I'm not talking about that bullshit Witness guilt, Margaret." I duck into the fast lane. The traffic barriers are three feet high and I do the math. At this speed and trajectory we'd flip on our side and sail into the pig truck. A massive fireball. The smell of bacon for miles. "I'm talking about the guilt of abandoning me when Dad was dying."

She sniffles, unfurls her Kleenex and blows. "There wasn't a day that went by that I didn't think about you, didn't regret leaving you. I did the worst thing any mother could, and I have to live with that for the rest of my life." She's using her shaky voice, it warbles like a lamb's, and I know she wants me to turn and look. Her eyes will be wet and glowing and she'll expect a feeling to stir inside me, a memory, perhaps, of maternal tenderness.

"You're grinding your teeth," she says.

"It's this traffic," I insist.

"Your father used to grind his teeth. His emotions caused him real problems, you know. As a matter of fact, I think his stress and anger and resentment gave him cancer."

I laugh. "That's not why he got cancer."

"I've read some articles."

"And I'm sure they're rooted in venerable science."

"Keep an open mind, Avery."

"You're belittling Dad's memory. He battled that disease until the very end, and he did it without you."

"He didn't have to."

"Yes, he did! You left him, remember? Over a lousy blood transfusion!"

"Avery—"

"The chemo attacked his white blood cells. He had no choice."

"That's not why I left."

I turn away from the road and to her. She flips down her mirror, twists a Kleenex into a point and dabs at the corners of her eyes like a beauty queen.

"I hoped he wouldn't do the transfusion, of course. 'If any man of the house of Israel or any foreigner who is residing in your midst eats any sort of blood, I will cut him off from among his people.'"

I looked at her and away from the road and so I've breached the social contract; the other drivers don't trust me now. *You're going to swerve and force me into oncoming traffic. Going to close your eyes and murder my children. Going to answer a call from a federal prison robot, slam on the brakes, flip over the guardrail and take me with you.*

"I didn't leave because of the blood," she says. "I left because your father was cruel and spiteful."

"He didn't even tell me he was dying, Margaret! He suffered alone! Died alone! To protect me! That's what kind of man he was. *You* were cruel and spiteful. My father was a hero."

"Oh, Avery. Your father was no hero."

"How the hell would you know?" I shout. "You weren't even there!"

Margaret's fingers are entwined in prayer. She's squeezing so hard they've gone bloodless from the pressure, bone white. "Because he forced me to leave you," she says.

I wrench the wheel and pull off to the shoulder. "You're lying."

"The day of the transfusion, he was so angry. He said I was brainwashing you with Watchtower doctrine, that I was going to ruin your life. He was like a wild animal, screaming and stomping. He threatened me. He told me I had to give you up, disappear and never come back."

My head falls to the steering wheel, daring the airbag to explode.

"It's not what you want to hear, Avery, but it's the truth," she says. "We were riding a thin line for our entire marriage; interfaith couples always are. You know that better than most."

The cars around us slow to a crawl to give their drivers a view. Margaret and I are disrupting traffic, turning lines red on Google maps, delaying deliveries, overflowing bladders, draining gas tanks dry. Finally, the mess of my life has spilled into the greater world, making it less of my burden alone. I feel relief, if only for a second.

"And so you chose your religion over me?"

"He didn't even give me the option. He said if I didn't leave right away, he would tell the police about all the jewellery and clothes and things."

"What about them?"

"He didn't tell you?"

"What are you talking about?"

"Your dad was —" She stops herself and forces her fingers apart. As if prayer hands are her microphone to god. She leans in to me and whispers. "He was going to tell the police I stole it all."

"Did you?"

"Not for myself," she says. "For a Kingdom Hall in Ethiopia."

"You've got to be joking."

"I'm not proud of it, of course. I was young and unhappy and naïve."

"What the hell is wrong with you?"

"Me? What about your father? He would have sent me to prison! His own wife!"

"Oh my god. Your dress. The plum Prada dress. Did you steal that, too?"

She looks away, nods.

"You make me sick," I spit. "You're blackmailing me but you're just as bad. Actually, you're worse."

"Me? You can't be serious."

"Dead serious." I pick up my phone. "I'm calling the police."

"I stole some gaudy trinkets and clothes over a decade ago," she says in her calmest voice. "A Crown attorney wouldn't even blink at that. But you? You committed grand larceny yesterday. Of a national treasure."

I hurl my phone into the back seat. I debate swerving into traffic, but the road is unnervingly clear, like a snowplow bullied away all the cars.

"Your father was worse than both of us combined," she says. "He stole you."

48

Kingston Penitentiary hugs Lake Ontario like an all-inclusive resort, sharing the shoreline with beaches, bars and tourist pontoons. But at 175 years old, the oldest prison in Canada, Kingston Pen looks its age. The walls, maybe twenty feet high, are crumbling into a doable scale for escape. The guard towers, unmanned but for pigeons, tilt left and crawl with scaffolding. Only the visitors' entrance inspires the kind of fear a prison should, with imposing wooden gates that look reclaimed from a castle where impaled heads were part of the decor.

"You're really going to make me do this?" I say to Margaret.

"Listen, I know poor Bryan needs this," she says. "But do you really think I would insist—"

"You mean blackmail."

"—if I didn't think it would be good for you too?"

She takes my hands and looks up to the clouds. One stands out above the rest: an enormous sky-eating cloud that's blocking out what it can of the sun. It's a dense, vertical tube of white that spreads and flattens at the top. Like an atom bomb set off in space.

"'And when you stand praying,'" she recites, "'forgive whatever you have against anyone, so that your Father who is in the heavens may also forgive you your trespasses.'"

"But you don't understand what happened," I say. "What Bryan did."

"And do you?"

Gulls pour out of the sky to caw and bicker at the edge of the parking lot. They fight over spilled Burger King French fries: one man's trash now their treasure. The gulls carry off what they can and soar over Lake Ontario. What's left of the sun skips off their backs, off the waves, and gets sucked into that mushroom tower of cloud.

"Because I look at you," Margaret says, "and what I don't see is a woman who understands herself."

The brooding castle gates are decommissioned, so Margaret and I enter through a standard metal door. The room we walk into is a mix of modern and gothic, with a soaring ceiling and transverse arches, and no-smoking signs fixed at eye level.

One wall is hand-cut limestone and across from it, an enormous cathedral window revealing not the majestic view it deserves, but a long, damp hallway lined with security cameras. The visitors' notice looms large like a menu at McDonald's, defining contraband as

a) An intoxicant;

b) A weapon or component thereof, ammunition for a weapon, and anything that is designed to kill, injure or disable a person, when possessed without prior authorization;

c) Currency over any applicable prescribed limit;

d) An explosive or bomb or a component thereof.

Margaret pulls me to the check-in and a guard behind bulletproof glass. The guard's body is square, with centre-of-gravity-defying breasts, and even though she's sitting, I can tell she's short. She doesn't need any more inches, though; she's as intimidating as the job requires.

"I called earlier," Margaret says to her. "I'm Margaret Stanford?"

I bristle at the name I don't know.

"This is my daughter, Avery Gauthier," she says. "She's here to see Bryan Milford."

"You're not coming?" I yelp.

"Oh no, I can't go in there. I can't see poor Bryan like that."

The guard flips through a legal pad. "Take a seat, Ms. Stanford. Be with you in two shakes."

"So it's Stanford now?" I say. "As in the university?"

"As in Frank Junior," she says. "We met at a Watchtower convention in New York."

"Have any kids?"

"Oh no. We have a Bichon Frise named Pepper, though, and a small house in Vancouver. Our Kingdom Hall has a view of the Rockies you wouldn't believe." Her eyes soften. They carry her far away from these limestone castle walls. "It was almost a perfect life, except for you, of course, the lack of you. Frank used to push me to reconnect, but I was too scared. Until now I didn't have the strength to face you."

"Divorced?"

"He died last year. Bone cancer. And I know, I know; the irony isn't lost on me."

"Found ya," says the guard, checking off her list. "Avery Goacher."

"It's Gauthier," I say. "Go-tee-eh."

She taps her drag queen nails on her desk. "Darlin', I ain't ever gonna be able to say that." Her accent is southern US and I wonder how she ended up here of all places, this bus station of a city, where waspy university students mix with the luckless locals. Kingston is regal in June when the tall ships float in, but it smells sour to me, like expired beer.

"You don't have any contraband on you, right?" the guard asks me. "No weapons? Ammunition?"

"No," I say. "Unfortunately."

She tsks me, wags her finger. "You can't say shit like that here. It's like joking about a bomb at the airport." She huffs her way out of her toll booth office, her keys clanging.

"Sorry."

"Spread your legs, darlin'." Her nails claw through my clothes. They're long as a stripper's and luminescent purple. "Hot colour, right?" she says. "My baby girl did the rhinestones." Her hands are fast and firm, but not very thorough. I could have hidden a razor in my sock or under my left ass cheek. She makes it to my shoulder and plucks out a feather. Café au lait, *Somateria mollissima*. She hands it to me. "What are you? An angel?" She winks and presses a comically large red button.

I hear the unscrambling of an enormous lock, and half-expect a dragon to come lumbering out. "You're good to go."

"Down there?" My words echo off the walls of the cavernous hallway. It's empty but for cameras that dip and rotate, and more red buttons, large enough so they can be found in any sort of melee. Power outage, riot, fire-breathing lizard, etc.

"Yep. Walk straight to booth number five."

I look for my mother but she's nowhere. "Like by myself?" The feather soaks with my sweat. It's grounded in my palm until conditions improve.

"Yes, darlin'. All by yer lonesome."

"You're not coming with me?"

"Course not," the guard says. "This is my post."

"No other guard can fill in for you?"

She folds a stick of gum into her mouth. "We're running on a skeleton crew."

"Short-staffed at a prison?" I say. "Doesn't seem very safe."

"Never been safer," she says, chewing. "All the serial killers and rapists are gone. Just some armed robbery pussycats left."

"Where did everyone go?"

"You live under a rock or something? KP is closing. Government's selling off parts and turning the rest into a museum."

"Seriously?"

She nods. "I got a job at the gift shop."

"Congratulations."

"Thanks, darlin'."

"Will you sell T-shirts?"

"I'm gonna sell your ass if you don't quit stalling."

I take a step and nearly slip. The floor is frosted. There's a tapping at the base of my shoes and a tickle, then the snow begins. It falls in the most unnatural way it knows: Up. From the laundry rooms and escape tunnels below. The flakes surge through the limestone like it's cheesecloth, hitting the soles of my shoes, ankles, calves, knees, hands, waist, chest and face. Even though the snow hits her just the same, the guard doesn't notice. She doesn't bend her head to marvel at the horror of the weather happening to us from the bottom up, doesn't brush away the flakes landing on the underside of her lash extensions, her double chin, the soles of her orthopedic shoes. She doesn't even look cold. She smacks the red button again and seals me in and that's it: there's no going back.

I close my eyes and feel my way down the hallway, try to experience the snow as my father did, use it to quiet my mind. "Because snow quiets everything, Ave. It surrounds and insulates all the sounds of the world, dulling them, taking away their sharp edges, their moans and cries. It soothes every noise that sinks into its depth. The rusty gears of an ancient castle lock. A dragon clawing at the walls." I cling to the feather and it pierces my palm. If I need to escape, it will fly me away. The snow is gone when I open my eyes, gather myself together — my past, present and future rolled up into one singular, sad, weak, shrivelled little man in booth number five.

The visitation area has all the smells and coziness of an emergency room. But at least I'm not alone. Two women talk into phones attached to tattoos and beards behind the Plexiglas. They press themselves close, their voices low, practiced and familiar with this routine. I can only see the backs of their heads and bodies. Damaged blondes, with hair pulled in clumps or fallen out from stress. Slumped shoulders, bras strangling rolls of back fat. A yawning guard points me to a stool. No legs: it's bolted into a beam and juts out, daring me to sit on it like a booby trap. And then I look up, through the soundproof window, blotched with grease from cheeks of women like these, and I remember. Bryan's been the trap all along.

A wide smile pushes his wrinkles out of the way. Wrinkles deep as tire grooves. They swallow the light. His hair is too thin to hide his scalp and one of his eyelids is hampered by a wet sore. A scraggly beard blotches the rest of his face and I am grateful for that. I don't want to see any more of him than I have to. He picks up the phone, clears his throat into the receiver. "Look at you," he says. His voice is sandpaper. It scratches at my brain, filing away the calluses I've been building up to protect myself from him. "You're all grown up."

"And you're an asshole," I say.

"I'm trying not to be," he says.

I laugh.

"You don't think your old uncle Bryan is capable of recovery?"

"I think you like drugs too much."

"I won't deny that." He smiles again, wide and square as a clown's.

"Why the hell am I here, Bryan?"

"Language, kid."

"You've got to be kidding," I say. "You're in a maximum security prison, and you're lecturing me for swearing?"

"I never said I was perfect." He leans back in his chair, smug. "Thankfully, Jehovah can forgive us even when our own hearts condemn."

"No praying." The guard's order comes like a whisper to me through the phone line, but like a yell to Bryan.

"Come on, Ray, I wasn't —"

The tips of the guard's fingers tickle his gun.

"If you're going to waste my time —" I stand up to leave.

"Don't go!" Bryan cries. "Please!"

I turn back and I wish for three things. One: to never have been born. Two: for Margaret to get sucked up into that awful cloud. Three: to relinquish the power the Plexiglas has given me. I don't want this power, the kind that makes another human beg. The kind Bryan had over me for years. I sit back down.

"Thank you," he says.

"Just spit it out," I tell him.

Bryan peers into the receiver, around the corner, at the water-stained ceiling, under the table. The guard taps him on the shoulder. "No paranoid schizophrenia OCD bullshit."

"Sure thing, Ray. You're the boss." Bryan fiddles with his nose. There's sweat mixed in with the hair above his lip. "Let's just say that a friend here at this lovely establishment used to supply me with . . . medicine," he whispers to me. "Sometimes I'd pay, sometimes I'd forget. And now this friend wants me dead. And he's very close to accomplishing that goal because he's a goal-oriented person." Bryan rolls up his sleeve. A lightning scar, red with infection, changes the topography of his track-marked arm. "He likes to practice, this pal o' mine. Because he's not just goal-oriented, he's a perfectionist. A real A-type."

"If you think I can save you—"

"Kid, no one can save me; I'm going to die in here. That's why I needed to see you." Bryan leans in, so I pull away. "Because if you don't forgive me, I'll never make it to God's side."

"After everything you did, you think—"

"No, *I know*. I know I'm one of God's anointed 144,000."

"You're insane."

"No, I'm changed."

He is a different man sitting in front of me, that's true. It was more than the dull greenish lighting that transformed him into a nearly unrecognizable stranger, more than time, even. He used to look so much like my father, a family joke that my mother tired of — in love with her brother but she had to settle for my dad. Back then he had the same square jaw my father had, same thick hair he'd run his hands through, checking that it was still there. Bryan didn't look like my father anymore; he barely looked human. I knew what it took to change a face from one kind into another, the kind of poison you had to consume, the lies, the violence, the fear. He points at me, his finger tapping soundlessly on the glass. "Your mom told me you're having problems," he says. "So if you can't forgive me for me, then do it for yourself. Don't you want to move on? Get your life back?"

I wonder about the nature of the glass between us. Will it shatter if he keeps tapping? Will I reach my hands through the shards, grab his neck and squeeze until everything he knows about me exhales from him like his last choking breath? Bryan can read my mind, he always could, and so he coughs, pressuring me for a response. He's trying to take his power back, but I hold it tight against me. I let myself feel like he must have all those years ago, in that bedroom with the walls as pink as my skin: the control and justification, the taking of what the universe owes me for some yet-to-be-named wrong. I tap on the glass where Bryan did, only my finger's on the outside. The guard motions for me to stop, but I do it once more. The glass is thick and the guard's gun is there for Bryan, not for me. I'm in a prison, there are dragons in the basement and shivs hidden in porridge, and I'm the safest I've ever been.

"You want me to forgive you," I say. "But you've never even admitted what you did."

"I told you a million times," he whispers.

"Tell me again."

"And the elders told you a million more."

"Tell. Me. Again."

"I was high as a kite that night." He turns around in his seat, checking the other guard who's checking his phone. "I thought you were Gloria."

"It's a good story, Bryan."

"It's the truth."

"And what about the second time?"

"I . . . I don't know what you're —"

"And the third, fourth, fifth, sixth —"

"I, I don't remember. I don't —"

I can't watch Bryan babble excuses; his weakness makes me sick. So I look to my left and the woman next to me, catch her from the side. Her eyes are watery with love, lips pink with Code Red Mountain Dew, jaw pumping with Nicorette. She's smiling at the neck tattoo and black eye on the other end, cooing words of devotion so terribly misplaced. Hers is a man who will continue to disappoint her in the grandest of ways, and she will let him. She's just like Gloria, just like I used to be. I open my fist. The feather is crumpled, but it slowly unfurls. I stick it in the woman's shoulder, but she doesn't look away from her man behind the glass. She never will.

Bryan panics. "You want me to get on my knees?" He drops the phone and sinks to the floor, his fingers knit together in prayer. I can't hear him, but his lips are moving slow so I can make a reliable guess. *Forgive me, Jehovah, for I have sinned.* The guard pulls him up, moving his own mouth. *No praying!* Deposits him back in the chair and forces the receiver on him.

"Why are you asking god for forgiveness, Bryan?" I say. "Did you ruin his life?"

Bryan's eyes are wet with tears that I know are for him, not for me.

"It was an accident. It —"

I hang up. Bryan slaps his palm against the glass. His lifeline is sawed in half by a weapon carved from a toothbrush.

I walk as fast as I can through the damp hallway, the security cameras not bothering to follow me because what's the point, really? The American guard is wrestling with the decommissioned castle doors, flexing and sweating to pull them open. The ancient wood groans against rusting hinges the size of records. "They're gonna cut these big boys up into kitchen cabinets," she says. "Might as well let 'em stretch their legs one last time." With a grunt the doors crack open like a book. There's the parking lot, the towers, the pigeons, Margaret and her knitting needles, the stair runner to nowhere else I can see it leading but up a vertical mile to that vast and threatening atom bomb cloud.

49

Cumulonimbus. I looked it up as soon as I got back to the apartment. It followed us from Kingston to Toronto last night, stalked me along the 401. Cumulonimbus clouds can grow ten kilometres in height, so tall the wind flattens their tops like anvils. The weather they reap is severe and unstable, thunder and tornadoes and hail the size of tumours. I stare at the cumulonimbus from my window. If Margaret wasn't sitting on her air mattress compulsively knitting, if there was a proper door on my bedroom, a lock on my bathroom, a shower wall without that maddening gap, if I had some source of privacy whatsoever, I would call Calvin and ask him if he could see the cloud too.

"You've been quiet," Margaret says. She's so thin she doesn't even dent the mattress. "Not a word out of you since the parking lot yesterday."

The cloud sweeps slowly into the city. A plane flies through it. I hold my breath. One.

"What did you and Bryan talk about in there?" Margaret asks.

Five, six.

"What happened between you two?"

Nine, ten.

"I need to know, Avery."

Twelve. The plane doesn't break through the other end. The cloud moves closer. Like it's coming for me next.

"It started after Dad died," I say. "When I moved in with Gloria and Bryan."

"Before all poor Bryan's troubles with the police?"

"It was after midnight when he came into my room."

"Who? Bryan?"

"He was high on something. Shaking. Talking fast. Sweating."

"And you argued?"

"No, Margaret," I say. "He raped me."

She stops. Aims her knitting needles recklessly at the air mattress. "Of course he didn't."

"I thought I was dying."

"You must have imagined it. You were always imagining things." Margaret stabs the needles into the wool. She's making knots instead of knits; she's ruining my stair runner. I take the wool from her. My hands are sweaty so the dye bleeds onto them, staining them into something entirely new.

"The pain of him pushing inside of me," I say.

"Stop!"

"And afterwards too. I couldn't get rid of the pain."

"Avery!"

"My body throbbed so intensely I worried something monstrous would come tearing out."

"Enough!"

"I ran to the bathroom, it was the only door in the house with a lock, and — you'll be proud, Margaret — I said a prayer."

"You're trying to shock me —"

"I looked in the mirror and with every word, every Jehovah-save-me-forgive-me-for-my-sins I watched myself vanish in chunks: my feet first, then my stomach, chest, my neck, mouth, nose, eyes, hair. From the bottom up I disappeared —"

"— and it's not going to work!"

"— until there was nothing left of me in all the world but a raw voice."

Margaret scrambles for the remote and snaps on the television. A nature documentary. A dozen zebras packed together in a pond, lapping up water. It would have been a relaxing scene if that was the whole story, but there's a narrator, a British one, and a team of cameras capturing the herd from a variety of angles, so there is, unquestionably, more to come. The tall, blonde grasses part and, through them, a lion appears, his mane indistinguishable from his environment. The zebras, with a flight response honed over millennia, don't need to see him to know he's there. They leap from the water, stripes and legs and manes tangled in panic.

"Bryan raped me," I say. "Many times. Until he got arrested for robbery." One zebra remains. He's standing in the pond drinking away with his black tongue when the lion pounces and grabs him by the throat. The zebra doesn't try to escape or fight back. He just stands there, dumbly, as the lion hangs off his body, all three kinds of teeth — incisor, molar and carnassial — digging into him. Devouring him alive. "Bryan knew I was weak after you left and Dad died, and he took advantage. He knew I was desperate to be loved."

Margaret shoves past me and presses herself closer to the screen, her eyes wild as the zebra's — as if they've both awoken from the most horrible dream. The zebra searches to the trees, the hills, the nettled bushes only a few gallops away, until he settles back on the river again. The lion tightens his grip, setting his right paw on the zebra's face. It looks like an embrace, like old army buddies whispering jokes.

"You made me swear not to tell Dad about Bryan's drug problem," I say. "If he would have known . . . or if he wasn't stubbornly denying his own death . . . that I would end up with *them*. Or if you would have just come back for me." The zebra makes a move, sloshing his way through the river as the lion hangs on to his cheeks, drawing blood that runs diagonally across those white-and-black stripes. In one fell swoop, the zebra twists his body down toward the water. "I told the elders at the Kingdom Hall. They said it was my fault. Made me feel like a whore. Bryan was helpless against my sexual manipulations, they said. A *thirteen-year-old's* sexual manipulations."

The lion is still hanging on to that delicious bit of face, only now he's on his back, his mouth just above water level. As the zebra pushes him down with his hooves and his massive, powerful head, the lion's grip loosens, his claws withdrawing from the black and white and red. The zebra drowns him. Slowly. With pleasure.

"They told me not to tell anyone, that no one would believe me over a man who used to serve at Brooklyn headquarters. Swore I'd lose the little I had left. My home, Gloria, any hope to be made whole again through god." I kneel next to Margaret and the air mattress deflates, hissing us both to the floor. "Then they drove me to the abortion clinic."

50

Nav's ice cream parlour is an art gallery. Candied pear, cherries jubilee, vanilla bean and black pepper, lemongrass, fig dream, almond, tomato basil, apple cinnamon, mojito. All the world's colours represented in gelato. And chocolate, of course. There will always be chocolate, no matter how upscale the clientele. The shop is little more than an elongated bus shelter with a marble bar and stools for six. Blue and white mosaic wall. Display case for Nav's handmade ice cream sandwiches. I make myself comfortable and scan the dozens of celebrity photos hanging on the front wall. Kardashian, Clooney, Witherspoon, Carrey licking ice cream on cones, provocatively or comically, depending what genre they occupy. I've been inside the shop for one minute but the bell on the door is still ringing, the sound spoiling the scenery. I blame the Doppler effect, but that can't be it. I reach my fingers inside the hollow metal shell of the bell and pinch the gongs.

Nav emerges from the back room. "Avery?" His white cook's apron dusted in what looks like cocoa or cinnamon. It matches his skin exactly. "Is it time for one of our top secret ice cream sessions again?"

"When did you go all Hollywood?" I ask.

"We're a photo op for the film festival crowd now."

"How did that happen? You're not even downtown."

"Let's just say I helped a certain actress out of a certain Scientology situation." He winks at me.

"Scientology, too?"

"Scientologists, Jehovah's Witnesses, Catholics, Muslims, Jews, Hindus, even Buddhists. Pretty much every kind of religion when it goes wrong. I got a call from a Yogi the other day."

"Interesting business to be in."

"Ice cream is my business. Religious recovery and intervention is my calling." He reaches for a coconut and a cleaver. "Does Henry know you're here?" he says, his neck craning to the window. "Because I'm trying to stay under the radar a bit. There's a movement within the Watchtower to ban sugar. A Witness comes here once a day, twice on weekends. Leaves flyers on my customers' cars."

"Henry's gone," I say. "He left me."

"He'll be back." He cracks the shell with the dull edge of the knife.

"No, Nav, he won't."

"Then you need this more than I do." He pulls me behind the counter and slips the cleaver into my hand. "Go ahead."

I hack at the coconut. The mosaic shakes, I shake too. Hack it again and again. The coconut lops in half. The slimy juice spills onto my shoes.

"There she goes!" Nav says. He peels away the hairy shell. Dumps the meat in a blender. He reaches into the freezer and pulls out a bucket of dry ice. It's steaming like a witch's brew. "I used to specialize in cults. Did I ever tell you that? But after a year or so, I found out it wasn't necessary to be so . . . fringe. The more mainstream the more interesting the deprogramming, actually."

"I thought Henry was deprogrammed."

"So did I at first," he says, pouring the dry ice into the blender like it's a river of smoke. "But sometimes they just can't fit into the real world."

"I know the feeling."

"You want an ice cream?" Nav asks. "Or one of my sandwiches maybe? I'm using walnut flour in the mix now. It'll blow your mind." He turns on the blender. Hunks of coconut spin madly. Cows in a tornado.

"You know that secret I told you?" I shout. The blender is as loud as a lawnmower. "And only you?"

"Pardon?" Nav yells.

"About my uncle?"

Pieces of coconut leap from the blades, clinging to the side of the plastic jug. They're desperate. But there's no way out.

"Avery, I can't hear —"

"My uncle! I saw him!"

Nav shuts off the machine. "Your uncle? *The* uncle?"

The blender hums as it powers down.

"Yeah," I say.

"So you went to the prison?"

"I did." I touch the base of the blender. It's motor hot. I don't know how the plastic can stand it.

"And what did he want?"

"He asked for my forgiveness."

"Wow."

"Yeah."

"And did he admit what he did?"

"No."

"Then I hope you told him to go fuck himself."

"That's your professional opinion?"

"Yep." He stretches out his hand. "Now pass me that spatula."

I slap it into his grip. "Aren't you supposed to be a sort of therapist? Shouldn't you be, I don't know, more Socratic instead of declarative?"

"I'm just a humble ice cream scooper, my dear. With a PhD."

I sink to the marble counter. The room itself is warm but this surface is so cold. Something about the conductivity of metamorphic rock.

"Listen, I'm not trying to be trite or cute." Nav scrapes the coconut cream into a metal bowl. "'Forgiveness is the attribute of the strong.' 'Forgive us our trespasses, as we forgive those who trespass against us.' 'Where there is forgiveness, there God resides.' All the religions have it, and it's a beautiful, therapeutic thing—especially for the victim." He hands me the spatula; I lick it. "But how can you forgive your drug-addicted pedophile uncle, like I mean truly forgive, when your drug-addicted pedophile uncle won't admit what he did?"

My tongue is numb now. I can't taste a thing, but I keep licking because there's the memory of the flavour that was or there's the hope that some sort of feeling will return. Nav clenches a scooper, dips it in hot water and reaches into the freezer. He digs into a tub of mocha so rich it's nearly black, with golden ribbons of peanut butter swirling through it. His forearm flexes as he sculpts the dark, rich ice cream into a rose. He hands over my cone, a homemade waffle fragrant with vanilla. I sweep a dark chocolate curl into my mouth. The southeast ridge of my tongue can still taste and what it tastes is too good for words so only noises come out of me. *Filthy nasty disgusting* noises.

"Okay, so you don't like it," he says. "But do you have to be so mean?"

"What are you talking about?" I say, my mouth coated in cocoa.

"Filthy nasty disgusting." He says it.

"Don't be weird," I tell him. "I didn't say that. Not out loud."

He looks at me sideways. "You did; you just licked my ice cream and said it."

"Shit," I say.

"What's going on, Avery? What's wrong?"

I feel a weight in my hand. "It's nothing."

"It's not nothing."

I look down. The cleaver. I'm still gripping it; I had no idea. I hand it to Nav handle first: the way a sane person passes something sharp. "I've, I've been seeing snow," I say.

"What do you mean seeing snow?" he says.

"I mean *snow*."

"Actual real snow?"

"Flakes and crystals and cold wind and sometimes full-on storms inside and—"

"*Inside?*"

"—and outside. It depends."

Nav laughs.

"I'm serious."

"I see snow too." Nav digs his hand into a tub of powdered sugar, flings it in the air like confetti. "And num num num it's delicious."

"It started when my uncle called me two weeks ago," I say. "Well, the ice started then. The snow came later."

"Holy shit, you're serious." He runs to the window. "Do you see it now?"

I look outside. It's summer. Kids are skipping down the sidewalk. Trees are leafy and every shade of green. The cumulonimbus is there, hulking over everything, but it isn't snow. At least not yet. "I haven't seen snow since yesterday. Not since I confronted Bryan."

"Really?"

"Really."

Nav takes my cone and tosses it in the trash. "Fuck ice cream."

"Hey!"

He pulls a joint out from his apron. Lights it, takes a drag. It smells damp, like spring. "I've heard of visions before," he says, "but it's usually in the realm of Jesus's face in toast."

"And then there's the coats," I tell him.

"Coats?"

"Yeah. Winter parkas. My dad's in particular."

"Your dad is dead."

"He is."

"I'm not following," he says. "You kept his coat?"

"No, but I just sort of find it sometimes," I say. "Or it finds me."

Nav hands me the joint. I cradle it between my middle and index finger like Bryan used to. "No thanks," I say, passing it back.

Nav stubs it out. "I guess you don't need drugs if you're seeing a dead man's coat."

I reach into the glass case for an ice cream sandwich.

"And where do you see this coat exactly?" asks Nav.

"On furniture or the floor," I say. "But eventually it ends up on me." The first bite is always the worst so I brace for it. The ice cream hits the top of my mouth and the pain is immediate. A needle through the brain.

Nav leans against the counter, his arms barely crossing over his belly. "I think I know what this is."

"Really?" I say, sucking in air, putting out the frozen fire in my mouth. "What?"

"I think it's your father."

"My dead father."

"That's the one."

"If you mean he's haunting me, then I'd rather be crazy."

"All I'm saying is that these types of apparitional inter-ferential events and communications are well documented.

They take on all kinds of forms: voices, smells, even feeling the person's touch."

I polish off the sandwich. My fingertips are sticky with cookie film. Like a second skin. "And how about the weather?" I say. "These *communications* don't normally happen through snow, do they? They don't usually take on the form of winter coats?"

"That's true. That's definitely a new one." Nav takes my hands, wipes them clean in his apron. "But whatever it is, you shouldn't fear it. Just accept it, and learn what lessons you can. These things are supposed to accelerate emotional healing. Think of it as a spiritual intervention. Sort of like what I do, in a way."

"You're crazier than I am, Nav."

He lets me go. "I'm just giving you my professional opinion."

The cookie film is gone, but my hands aren't clean. They're blotted with cinnamon or cocoa. I smell them. Nutmeg?

"I think your father is trying to protect you," Nav says. "Just like he used to. Or maybe, just maybe, this is his way of making up for the times he couldn't."

"How can you even believe in this stuff anyways?" I say. "The afterlife? Spirits? After everything you've seen religion do to people. How it manipulates them, breaks up families, how it ruins lives. I mean, Jesus, Nav, after all the messes you've had to clean up, how do you even believe in god?"

Nav takes off his apron, hangs it near a photo of Kim Kardashian. Puckered lips. Arched back. A cup of mint chocolate chip balanced on her ass. "It's not God I have trouble believing in," he says.

51

A haunting coat? Impossible, no matter what Nav says, but I wish I was wearing it now, standing outside my building working up the nerve to walk inside my apartment. It was taking a lot of pacing, a lot of deep breaths. Margaret is gone now; she grabbed her purse and ran out the door when the credits began to roll. David Attenborough. The BBC. Special thanks to someone named Pompillio Campos Chinchilla, which made me laugh so hard I cried. So I'd rather stay outside because I know what I'll find when I open my door: all the characteristics of loneliness writ large. The apartment will be exactly the way I left it this morning; nothing will have been moved. Coffee grounds and Rice Krispies still in the kitchen sink, pajamas balled up on the bathroom floor, the bedroom closet wide open, clothes tumbled out, unmade bed, pillows unfluffed. Everything will be as I left it—the same. Which means that everything is now very different.

I drag up the nerve while that old loneliness seeps back like those bathroom sounds and smells seep through the gap in the wall. It's the brand of loneliness that drove me to find Henry and hold onto him for dear life. I thought marriage would cure my loneliness, but it didn't; it made my isolation more pronounced, unjust even, because it was Henry's legal obligation to spend time with me but he did not. I had such high hopes when I found him, someone just like me. A twin consciousness, he said, and I believed it. I thought his eyes were the kind I could look into and he'd look back and know what it felt like to be me. I wouldn't have to describe the sensation in words or stretch my arms as wide as they could go, reproducing my outsized perception of aloneness. I know now that he could only gather my loneliness like a vessel and then pour me down the drain. But I clogged the pipes, with my endless strands of knotted hair, and he gave up, stopped pulling me out. And I was forced to write the one biography I never wanted to:

GAUTHIER, AVERY: LOSER

Ms. Gauthier will live a lonely life, unloved and unwanted, with only her drain hair, shitty Ikea carpet and television for company until she meets her untimely death when a window—a tempered pane treated with a nanotech sealant that makes the window a self-cleaning window, the most advanced fucking super window in the world—comes crashing down on her—

"Shit," I yelp. "My job!" I rush to my computer.

Boss: *Yer fired.*

Avery: *Please don't. Please! I need this job!*

Boss: *You fucked up! Cost me 50k!*

Avery: *?*

Boss: *I had to reprint the hole yearbook!*

Avery: *?*

Boss: *Sound familer?: "Wright has a broad range of experience in commercial, regulatory and cockstroke brag back brag."*

Avery: *?*

Boss: *It went 2 print!*

Avery: *I didn't write that.*

Boss: *How bout this?: "due diligence and sticking his thumb up his ass." ???*

Avery: *But I didn't actually write those things.*

Boss: *You did!*

Avery: *No, I only thought them. Inside my head.*

Boss: *UNAVAILABLE*
Avery: *Hello?*
Avery: *Are you still there?*
Avery: *Are you still there?*

Right foot, steady. Right arm against the tile. I step in, differently now because it's dangerous. Left foot next to right. All right. All right? You're all right. I used to move more quickly, back when I had Henry, but I will not be one of those abandoned women who slip on soap, grasp for the curtain and slice open their heads. I will not go down, naked and bleeding, unsaved. I unwrap a pink Dove bar that won't lurk in the white of the tub and insist on a bath instead of a shower. Since Henry left, my already-dry skin has seemed to worsen and my scalp requires more frequent doses of my medicated shampoo. I let the vile stuff seep into my roots for two to three minutes *pour obtenir les meilleurs résultants.* The only school French I retained was what I can read on the backs of shampoo bottles.

"What is that stench?" Billy Pfeiffer through the wall. "Road tar?"

"Denorex," I say, and it sounds like a sigh.

"It's been a while since we talked."

"It's been forever."

He's fumbling with his guitar, his fingers brushing the frets. *I would do anything for love.* I sink under the water and rinse while he plays my favourite part, breaking his voice in two or the song will fall apart: the woman posing the questions, pleading and frantic; Meatloaf answering, obstinate and cold.

Silence. Then a guitar plinking down on a bathtub.

"I hate Meatloaf," he says. "It's not even a guitar song."

"So why play it?" I ask.

"My girlfriend likes it. *Ex*-girlfriend."

"Sorry to hear it."

"She called me a loser. Said I never did anything after winning *Idol*."

"She sounds like a bitch."

"She's right; I am a fucking loser."

"You're not."

"I only sold 1000 albums," he says. "And it wasn't even *my* music. Just a bunch of shitty covers. Like fucking Meatloaf. Not even my girlfriend wanted to hear my own stuff." A metal ding. He's punched the wall. He wears several rings on each hand, I remember from the show. He would alternate fingers every now and then, and the green tinge they left behind made his hands look sickly on camera. He punches again, harder this time. The bathwater sloshes, the wall quivers. His knuckles must be bleeding.

"You miss her," I say. "You loved her and you miss her."

Silence. And then: "This shit is getting too personal."

"Oh, come on."

"No, really. I don't think it's any of your business."

"You make it my business," I say. "The fighting, the weed, the rough sex — all of it comes through that crack up there like a fog."

"This fucking stupid goddamn wall!"

"I know how long it takes you to poo in the morning," I say. "How you feel about breaking up with your girlfriend is the least personal thing I know about you."

The wall rocks. A thud. Then another. A tile tumbles into the water, the drywall behind it so cheap and porous his rings leave impressions. A skull. A cross. "I hate this fucking shitty ass punk wall!" Tiles rain down into the bath. So this is how the sky falls, I think, as I tiptoe away from the carnage.

52

Margaret's stair runner is heaped by the television. I unfurl it. It stretches from the living room into the kitchen, but it's impossible to know if it's finished. Depends on my mother and the stairs, two things I don't have. "Oh my god," I say. "I think I miss her." I wrap the runner around my shoulders. The wool is itchy and smells of barn so I drag my feet to the closet and Margaret's plum dress. I step into it and struggle with reaching the zipper, nearly dislocating my shoulder. I want to ask Billy Pfeiffer to help me, but he's swearing and throwing two different things — his shoulder? handfuls of ball bearings? — at the wall, so I decide against it.

A knock at my front door.

"An old man let me in. He looked about a hundred?" Kristie's wearing a lot of makeup. "Too much?"

"No," I lie. "You look pretty."

"I did one of those YouTube tutorials," she says, scrolling through her phone. "You know, where they start off naked-faced and then add on all the layers in fast motion and then show the before and after and it's like wow?" She presses play. A Korean man highlights and contours himself into a Scandinavian woman.

"I'll have to check them out."

"You should," she says, scanning my face. "And you should try one."

"Not enough?" I say, my fingers on my face. I didn't put on any cover up or BB or CC cream or tinted moisturizer or *teint encre de peau* or serum or double-wear maximum cover or liquid foundation or colour-correcting S P F or fluide or mineral powder or pressed power or self-tanner or any other manner of salve and lotion assigned to hide women's hideous faces. It's just me out here in the hallway. A piece of raw meat.

"No," Kristie lies, walking into my apartment. "You look pretty too." She's wearing an oversized hoodie, but there's no hiding that bump; it stretches out the pocket that I'm sure she hoped would obscure her pregnancy. It would take something far thicker to hide her secret, though. It would take a ridiculous Frankenstein coat.

"What's that?" Kristie asks.

The shower wall is alive and rocking.

"Just my neighbour," I say, closing the bathroom door.

That answer is enough for Kristie's Snapchat-generation attention span. She's already moved on. "Nice dress," she says. "Plum's my favourite colour."

"Plum?" I say, surprised. "Nobody ever thinks plum but me."

"Well, I do."

"Why not purple?" I spin around. Show her one of the problems I have with this dress.

"I don't know," she says, zipping me up. "Because it's, like, plum?"

"It's my mother's dress."

"That's cool that you're the same size," she says. "You two look so much alike."

"No, we don't."

"Are you kidding? At the last meeting, I thought it was you walking through the door. But only like twenty years older."

"Twenty-eight."

"Anyways," she says. "I came over because I wanted to apologize for the other day. For eavesdropping on you with the doctor? And all that mean stuff I said about you having a breakdown?"

"Don't worry about it."

She's upset and the makeup accentuates it. Eyebrows, fuller and darker with pencil, cramp. She bites her lip, smudging a tooth crimson. "But I did worry about it. Like a lot. I was going to apologize at group, but you didn't show up. So your mother gave me your address and—"

"Did she make you uncomfortable? She can be very . . . preachy."

"Are you kidding? She's the reason I decided to keep the baby."

"Really?" I say. "How is that . . . What did she say?"

"She said even though you and her didn't agree on Jehovah anymore, and even though you had wandered away from the flock, she loved you and wanted to make things right."

I slump down on my shitty rug, my fingers tracing the bold concentric circles, coaxing hairs out of their hiding places and the colour out of the fibres. "She said that?"

"Uh huh. And it made me rethink everything about my situation. I mean, you two must have gone through some rough times, just like my parents and me. So it gives me hope, you know?"

"Then I guess that's great, Kristie," I say. "Congratulations."

"Whoa." She takes my hand—it's blue with the indigo from my rug—and places it on her stomach. "Feel that?" It's soft, the flick flick flick of this creature who has no control and yet so very much. I never felt that, with Bryan's fetus. I got it out of me long before it grew feet for kicking. "I'm going to name the baby Avery."

I pull my hand away from her—from it—and turn to the window. The cumulonimbus is growing darker. Veins of lightning prickle through it.

"I know it's a bit weird," she says. "But I feel like you saved my baby's life, in a way, and that deserves something major, don't you think?"

"I'd really rather you didn't give it my name," I say.

"Why?"

The cloud pulses with thunder. I flinch but Kristie doesn't. Of course she doesn't. The cloud isn't there. It never was. I'm stuck in this weather system forever. I am the angel of Armageddon, the pestilence and locusts all mine. "Please, Kristie," I say. "Just choose something else."

"Fine, whatever." Kristie shrugs. "You're being like way dramatic, though. Anyone ever tell you that?"

I switch on the TV. Calvin stands in front of the weather map, his shoulders obstructing the province of Ontario. *"Buckle your seatbelts, weather watchers,"* he says. *"A spectacular system is on the way."*

"Is your mother here?" Kristie asks.

"Nope."

"Oh. Well, when will she be back?"

"I don't know," I say. "Maybe never."

Kristie rubs her belly and walks to the window. "That used to be my Kingdom Hall, you know. Where it all started."

"Uh huh," I say, turning Calvin up.

"It's rare, ish, this weather system, and it's basically porn for meteorologists." Calvin cranes his neck off camera. *"Okay, apparently you can't say* porn *on television. What's that, Mike? Oh, just not on the Weather Network. Thank you, Mike, for that info. Anyways."* Calvin swings his arm northward just as I taught him, *"As I was saying, this particular type of unstable weather system usually sweeps in from —"* then manages to tangle his shirtsleeve in his lapel microphone.

"Worst. Weatherman. Ever." Kristie mutes the television. "But he's right about the forecast." She presses her forehead against the window. "That cloud, I mean, wow. Very Armageddony."

"Wait, what?" I grab her by the arm. "You can see it? You can actually see it?"

"Of course I — oh no." Kristie pulls open the balcony door. "Oh no no no."

I follow her outside. The noise of wind chimes, like a cat walking across a piano. The sun is gone, birds gone — all of nature making way for the cumulonimbus, brooding and moody and striped with lightning. The Kingdom Hall empties and the Witnesses look up. They'll agree with Kristie: Armageddon indeed. Christ and his army will pour from the cloud and smite the earth with earthquakes, floods, fire, sulfur and disease. Only the Witnesses with the truest of hearts will remain when he's done with his righteous war, and I worry for them. Who will they hand their magazines to?

"Avery! Would you look?"

"It's scary, I know, but like Calvin said it's —"

"Not the cloud!" Kristie points at the Kingdom Hall. At the person on the edge of the roof.

"Margaret?" I croak.

53

A cabbie hangs out his window, honking wildly, as though celebrating like he used to where he came from, firing bullets off into the sky. He's honking at me because I'm tearing across the street. The cab swerves around me and other cars too. An SUV with squeaky brakes. A minivan loaded with soccer players. A truck with a poodle in the passenger seat. He barks a warning I don't have time to heed because I'm running toward her, waving my arms in bold concentric circles. She pretends not to see me. Looks right through me like I'm not real. But I am real. "Margaret!" I scream.

She takes another step. Her feet are more in the air than on the building. The crowd of Witnesses gasps and there's some encouraging noise involved in trying to talk her down, but no one calls 911. They pray instead, with a ferocity that rivals the wind — *Jehovah, protect this sister for she not knows what she does wrap her in your arms and pull her down to safety protect her from her strife and numb the pain of suffering.* I'm not sure what they expect: that God will reach down and pluck her from the roof or that their sound waves will push Margaret back from the ledge? We're all staring at Margaret when a bird flies into the window right below her feet, bounces off and lands on the sidewalk. There's no blood or brains coming out of it, so we all take a breath, watch its chest rise and fall. That glass, so shiny and enticing — maybe I should fly into it too, knock myself out, wake up and have the chance to start all over. A commotion startles the crowd. A bark and a scuffle. The poodle snatches the bird and shakes it dead. "Sparkles!" its owner screams, "you get back in this goddamn truck!"

I run into the hall, wind up the four storeys, past the signs warning me to turn back: *Caution: Fragile Roof!*, *Maintenance Staff Access: Keep Out!*, *Authorized Personnel Only!* The elders don't want their congregation to get close to heaven. Do the Witnesses need more proof than this? The door to the roof is open and I see Margaret through it, her body thin as a sail in the wind. I don't want to scare her so I think like that lion on the zebra hunt. I check my surroundings for camouflage. There's not much for me to blend in with up here. Grey pebbles. Navy solar panels. They're both in the same family as my dress, a few pie pieces away on the colour wheel. I take my chances and step on to the roof. The gravel crunches under my feet — which I notice are bare and scratched and bleeding — and Margaret's head swings round. She doesn't see me though, because I'm a stealthy hunter now. All those lessons I had when I was prey.

Margaret's eyes turn fierce for a moment and then buckle, dropping to her shoes and the street below. I inch my way to her and scoop up some pebbles. I toss them to her left. She looks and I grab her from the right, pulling her down to the roof. She screams and lands on top of me, the back of her head clonking the front of mine. She scrambles up but I've got her by the wrist.

"Let go of—" She freezes. "Avery? My goodness, you look awful!"

"Oh, I'm sorry," I say. "Should I be in full makeup for your suicide?"

"What happened to your eye?"

I look into the solar panel. My eye is green and yellow now. Too bad. The purple it used to be would have gone so well with the plum. I turn around and Margaret's back on the ledge. "God-dammit! Get down!"

"You know I almost did this before?" she says, in a daze. She's hypnotized by the height — I'll never forget the dizzying conflicting feeling: so powerful and yet powerless — and the only two choices laid out before her. Life or death. "I almost did it after your dad made me leave you."

"Margaret—"

"I went to the cliffs, the ones near the Parliament buildings that look over the river to Quebec. I was wearing a summer dress. It was floral and so light and thin it moved wherever the wind wanted to take it. I walked to the edge and stared down into the waves as they lapped against the rock. I thought about diving into it."

"Margaret, don't."

"That dive was all I could think about. My graceful leap, my arms up and over my head, and tight against my ears. My toes pointed. My dress flying over my face, revealing one shame, hiding another."

Cell tower, rack of solar panels, cigarette butts and crumpled beer cans. There's no tool on this roof I can use to bring her away from the edge. No magnets or rope. No oversized vaudeville canes.

"I was weighing the idea of dying like that," Margaret says, "when I felt the earth shift beneath my toes. I stepped back and as I did," her head is turned sideways, she's talking loud, over the wind, "my part of the cliff crumbled into the river. I turned away from the water and looked up at the sun the way they say you're not supposed to, the way they say will make you go blind."

"You didn't do it then," I say, "and you're not going to do it now."

"Why shouldn't I?"

"Because if you displease god, you lose your rights to a happy Armageddon."

She laughs. "A happy Armageddon."

"A happy Armageddon, a happy beginning. You told me that."

"It was never me who told you anything; it was the elders. The men who make the magazines, men like Henry. Men men men men. Always men telling us what to do."

She creeps closer to the edge.

"Don't, Mom! Please!"

Margaret stops. She's an inch away from falling. Her feet are impatient, but her centre of gravity is fighting against it, leaning her backwards toward the roof. "What did you just call me?" she says.

The wind moans and the trees bend like straws. The cumulonimbus cloud attacks, dropping bombs of ice like a zeppelin in war.

"What did you—"

A stone of hail clunks Margaret on the head. She crumples and I pull her into my arms.

"Jehovah," she moans, "if this is a sign—"

I look over the edge. I shouldn't look over the edge. The crowd is taking cover. Bus shelters. Sleep Country Canada. Burger Shack. Ice pings the roof, crashes through windows. The cloud shakes out hail, huge pellets the size of fists.

I drag Margaret under the solar panels. Saved by the light of god.

"What did you call me?" she asks.

"Nothing," I say.

"You called me Mom." The word makes her cry and her tears clog up her throat. "I haven't heard that since you were twelve," she says, all nasally.

"Yeah, well, it just slipped out."

"Mom."

"Why would you even consider jumping?"

She rakes her fingers through the pebbles like a Zen garden. "Because what Bryan did," she says, "it's an unforgivable sin."

"But it wasn't your sin," I say.

"If I'd just come back, if I'd called . . . if I wasn't so afraid of being rejected."

"It's not your sin," I insist. "It's Bryan's. And it's the elders who covered it up. And Gloria's for not protecting me. But it's not yours. And suicide won't fix it."

"It would balance it out."

"How?"

"My unforgivable sin for theirs."

I feel a hand on my shoulder and I jump, my fists curled and ready. I don't know who I expect to fight, or whose ghost I think I'll punch a hole through. It seems there are so many. It's Akono under a golf umbrella. He's smiling, closed mouth, no teeth, the smile of the self-satisfied. In this grey end-of-the-world light, his face has the eerie symmetry and prominent bone structure of something not quite human, more humanoid, and his eyes are so focused and confident, even under the pelting hail and Armageddon unfolding around him. If he served a different cause, and was taller, I might have followed him.

"Good job, Avery," Akono says. "Now come with me, Sister Margaret."

She takes off her shoe. "It's because of people like you!" Whips him in the leg. "You people did this to her!" Her other shoe. Whips it at his crotch, but he catches it.

"Whatever this is about," he says, "forgiveness is the path to healing."

Margaret picks up a pebble of ice and tries to throw it, but it melts in the heat of her hand.

"Look to the Bible," Akono says.

"I have," Margaret says. "I spent all day here in the library."

"And the Bible tells you to forgive."

"Not all of it." Her need to throw things recedes, but she doesn't look any less dangerous. "Not the Book of Nahum."

Akono ducks the cloud's biggest hail bomb yet. "You don't want to turn to this particular book, Sister Margaret. I can point you in a much better direction if you'll just—"

"'Jehovah is a jealous deity and takes revenge,'" she recites. "'He takes revenge and is fierce in temper.'"

"Nahum the Elkoshite was a minor prophet," says Akono. "He was burdened and pained, and he was most certainly overly dramatic—"

"'Jehovah takes revenge on his foes and bears his enemies in mind. He is patient and powerful, and does not acquit an offender.'" Margaret raises her arms to the cloud. "'His walk is in gale and tempest, and clouds are the dust of his feet.'" The cumulonimbus pulses overhead and unleashes more hail bombs so huge and solid they can't possibly be frozen water. They have to be rock. Chunks of the moon. "Screw forgiveness!" Margaret's on her knees. Her eyes have a direct line into mine. "I want revenge."

54

The hail falls hard and fast, puckering dents into Steve's Smart Car. I speed past lines of drivers clutching at the wheels like life rings. They aren't as prepared as I am, haven't the practice with unseasonable weather. Calvin's forecast is being simulcast on the radio. *"Summer hail is not a freak occurrence. The warmer and more humid the air is the more unpredictable—"* His shirtsleeve must have connected with his lapel mic again. The sound like a muffled series of punches.

"What the hell are you doing here?"

"I brought you gifts," I say, swinging a bottle of whiskey like a pendulum.

The door chain falls away.

"You said gift*s*," Gloria says, putting extra spit into the *s*.

"The other's a surprise."

"Let me put my face on." She wobbles off into the bathroom, leaving a scent trail of coconut hand cream and White Diamonds.

I set down my tote bag and let my body get swallowed whole into the musty lips of her chair. Familiar garbage haunts the house. Pizza boxes and beer cans. An orchestra of flies. A battery-operated air freshener pumps out chemicals at an exhausting rate, every piña colada puff a sigh. A romance novel does the splits on the armrest. *The Scoundrel King*. The cover is bent and abused; so is the woman on it. Forlorn near an Umbrian vineyard and castle, she gazes off into the sunset, her breasts tumbling out of her corseted blue gown. A shirtless man grasps at her hips. His knees in the calcareous soil.

He was a bad man, the worst kind: a thief, a murderer, a liar. Oh but how Elisha loved him so, how she burned for him. She knew it was wrong, that she was throwing everything away to be with him: her family's honour, her innocence. But she had to have him. Now.

Gloria re-announces herself by stumbling into one of the ridiculous faux columns that separate the kitchen from the living room. Her blonde hair is down, the ends crispy. She wears a frumpy housedress I can't imagine someone going to the trouble of designing, sewing and shipping across the world. Stacks of gold bangles jangle up and down her thin wrists as she makes her way, unsteadily, toward me.

"Now that's better." She smiles at her reflection in the window. "A little rouge works miracles."

What's a miracle is that she's managed to hang on to that face of hers. If she was a stranger on the street I would have assumed plastic surgery, but I know all Gloria's savings went to Bryan's drug habit and lawyers, the one feeding the other. Her skin is still tight and dewy. It could have taken her to so many places that were better than Etobicoke, to so many men better than my uncle.

"I'll make us a drink." She tears the bottle from me then cradles it into the kitchen.

I flip to the end of the romance novel. I'll never come back to Gloria's living room, so if I'm going to find out how this story ends, it'll have to be now.

"I must warn you," the Marquis said, the sweat glistening off his chest like a sunset off the Mediterranean. "I am a dangerous man, a violent man. A sinner." Elisha could feel her desire growing. It hurt; it was that ferocious. "I know what you are!" she cried. "I know, I know!" She fell into his arms, helpless and hopelessly in love with the wrong man.

Gloria hands me my drink, which is her drink: whiskey and water and lime. "Why are you here?"

"I'm worried about you," I say.

She takes an enormous gulp, the gulp of a runner, a boxer, a zebra in the Serengeti. "You don't give a shit about me."

"That's not true," I say.

Gloria flutters and darts from one end of the room to the other. I feel nervous for her, expecting her to trip over her dressy slippers, the pair with sequined leopards sewn into the hand-towel material. Her hummingbird focus shifts from me to her glass to my tote bag. I pull it into my lap.

"I asked one favour of you," she says. "One! And you wouldn't even do it!" She lands too hard next to me, as if she's forgotten the unforgiving stiffness of her own furniture. "All you have to do is say three words to Bryan: I. Forgive. You."

"But I don't."

"So fake it! It's not hard!"

"You would certainly know."

"Why are you being so selfish?"

"I'm selfish? Me?"

"Yes, you!"

"I didn't press charges against Bryan *because* of you. I did that for *you*."

She waves my words away like a bad smell, her bracelets jingling. "Don't make yourself out to be a martyr, honey bun. You didn't press charges because you knew that whole thing was a misunderstanding."

She's talking with her hands and the sound of her bracelets, like jolly sleigh bells, makes this conversation inappropriately cheerful. I grab her by the wrists to shut them up. "You actually believe that," I say.

"I always believe the truth." She pulls away.

"You just can't face the possibility that Bryan is a monster."

"You want to talk about monsters? Do you know what's going to happen to him if he dies in jail without your forgiveness? He'll be locked up again! In an abyss with Satan! For 1000 years!"

"Give me a break, Gloria," I say, flopping back on the couch. "You don't even believe any of that. You just faked it around Bryan."

She picks at her fingers and plucks off a lemonade-pink press-on nail. "Well, it worked, didn't it?" She stuffs it in her pocket. "He stuck with me."

"He cheated on you relentlessly!"

"At least I still have a husband."

I leap up, banging my shin on her Lucite coffee table. The original bruise had healed and now I'll have to start healing all over again. "How did you know?"

She pulls a bedazzled iPhone out of her pocket, her lemonade nail stuck to it. She strokes the screen until it gives her Facebook. "It's called 'privacy settings'," she says. "Look it up."

"No! How do you know I don't have a husband *anymore*?"

"Because I know you," Gloria says. "Your posture's all sunken. Dark circles under your eyes. And skinny. It's the same look you had after your father died. That, and you're just like me and—"

"I'm nothing like you."

"—when our men leave us, the light inside leaves us too."

"*Your man* robbed a Peoples Jewellers and got locked up in prison."

Gloria sees the romance novel and swipes it from me, pressing it against her chest. "Men are complicated," she says. "Sometimes they just need space. To think and experiment and solve the problems of the world."

I laugh. "You're living in a fantasy, Gloria. Bryan is a drug addict and a—"

"If you *really* knew Bryan, you'd—"

"I'm the only one who does!"

"Oh aren't you just Miss Perfect then! Just like Bryan thinks you are!" Gloria's rose liner had wandered away from her lips, widening her mouth by the centimetre it takes to go from pretty to freak. "He never shuts up about you. Like you're his goddamn princess. Avery this and Avery that. It's enough to make me sick. But he married me, okay? He married *me!*" She wags her ring in my face, those hideous bees. The way the light catches it, the way her hand is swaying, they look sinister and alive. Like if I try to run they will fly off her hand and attack. "I stood by him through all of his crapola. Twenty-nine years of his messing around, lying, up to who knows what with who knows who. And here I've been, sitting at home like a Housewife of Beverly Goddamn Hills while he's out all night partying, never calling or apologizing when he decides to finally drag his sorry ass home. And for what? For his idiot thugs to *steal* me a ring? As if that's all I deserved? After everything?" She makes a terrible glug as she tries to drain the dregs of the glass, but there's nothing left. She's sipping fumes. "You know what? Take it!" She pulls her bee ring from her finger and throws it at my face. It stings like the real thing. "You probably think you deserve it, don't you?

You probably think Bryan loves you more than me anyways."

"I think you've had enough to drink," I say.

"Oh please. I've been drinking all day! That whiskey was like a cup of tea to me!"

"Let's just—"

"He trapped me in Etobicoke. Etobicoke! And he has the nerve to complain, to call me and whine like it's his life that's ruined, saying that I wouldn't understand. And never shutting up about you. But I get it all right, because when you fall in love with someone with your family's blood, your DNA . . . Ho ho ho! Oh boy! You're in for quite a ride! I could have had a big life if it weren't for him. Men flocked to me! Rich, beautiful men! I could have stayed in New York, been a success. But you lot get into our hearts with your claws. Scratching and cutting 'til we've been bled dry. We're too weak to run!"

She whimpers like a dog and melts off the couch into a pile on the floor, her ass ending up in a pizza box. The cardboard hisses, flies scatter. I help her back on to the lips, easing her limp, clammy body into the kiss. She relaxes into a blackout, and her hair falls away from her face. There's a glistening behind her ear. I move closer. It's tape, the clear medical kind for sealing seeping wounds shut. Beneath the tape is a collection of wrinkles crammed together like an accordion. The more I search her face, the more tape I find. Lift her hair back: a two-inch piece near her temple where her hair normally hangs. An elastic band fixed to it trapping more wrinkly flesh below. I follow the elastic like a trail of breadcrumbs. It's taut and goes all the way around the back of her skull, connecting to yet another piece of tape, which adheres to her other temple, pulling even more wrinkles smooth. On and on and on. Gloria's entire face stretched and held together by gift-wrapping supplies. I pull on a piece of tape and Gloria's face comes undone. Her neck sags from behind her ear, the wrinkled folds of skin sighing as they droop under gravity's pressure. I peel back another. Her once-taut cheeks descend and transform into jowls. She makes a gurgling noise and says my name, croaking it three times. I answer her, but I can't look at her.

"Give me back my ring," she says.

"I don't have it," I tell her.

"Please."

"I told you I don't have it."

"But I threw it right at you."

"You must have imagined it," I tell her. "You've always been so good at that."

Gloria forces a smile and I wish she hadn't. I see all of her teeth, even the dying back molars her bleaching strips can't reach. "Did you know that your uncle, when he proposed to me, we were standing outside a castle in Italy?" Gloria's slurring and spitting. I inch away so I don't get hit. "I was wearing this beautiful cornflower-blue dress and the sun was just beginning to set, it was shining off your uncle's chest like the sun off the Mediterranean and—"

She blacks out. Her eyes flutter, eyelids unrecognizably crinkly like rice paper lampshades. Somewhere an elastic snaps and the rest of her face comes tumbling down. There's enough skin to make a second.

I rip down the print of *Snow*. When I tacked it up over my hand-drawn vortex all those years ago—long before Henry and I, before the dinosaurs roamed the earth, when it was just bacteria and humid swamps and dragonflies—I used the wrong tape for the job: duct. Because of my ignorance, the metallic grey will stain this wall forever: leave behind a stringy, cloth-like fossil. Now that I know what the real thing looks like, this

Snow print is all wrong. It's too smooth. The brush strokes look like photocopies, which perhaps they are; my understanding of the print-making business is zero. All that texture wiped out is upsetting. The image, normally so alive and vibrant, looks dead. When my nose touches it, I back off. It smells like Gloria's cigarettes.

I lean into the vortex. The scraggly crayon going round and round and round. It was soothing just drawing this circle. I remember when I made it, because it was the same day Bryan got arrested — not for me, but for the Peoples Jewellers next to the PetSmart at the mall. He bought a gun from a farmer in Caledon and bullets from his drug dealer and stole $200,000 worth of engagement rings, pearls and those hideous Mother's Day charms. He was going to use the money for cocaine and pills, for the high fives among thieves and for everything he thought the universe owed him. At the time, Bryan was still an active Jehovah's Witness of some regard, if only nostalgic. His Kingdom Hall was in a leafy residential neighbourhood, but the houses kept their distance, as though the building had a virus that made eyes bleed. A week after Bryan's arrest, Gloria, drunk on Long Island Iced Tea, let it slip that the elders counselled Bryan against a plea deal because his guilt would, by association, be theirs. So he pleaded innocent, went to trial and — finally — got what he deserved. "Joho bastards just wanted to protect their own asses!" Gloria had said. "But who's going to protect *me* from them?"

I forgave her this narcissism, because she took the news of my pregnancy better than I expected. Slapping me only once and then blubbering an apology through the bathroom door. She made the arrangements swiftly, and very little was spoken about it until we were seated, one empty chair between us, in the waiting room at the Morgentaler Clinic. "It was very nice of

Elder Mark to drive us here, wasn't it, hun?" She paced the coffee table with her press-on nails. "I could have managed, of course, but I'll take a helping hand now and then." A rattled teenaged boy tried to sit between us, but Gloria slapped her pink suede purse down. "Taken." We needed three chairs because there were three of us. Me, Gloria, and this thing inside of me. Breathing eating living off me. It would have had Bryan's feet. Hairy on the tops, long yellow nails. Scratching nails. "I just want you to be prepared, hun, for the reality of this situation." I looked for a distraction. Found none but the sign on the wall. *The Morgentaler Clinic.* The only stuff for me to play with was that name. "I understand you're young and you're in a pickle, but you need to know that this . . . *sort of thing* leaves a mark." How to pronounce it? Morgenthawler? "After all, hun, technically, after today, you will be a murderer." Thaw? Like ice? Like the doctor's hands? Are you Dr. Morgenthawler? *No, my dear. I'm Dr. Sangeet.* A paper gown. No underwear or bra. *I'm going to give you something that will relax every muscle you've got.* A needle in my hand. Kettle water through my vein. *You have very good veins, my dear.* Through my very good vein. Pressure. *Just a little.* A cramp. The worst cramp in the world. A knot that my body tried to undo. *All done, my dear. You did brilliantly.* The snap of latex. The scrape of a curtain opening. My aunt Gloria lighting a cigarette in the parking lot, holding it between fingers crooked with arthritis from holding cigarettes.

The security guard rolled me out but then Gloria pulled me away, the wheels on the chair making it so easy. Protesters surrounded the building in a semicircle. Catholics. A priest, a nun and a couple fanatics. The rest maybe meant well. "See, hun? It's that mark I warned you about. Everyone can tell." Shouting and chanting and loudspeakers and my head banging like dropped pots. Protest signs in uppercase and superfluous exclamation marks. DOCTOR SANGEET IS NOT GOD!!! YOU ARE NOT GOD!!! ABORTION IS MURDER!!! YOU = MURDERER!!!! Horrific props. A cross with a Jesus tacked up, all blood and thorns and ribs. A fetus formed of chicken breasts and gristle. How did the Catholics slip inside of my nightmares and pull them out?

Gloria pushed me down the ramp, but not fast enough. The red paint hit me on my back when I stood up to run. I was not supposed to run. Security guards and nurses and even Dr. Sangeet. But the paint was in my hair—gooey from split ends to scalp. "Hun, don't be mad at me, okay? But Elder Mark can't have you in his car in the state you're in. The seats are leather. So I'm going to have him drive me home now. You wait inside. And I'll come back with some clean clothes."

Sitting again, somehow. Wheels, uphill when they should go down. Brake.

Morgentaler.

Gental. Gent.

I laughed. I couldn't help it. I laughed and I shook.

The Catholics banged on the windows. The cops were called. Sirens, officers in uniforms. Dr. Sangeet knelt in front of me with her mask pulled down to make things fair between us—she sees me, I see her. Her skin creamy like peanut butter. Her teeth the straightest whitest, teeth like my mother and like me. *Do you want to press charges, my dear?* For which thing? I answered.

I don't want to wake Gloria, but I don't owe her peace and quiet or anything else. Plus, the appeal of hammering into this wall is so great. I want to make a hole, a real one, and then fill it with something. I reach into my tote for the hammer and nail, wrapped like it's dangerous in a Home Depot bag, and for the painting. The real one. *Snow* by Lawren Harris. It will cover my hole, I realize, when I hold it up for as long as I can until my arms change from muscle to tired to only sleeves. I nail the painting up like Jesus on that cross, like the Catholics and the nightmares that Gloria fed me to. It looks more like a window than a painting, a view to a winter world that everyone can see, not only me. I wonder if Gloria will notice the difference between the fake thing and the real? In a year from now the police will show up at her door in response to an anonymous tip about a hijacked national treasure, stolen by proxy by her convict husband, his band of thieves doing him one last favour. I wonder if Gloria will even be alive to open the front door?

Margaret's knees must be shaking because the Smart Car is bouncing on its go-kart tires. When I left her in the driveway, she must have tugged the emergency brake into position and turned the engine off because I intended to keep it running. But Margaret? She didn't want to feel like a criminal or a fugitive, even though we were. Even though that's who we've always been.

"Did you get Gloria drunk?" she says.

"No need." My body tucks behind the wheel. "Well, I helped."

"And did you swap the print for the painting?"

I hand her the print of *Snow*, rolled up into a tight tube.

"Oh my goodness." She unfurls it, examining it like it's a Dead Sea scroll. "Oh my goodness goodness gracious."

I belt myself in. As if it will make any difference if a semi decides to eat Steve's car for a snack. My mother checks the mirrors, for cops or targeted lightning bolts. I check for the cumulonimbus. It's spread further across the city like wine spilled on a plush blue carpet. The hail has evolved into a pissing rain.

"It's justice what we did," Margaret says. "'For Jehovah has brought back Jacob's pride like Israel's, because riflers had rifled them and had wrecked their branches.' And I feel good about it. I think."

I make incremental twists on the radio dial until I find Calvin. *"Some fun facts for you weather watchers. A single cumulonimbus has the same energy as ten atom bombs. Sort of like my producer Mike after Taco Bell."*

Margaret tries to snap the radio off, but twists to the right instead of left.

"AND UNLIKE MIKE THEY CAN LAST FOR HOURS!"

She corrects the knob and the car is quiet but for her fast short breaths and the rain bruising the roof. "Oh but now I feel guilty about not feeling guilty. Should I feel guilty? Does anything I'm saying make sense?"

I shrug and turn the key. The lawnmower engine spits and rumbles like the sky.

"What about you, Avery? Do you feel bad at all?"

I release the emergency brake and roll backwards down the driveway. "For which thing?" I turn on to the road, trusting myself to get us home.

55

Margaret lowers herself face-first onto her air mattress. The mattress is extra soft, but she can't see why. I can, although I wish I couldn't because I thought I was better now, cured, thought I didn't need it anymore. My dad's parka. It's under her, adding a comforting extra layer. It poofs as the air around the feathers and Gore-Tex moves in space to adjust to her weight. When it deflates back to normal, the rushing sound of the air gone with it, my heart aches and then speeds up.

"I feel hot," Margaret says. "Why am I so hot?"

The feathers and the Gore-Tex.

"It must be The Change," she says. "All the stress from today probably unleashed my old-lady hormones." She turns over, stretches out. "Or maybe all the stress from life."

I cry like a burst pipe. No warning. Everything wet inside of me, my blood, my bile, my digestive juices and enzymes, gushes out through my eyes and nose. I think of the peace that Margaret was aiming for on the roof, that I was aiming for in Brooklyn. The bliss of nothingness, of blackness. But I don't want that, not really. What I want is to be connected to reality or be completely disconnected. I can't live in the middle anymore.

"I know," Margaret says, rubbing my back like she used to. "I know the feeling exactly."

I tidy my eyes and nose on my sleeve, do the best I can to sop myself up. But then more wet streams out and I have to tidy all over again. I'm going to need a fresh shirt or a palette of Kleenex or a maid service. "Do they make maids for faces? Nano-maids? With micro sponges to absorb the tears and cell-sized Dysons to suck the tissue dust from my upper lip?"

My mother is staring at me.

"Because if they can make self-cleaning super-windows, I don't think it's an unreasonable idea."

"You really are weird, Avery," she says. And even though we're a little bit better, her and I, I still don't want to hear it.

I'd turn on the Weather Network but it never turned off. Calvin's still on my screen: been there all this time. He's outside his office building getting bullied around by the high winds and rain. He's nervous. Keeps eyeing the sky. *The hail is over, but the storm is still near hurricane-force levels.* He's white-knuckling a waterproof mic but he still has to shout, the storm and traffic roaring. His yellow Weather Network rain slicker tears in the gale. *"If you absolutely have to be outside — like if your heart-less producer, Mike, makes you, for example, go into the storm of the century because the daily humiliations aren't enough, oh no — for the big ratings you put Cornell-educated climatologists in life-threatening situations and cross your fingers that something smacks them from behind."* He's yelling now, in full tantrum. *"How about a rogue wave, Mike! Or balcony glass! Or maybe an industrial air cond —"* The windscreen whips off his microphone. A producer, Mike?, chases after it. A loud crack. Margaret and I jump. The whistle of sliced air. Calvin looks up as a window hits the ground, shattering behind him. He screams and the screen goes black. Did the feed cut? But then it clears and there are Calvin's feet, the camera on the ground, level with his worn loafers. *"I quit, Mike! I fucking quit!"* The screen goes dark again as they cut to commercial. A cream that soothes sore backs. An elevator the infirm can connect to staircases.

"Well, hallelujah to that," Margaret says. "He's just the worst weatherman ever."

Thunder. Flashes of lightning. Margaret and I duck for cover under the air mattress. Boom! The power cracks out. Quiet takes over like it's a sound. Then sirens. Car alarms. The howls of dogs. The emergency hallway light strobes red into the living room. Steve comes in too. "You okay under there?" His flashlight shines in our faces.

"Super Steve to the rescue!" Margaret says.

He puts the flashlight in his mouth and flies over to us.

"Perfect!" Margaret says, flipping the mattress away. "You've got your tool belt on. We were just about to hang this."

She unrolls the *Snow* print.

"Just into the wall?" Steve says. "No frame?"

"I don't think it needs a frame," she says. "I think it'll do just fine on its own."

He hands me the flashlight. "You're the boss, Margie." Margaret holds one corner down and Steve hammers. "It's going to tear," he warns.

Margaret wraps her free arm around my shoulders. "It'll survive."

The print is crooked so I tug on it. Just a quarter inch to the left makes all the difference.

"You know," says Steve, "if you're looking for art, Ikea has these great big sushi roll pic —"

A thundering thump. Another. Like the pounding of fists the size of barrels. There's a giant in the apartment. A crash. The floor shakes, what's left of my furniture with it. The noise is coming from the bathroom.

"Oh, shit," I say, and skid across the floor, because I remember. There's no giant — only Billy Pfeiffer standing in his bathtub, in his bathroom, in the piles of drywall, tile and dust that were once joined together in the form of a shower wall, the most inadequate shower wall in the history of the world. And now he's done it; Billy Pfeiffer has gone and done it. Our two bathrooms conjoined into one.

"Why the hell did you do that?" Steve yells.

"I got tired of waiting for someone else to fix it," he says.

My side bears the brunt of his body slams. The busted tile cracks like ice beneath my shoes. Billy Pfeiffer wipes the sweat from his forehead, and the tile and splinters from his right side. He looks so different in person than he did on TV. His blonde hair is thinning, with a manicured beard rimming the edges of a softened jaw. Jeans held up with a skull belt buckle, his now doughy stomach rolling over its forehead. His left ear is still pierced with a tiny horseshoe, his trademark, and I recognize his T-shirt: black and silkscreened with white horses, the devil's stallions tamed by skeletons, demons and naked women. He wore it on the *Canadian Idol* finale. The nipples were blurred out by the network.

"And now what?" Steve says, punting my Denorex into the tub. "What's your plan, Mr. Tim 'The Tool Man' Taylor?"

Billy Pfeiffer looks down at the mess he's made. Ankle-deep in busted tile and drywall. His pride fades into worry, revolutionary zeal clamps into fear. He's like the emperor of fallen Rome. "I don't . . . I didn't think that far—"

"Of course you didn't, you stupid millennials and your fu—"

Steve and Billy Pfeiffer argue about generational gaps and Home Depot bills, and I tilt the flashlight under my chin and catch my reflection in the mirror. "Bloody Mary, Bloody Mary, Bloody Mary." Nothing appears; it's just me. It's been so long since I've seen my own face for what it is. Strawberry-blonde hair, my father's green eyes. Every single moment of every day lined and circled on my face. My black-now-green-and-yellow bruises. I look a great deal like my goddamn living room carpet.

I lean against the counter and Gloria's ring chafes my hipbone. I tug it from my pocket and hand it to Steve.

"What's this?" he says.

"For the hail damage to your car," I say. "And maybe a trip to Greece to make things right with Accalia. Maybe you two can fall in love again."

Everyone laughs but me.

"What's so funny?"

"Steve's gay," says Billy Pfeiffer.

"What?" I say. "How do you know that?"

Margaret shrugs. "How do you know anyone's gay? You just . . . know."

"Is it true?"

Steve nods.

"So that's why Accalia left you?"

"No," Steve says. "Accalia left because I was an asshole," Steve passes the ring back to me, "probably because I had to hide that I was gay."

"Or because she caught you sucking her brother's dick," Billy Pfeiffer says.

"Or that." Steve winks at me.

"Jesus," I say, dropping onto the toilet.

"Language!" Margaret yells. "Both of you!"

"That is one sick ring," says Billy Pfeiffer, eyeing the bees. "You've got to be crazy to give it away."

"I'm not crazy," I say.

"She's not," my mother says.

I hand him the ring.

"Seriously?"

"Yeah."

"Why give it to me?" he says. "Why give it away at all?"

"Because it's stolen," I tell him, "and I have to get rid of the evidence."

He laughs. "Very funny."

"I'm not kidding."

"She's not," my mother says.

Billy Pfeiffer crams the ring onto his pinky, next to the skull. "It'd pay for my next record," he says. "Mind if I sell it?"

"I'd be disappointed if you didn't."

He pulls the ring off. Slips it into his back pocket. "Maybe an album of covers that *I* like for once. Jeff Buckley and Nirvana and Elton John."

"That'd be good."

"Or some songs I wrote myself."

"That'd be even better."

A fresh chunk of drywall drops from the ceiling. Dust is everywhere, including our lungs. We step onto the balcony to cough it out. The cumulonimbus is gone; it must have blown itself up. I see the stars over Toronto for the first time, pulsing, racing the satellites. They share the same sky with me and yet are so far away their distance is measured in light years, a unit of time only a handful of people understand—people who use the stars to measure all the way back to the beginning of time before the dinosaurs. To what killed them. To what killed Henry and me.

"Who's gonna help me clean up?" Billy Pfeiffer says. "I'll pay you in music."

"I'll help," says Margaret.

"I'll go get the wet vac," says Steve, leaving and taking the light with him.

On the mattress, my father's coat raises an arm.

I grab my mother by the hand. "Do you see it?" I say. "The coat—"

But it's gone.

"What coat?" she says.

"Never mind," I say. "It's nothing."

"Do you remember your father's coat?" she says. "The Resolute, I think it was called. He was so in love with that thing."

The sky is milky rich with stars. I raise my hand to block the light because there's almost too much. It looks like snow that refuses to fall. How could it ever be cold in space with all that light up there? How could anyone ever be cold anywhere?

"I loved it too, I have to admit," Margaret says. "I used to wear it around the house when he was at work. Put the hood up and pretend I was an Arctic explorer."

I take a gulp of air, of stardust.

"I buried Dad in that coat," I tell her.

She pulls me into a hug, and I feel her warmth, finally. "He would have liked that."

END

Acknowledgements

To everyone at Freehand Books — from the editorial board to the sales team — thank you for taking this novel on. Anna Boyar, for shepherding me through the process with patience and a cool head. Kelsey Attard, for your careful copy edit and your work in bringing this book to publication. Natalie Olsen, for dreaming up such a beautiful cover. Thank you to the Ontario Arts Council for its support. To my very early readers Amanda Betts, Gabrielle Johnson, Kathleen Saso and Matt Schmidt — thanks for your notes, questions and encouragement. Thanks to Trena White from Page Two Strategies for your notes and honesty (and for Andre's too!), and your professional expertise; and to Becky Toyne for your feedback (and for being so nice about it). Nicole and Vanessa at Balance Fitness — thank you for literally saving my ass so I could keep writing. Thanks to Chris Bucci: your notes were bang-on, generous and transformative. Thanks to Lucy Scioscia and Melissa for sharing what you shared. To the Webster family, your Chad taught me innumerable lessons about creativity and compassion that, in so many ways, led me here. To my family and friends for being encouraging, even when you probably thought I was nuts. (For the record: I was.) Three cheers for Evadne Macedo! Thank you for being so supportive from afar — this book wouldn't have made it without you! Three more cheers for Deborah Willis (!) for championing my writing and making me feel like I was worthy. Rosemary Nixon, your insightful edit was an education and an inspiration — thank you. To Linda Epstein, you were the first person to believe in me and this story; I'm in your debt for the next 6000 years. To my friend Alana Trumpy, thank you for keeping Write Club alive and well, for your innumerable editorial insights, and for listening and commiserating. And to Anthony Tummillo. Thank you for being a lesson in strength and patience, for pushing away the dark clouds, and for making me laugh every single day.

References

While writing this novel, I read, watched and surfed my way through a mountain of material that helped me stitch this story together, but there were some standouts that deserve special mention. Canada Goose's The Resolute parka was the inspiration for Avery's dad's coat. Patagonia's Facebook post on feather leakage was exceptionally useful. For a how-to on building snow shelters, I turned to Norbert E. Yankielun's book, *How to Build an Igloo — and Other Show Shelters* (W.W. Norton and Co.. New York, 2007), and for information about baptism, I looked to YouTube and also to *Answering Jehovah's Witnesses: Subject by Subject* by David A. Reed (Baker Books; Reprinted edition, 1987). Last, but certainly not least, to the Office of Public Information, Jehovah's Witnesses — thank you for granting me permission to quote from watchtower.org.

EMILY SASO
writes fiction and screenplays. She lives in
Toronto and blogs at egoburn.blogspot.ca.
The Weather Inside is her debut novel.